# RYDER MANN

## Arizona Ranger

## James Domenighini

978-1-965552-69-8 (Paperback)
978-1-965552-48-3 (Hardback)

*Library of Congress Control Number:* 2025920821

admin@bookwrightshouse.com
☎ (213) 286 6700

# CHAPTER ONE

R ILEY MANN WAS UP before the sunrise, the sky a thin red strip to the east, while to the west it was still black and filled with stars. It had rained the night before and Riley could smell the dew in the dry grasses all about, giving them the impossible smell of newly mown hay. Standing on the cabin's front porch in his socks, his parents' soft snoring echoing from their room, Riley carefully put on his boots.

As quietly as possible, he stepped off the porch. He had turned thirteen the night before and his father had given him his grandfather's Henry repeating rifle, the one Grandpa Mann had carried in the Civil War. The gift was an honor and a testament that Riley was now a man, and he looked forward to hunting with it today.

He had fired repeating rifles before. His father had taught him how to shoot with his Winchester and his brother, Ryder, had carried a Winchester in Cuba with Roosevelt's Rough Riders. His brother was a hero, as had been his grandfather, and Riley dreamt of being a hero, too.

Out across the barnyard he moved, the Henry cradled in his arms. The tube beneath the rifle's barrel contained sixteen forty-four caliber shells, more than enough for this morning's hunt.

Riley had carefully opened and closed the fenced-in barnyard's gate as he passed through it. A hundred yards beyond it, he began climbing into the low rolling hills of his family's ranch.

A coyote had raided the sheep pen last night. It had dug a hole under the fence, got in and killed a ewe and then dragged her corpse out. The rain had washed away most of the blood and the coyote's scent, but the ground was muddy enough for it to leave tracks. And where it didn't leave tracks, the wet grass was still bent by the coyote dragging the ewe's corpse.

He wasn't worried about rattlesnakes. The cold rain last night would keep them safely deep down in old squirrel and rat holes. The wet grass robbed the rattlers of their body heat. After sunrise, when the grass dried, they might be a problem, as would tracking the coyote, but not now.

It was late October in northeast New Mexico, the month of change. It could be blazing hot one day, rainy and cold the next, snow the day after that, and be back to blazing hot the very next day.

Trudging through the grasses, dew beading on his boots, Riley was thankful his mother made him oil them so often. The wet grass wouldn't ruin them.

There was a wide, grassy gully a quarter mile beyond the house. Here the coyote had stopped to finish its meal. There was blood and wool and the boney remains of the unfortunate sheep. The coyote had also left stool to mark its territory, though it probably wouldn't be coming back this way. The next time it approached the barnyard, it would come from a different direction. Most people thought of coyotes as stupid pests but Riley's pa had taught him that they were intelligent predators and it was important to respect them. In fact, his pa had taught him to respect all people and all animals. He said that when you stopped respecting them, that's when they bested you.

The coyote's droppings were still moist, still rank. It had left but recently.

It was lighter now, the sky behind him less red and more pink. The sun would be up soon. The cock would crow and he'd have to return for chores.

Riley followed the coyote's trail. There was no knowing how far ahead of him it might be. Nor could he know if it had found someplace to rest for the day. What he did know was rushing to catch up would alert the critter to his pursuit, so every step he took was careful and measured. However, every step was longer than a normal walking step.

His pa had also taught him that long stalking steps were faster than running steps. At least, sometimes.

Off to his left, to the south, he heard morning activity in the town of Brannan, almost two miles away. In a few hours, he'd be on his way to town, where he'd meet with some of his friends after church. They'd be so excited that he was the first among them with a repeating rifle, and that it was his grandfather's Henry.

Though his parents put a lot of stock in church, and though he liked the music and the singing, he found the long sermons boring. However, he had one special reason for attending church, to see Suzy Gleason.

He loved Suzy. She had a great smile and an easy laugh. They were close friends and she loved him, too. She had told him so.

Suzy's twin brother, Nate, was his best friend. Brother and sister both had blue eyes and blond hair, while their older brothers and parents all had brown eyes and brown hair. It puzzled him sometimes why this was so, but his ma had told him that sometimes people had blond hair when they were young but as they got older, their hair turned darker.

He accepted this explanation, not even wondering if they would keep their blue eyes but imagining that they would turn brown as well.

Suzy's pa, Vernon Gleason was a hard man, though. He didn't like her flirting with Riley and beat her often for it. Since their ranch was only a couple of miles further out than Riley's ranch, they often met out by the road at sunset or before sunrise. But never on Sunday mornings or evenings. That's when her pa was most alert for their sneaking off together.

They never did anything inappropriate. They sometimes kissed and often held hands and walked the hills or up and down the road. Someday, Riley told her, he'd save her from her pa. He'd take her away to some place safe, where they could get married maybe. They never talked about sex or children or anything else like that, because they were too young and couldn't even begin to imagine of such things. But they loved their little gentle kisses and holding hands. For them, that was enough.

Riley heard a faint shot somewhere. The thing with all the hills and gullies around him was that gunfire was often muffled by the terrain. It could be close at hand and yet seem far away.

He continued following the coyote's trail, which proceeded down the gully, toward the not so distant road. But as the sky and world lightened about him, he realized he had lost the trail. Backtracking up the gully, he found where the coyote cut to the right, his current left. How he had missed it, he didn't know.

He turned up it.

Once he made the little plateau where the hills popped up from and the gullies sank down into, he made better time.

The coyote must know he was being followed, for he had increased his speed from a walk to a trot. He moved toward the road that headed north from the town. It dipped and climbed and turned as it cut its way through the hills and gullies. In places, it etched along the hilltops and in other places it groveled through the gullies, but generally it just meandered a foot below the plateau.

The sun was just below the horizon now. Any moment, it would pop up. And their cock would crow. The cock usually crowed well before sun-up and Riley couldn't understand why it hadn't, yet, unless the coyote or one of its friends, had eaten the bird, too.

The coyote's track led straight for the road, a hundred yards away. As Riley closed, he resisted the urge to crank a round into the Henry's firing chamber. His father had drummed it into him since he was old enough to hold a rifle that Henrys didn't have safeties. Too many men who walked around with chambered rounds suffered fatal accidents.

Henrys were dangerous weapons and just as you should respect animals and people, you should respect the tools and weapons you used too, Riley's pa said. If your hand covered the muzzle and you banged the rifle against the ground, a slug in the chamber meant a hole in the hand, if you had any hand left at all. And a bumped weapon could kill you as easily as being shot by someone.

This rule applied to all rifles, though most rifles made after Henrys had built-in safeties. The same applied to pistols too, his pa said. A cylinder had six chambers for six shells. Keeping an empty chamber lined up with the barrel meant you kept a vital part of your anatomy safe.

"Besides," his pa had once said, concerning pistols, "if you can't hit a man with five bullets, you have no business gettin' in a fight with him."

Riley moved slowly and carefully along the trail, trying not to make any noise. Forty feet away, he spied his prey. It hid in the grass near the road's edge. Riley crept forward, slow as he could. He made no noise. The breeze was from the left, and away, so the coyote couldn't smell him, nor hear him.

Twenty feet away, he stopped. Stretching to his full height, he brought the Henry repeater up. It would be a downward shot, the ground he stood on was a full foot higher than where the coyote lay above the road. His sights were aimed at the back of the creature's head. A merciful shot, he thought, a quick shot.

Pressing the rifle's butt against his shoulder, he gently squeezed the trigger. Time slowed to single heartbeats. The hammer rose, fell. There was a thunk. The hammer fell on an empty chamber.

The coyote's ears stood up. Its head spun around. For a moment, a single breath, a heartbeat, it saw nothing, for Riley stood tall, thin, unmoving.

Riley cursed at himself. Then the Henry swung out. He cocked a slug into the firing chamber. As he brought the rifle up again, he saw the coyote leap for the road.

He fired.

The coyote disappeared over the edge.

Riley ran to the road's edge. He looked downward into the gully the road dropped through. The coyote was gone. But before him galloped a horse pulling an open buggy. A man leaned over the railing in front of his seat, a big, bloody hole in the middle of his back. Blood covered the buggy.

He had missed the coyote and had hit the man.

Riley watched in horror as the horse raced down the road towards the town, the buggy jerking and bouncing in every hole, on every bump. The man's body flopped around, almost falling out of the buggy.

Riley twisted right and ran, dropping the Henry. Man though he might be, he was still a boy, too. As he ran, he knew he'd never be a hero now. He had killed a man. He was a murderer, a villain. And as he ran, he knew he was a coward, too. He was only thirteen and he didn't want to die, but the penalty in the New Mexico Territory for murder was death by hanging.

Riley knew that when the buggy reached town, the sheriff would gather a posse and ride up the road. Searching about, they'd find his rifle in the grass. They'd find the spent shell casing ejected from his rifle. They would know it was him, because his parents had had his name etched on it, just below his grandpa's name. They'd know who to look for and, because he ran, that he was guilty. Eventually, they'd find him, take him back to town, toss him in jail. There would be a trial, with a guilty verdict, and soon he'd be dangling from a noose, either his neck broken or choking to death.

After a mile of terrified running, often stumbling and falling and getting up and running more, he stopped, out of breath. His legs ached. His lungs burned. He felt dizzy, both with shock and with the exertion of running full blast across the grassy hills.

What could he do? Where could he go? He wanted to go home. He wanted to feel his ma's arms around him. He wanted to cry against her shoulder and plead for forgiveness. To plead for her to save him. But how could she? He had killed a man and he must pay the penalty. He had broken the Commandments and on a Sunday no less.

Oh, if he had just turned back when he saw the sunlight. If he had just let the coyote be. If he had returned home, right now he'd be feeding the chickens and gathering their eggs. Maybe he'd be milking the cows. Maybe he'd be feeding the sheep. Or watering the horses and giving them their morning hay. He might even be hitching the horses to the buggy. Or washing up and eating breakfast.

If he had only done what he should have done! Then everything would be okay. He wouldn't be a killer, a murderer, an outlaw, a desperado. He'd have a future. School, Suzy to kiss, a name to make. A worthy name.

But, no.

He felt his heart beating, the blood rushing to his head, to his hands. He had killed a man. And for nothing other than missing a stupid coyote.

Still feeling dizzy, he began walking toward the northeast, away from the road. As he walked, he wondered who the man was he had killed. He hoped and prayed it wasn't someone he knew.

Far back behind him, he heard horses. The posse. They were coming for him.

Riley ran again. He ran all day, dropping sometimes out of exhaustion. But after catching his breath, he ran on. He ran and ran and ran, until the sun was low in the sky.

Just ahead, less than a quarter of a mile away, he spied a jumble of sun-bleached boulders. He was too tired and too sore to run now, so he walked. The little food and water that he'd brought from home was long gone.

Climbing among the rocks, as the sun set, he heard a rattlesnake's warning. He prayed that it would strike him. He prayed that he would die. He deserved it. He had killed a man. The dirty little coward that he was, he had killed an innocent man.

The snake never struck.

The rocks were warm as he climbed among them. But the night was cold and the heat from the rocks faded quickly. He shivered in the dark. He heard coyotes crying, mocking him. They called him a coward. They called him a dead man, asking if he wanted them to eat him, saving him from the noose.

At some point, he cried. No more a man now, but a terrified, lonely little boy.

While crying for himself, he also cried for his parents, especially his ma. She would be so lonely now, with him dead. He had ruined the family name and what would happen to his parents? Would they be driven from the

Territory? He knew they'd be branded as the parents of a dirty little stinking coward, a killer of innocent men.

And what of his brother, Ryder, a Ranger in the Arizona Territory to the west. Would Arizona let him remain a lawman or drive him out for having a cowardly killer in the family? Would Ryder still be a hero, known for charging up San Juan Hill with President Roosevelt, then Colonel Roosevelt, and his Rough Riders? Or would people only remember his cowardly brother, the back-shooter?

Somehow, Riley made it through the night. After long, cold and lonely hours, he slept. He slept until dawn.

Something jabbed him in his ribs. Waking, he yipped from another jab. His eyes popped open but were blinded by the morning sun. At first, he wondered how he had gotten out of the house. But when his eyes adjusted to the light, he saw two big black holes in front of him, the business end of a double-barreled shotgun.

"Don't move, boy," a gruff voice said. "Ah got ya!"

# CHAPTER TWO

A FEW DAYS LATER, HUNDREDS of miles to the west, Ryder Mann rode his horse into the town of Holbrook, Arizona Territory. He was on his way to meet up with a friend of his, a friend he hadn't seen in more than four years, since they had both mustered out of the now disbanded Rough Riders.

Sometime back, Ryder's friend, Bob McCorkle, had sent him a telegram at the Ranger office in Flagstaff, asking him if he could meet him in Holbrook on a certain date, today. When Ryder asked his Ranger boss if he could journey to Holbrook, his senior had told he could, provided that he kept an eye out for any of the hundreds of desperados wandering the Territory.

Arizona, like its sister territories, of New Mexico and Oklahoma, desperately wanted to become a state. The United States now consisted of forty-five states and several territories, including Alaska and Hawaii, and several new ones gained from the Spanish-American War just a few years back. To become a state, a territory had to have enough voters for a congressman. All the current territories lacked such voters, mostly because settlers wanted to remain in the safer states surrounding them. Killers, robbers, outlaw gangs, and all sorts of desperados wandered the territories, driving decent citizens out. In New Mexico, the United States Marshal service and local sheriffs fought off the villains, but Arizona had copied Texas, creating its own Ranger force, consisting of twenty-six men, mostly gunfighters and former soldiers, such as Ryder.

The reason the Arizona Rangers consisted of only twenty-six men was because that was all the territory could afford. These men wandered about alone, though sometimes Rangers were grouped together to handle larger problems, such as gangs. Yet most of the desperados remained loners. The more men in a group, the more it stood out and the sooner groups of Rangers, backed by a posse and often the Army, went after them. The Rangers preferred to work alone. Hunting a man was easier one on one, than with companions whose actions might be difficult to control.

Men became loners and introverts because society was so complex and competitive. Some men preferred to live alone, ignoring everyone else. Often it was because of guilt. Society was quick to condemn and slow to forgive. Most people felt that "once a badman, always a badman," refusing redemption for others while craving it for themselves.

Alone, a man or a woman had no one to worry about. They could do what they wanted, when they wanted. They found peace where there was no peace. By yourself, you were only lonely when around others. When you were by yourself, you always had yourself. And if you were fortunate to have a horse, a dog, or some other creature for companionship, that was enough.

Ryder had been like that, a loner, an outcast, a wanderer. He had once had a chance for a wife and a family, but he threw it all away when he went off to war.

He had wanted to be part of the war with Spain, and the Rough Riders were right up his alley, consisting of cowboys, ex-gunfighters, lawmen, Native Americans, adventurers, and even the occasional desperado. They came from everywhere, even the big cities of the East, but mostly they came from the West. He had craved such comradery, everyone working toward a shared goal, with a common purpose. He had thought of it as the greatest adventure of his life, being too young to realize that there might be a greater adventure still, something more civilized and less dangerous: marriage and family.

So he left his bride to be, Emily Walker, at the altar and ran off to join up. He left her, knowing she was with child, his child, and she suffered the shame of being an unwed mother.

His whole town sided with Emily against him.

When he returned home after the war, everyone either despised or hated him, including his own mother. And Emily? She hated him beyond words, both because of the shame she suffered and because their little baby girl died at just a few months old, and he wasn't there.

Emily hated him with such a focused passion, that she could neither forgive him, nor see any value in him. To her, he was beyond redemption. She would hate him until the end of time and argue in Heaven for his condemnation to Hell. So said she. So she behaved.

One selfish act, which at the time he thought was patriotic, cost him everything and everyone he held dear. So he left a second time, left a little brother who idolized him, who forgave him no matter what he had done. The only person, other than his father, who loved him unconditionally.

To be exact, he ran out.

Again.

He wandered the west for a while. He worked as a ranch hand, for a cattle rancher. Later, he worked as a shepherd, for a sheep rancher. And then as a farm hand. And finally, when there seemed to be no more jobs, no more chances, he swept out a saloon, cleaning out spittoons, carrying buckets of human refuse out of indoor toilets. He cleaned up vomit and blood. He did everything and literally became the Prodigal Son from the Gospels. But unlike the Prodigal Son, he had no home to return to, no one to welcome him back with tears in their eyes and forgiveness in their hearts.

Finally, he left the towns and farms and ranches behind and drifted the wilderness, keeping to himself, keeping away from the self-righteous, the cruel, the cold-hearted.

He admitted to his sins, but kept to himself.

Ryder never really developed a taste for alcohol. He drank the occasional beer, sipped at the rare whiskey. But alcohol was never his retreat; the wilderness was.

He liked the open spaces of the west, its emptiness. It eased the loneliness and filled the emptiness within him.

One morning, he awoke in the dry grass that had been his bed for the night. His horse, a mare named No Name, nibbled the grass. Yawning, rubbing his eyes, he smelled lard burning. He rolled over to the sight of a cowboy sitting behind a camp fire surrounded by rocks and with the dry grass scraped away.

The cowboy was but a few feet away and looking at him.

"Who are you?" he asked, reaching for his pistol. He only had a couple of bullets in it, the last bullets he owned.

"Ah'm curious," the man said.

"That's a strange name, but I'll accept it," Ryder replied.

The man chuckled. "It ain't my name. Ah'm just curious as ta why yer out here all by yer lonesome. An' Ah'd appreciate it if'n ya don't try ta shoot me. Ah don't mean ya no harm."

Ryder noticed that the man remained sitting cross-legged on the ground, his arms resting on his knees, his left hand comfortably away from the pistol on his left hip. So Ryder drew back his hand from his own pistol.

"What d'you want, then?" Ryder asked. He smelled biscuits and bacon cooking in a frying pan and his stomach lurched and growled. He hadn't eaten in days.

"Ta understand ya," the man replied.

"Why?"

The man reached up and drew back his coat's lapel, revealing a badge. "Ah'm an Arizona Ranger. It's my job ta hunt down criminals an' t'other vermin, an' Ah want ta know which one ya are."

"I'm nobody. No one wants me for anythin'," Ryder replied.

"Whadda ya mean by that?"

"I mean I ain't wanted by the law, I ain't wanted by society, an' I ain't wanted by my family. Nobody wants me. I'm a sinner."

"What kinda sinner? The bottle?"

"Nope. I ran off to war an' left behind my bride to be carryin' my baby. When I got back, my little baby girl had been born an' died while I was in Cuba an' everyone hated me. I got no place to go an' no one who wants me."

"Can ya shoot?"

"Yep."

"Can ya stand up t'other men?"

"I climbed San Juan Heights with the men beside me."

"Ya a Rough Rider?"

"Was."

"Then whadda ya doin' out here? The Territory needs men like ya. There's only a handful of us right now an' there's a lotta work ta do. Arizona wants ta be a state someday an' it can't 'til we git ridda all the killers an' t'other desperados."

"Why would you want me? No one else does."

"Ya climbed that hill with all those t'others while bullets burned by ya. Ya never gave up. Whatever happened before don't make no difference. Yer a man an' Ah think ya'd be a fine Ranger. That's why Ah wantcha."

Ryder sat up. "Can I have some of that bacon an' a biscuit while I think on it?"

"Sure. Ah made some for ya, in case ya was alive. Some coffee, too. Yer just skin an' bones an' Ah thought maybe ya an' yer hoss were on yer way ta the Afterlife an' jest got lost for a little bit."

Ryder laughed, the first laugh in a long time.

The man handed him a metal plate with three strips of thick bacon and a large biscuit on it. He also handed Ryder a cup of steaming coffee.

"You get fed like this in the Rangers?" Ryder asked, between mouthfuls of food.

"Sure do."

"Then where do I sign up?"

"In Flagstaff, 'bout twenty miles south a here. Ah'll show ya the way."

"Thanks. What's your name?"

"Johnny Sharpton. Yers?"

"Ryder Mann."

"An' ya thought my name was strange?"

"When it was Curious, it was."

Sharpton laughed.

And so it went. He became a Ranger, found out the pay was so-so, that you bought your own clothes, your own food for you and your horse, paid for your own room in a boarding house or a hotel, but that the Territory bought your bullets and whatever other equipment you needed.

You didn't starve. And while people respected you, some feared you. Some hated you. And some payed no attention whatsoever.

He could ride the wilderness all he wanted. He could sleep where he wanted, even on the open range. And in towns, if he wanted, he could sleep indoors.

He was a man again, though he really hadn't stopped being one. But he was respected and part of something bigger than him.

He wasn't whole. Pieces of him were missing, while other parts hurt. Worst of all, he could never go home again, even if he wanted to, which he desperately did.

# CHAPTER THREE

OLBROOK WAS TYPICAL OF most cow towns of the Territory. Lots of saloons, a few stores, most of the buildings made from adobe or brick. Few wooden buildings.

Everything looked weather-beaten and was. Money abounded in Holbrook, coming from the large cattle ranches surrounding the town for a hundred miles in every direction, but it wasn't used for making things look nice. There were banks, stores and trading posts, restaurants, a post office, stables, hotels, saloons, brothels, and a magnificent county courthouse.

Holbrook was the county seat for Navajo County, split off from Apache County only eight years back and was often called the meanest town in the west, considered too tough for decent people to live in.

But it was changing. Arizona wanted statehood and every town needed decent, family-oriented people. While Holbrook claimed it was "too tough for women to live in", Ryder saw wives walking with their husbands and gaggles of decent women moving up and down the streets.

The train station was active, with cattle trains rolling east, and immigrants moving west. However, the tracks didn't go everywhere yet and so there were still some stage coach lines. People had to get around and not everyone owned horses. The territories were the frontier, not quite yet developed.

The town's telegraph station was located beside the train depot and Ryder stopped there first. Entering, he pulled back his long coat's left lapel to reveal his Ranger badge.

"I'm Ryder Mann. Any messages for me?"

The clerk sorted through a stack of paper. "Nope."

"Thanks."

"Passin' through or stayin' a while?" the clerk asked.

"Don't know yet," Ryder replied.

"If yew stay, let me know where yer at, in case somethin' comes fer yew."

"Will do."

Returning outside, Ryder retrieved his horse, No Name. He petted her face and scratched behind her ears. With a gentle nudge of her head, she thanked him.

He mounted up, drew back the reins and pulled her out onto the main street. He moseyed into town.

Ryder had been to Holbrook before, mostly passing through while on the trail of some desperado here or there. He knew it wasn't a large town, but it was a growing town. Growth came in spurts and with pain.

Not a drinking man, Ryder nonetheless stopped outside of a saloon. He tied No Name to one of the three rails in front and went inside. At midday, the saloon was almost empty.

"Got any coffee?" Ryder asked as he entered.

"This look like a restaurant?" the barman said.

"Nope."

"Beer or whiskey?"

"Water."

"Cost the same as beer."

Frowning, Ryder walked back outside.

Part of the problem with finding his friend, Bob McCorkle, was the fact that Bob's telegram had not mentioned a meeting place. He only knew that Bob would be in town today. Yet another problem was that Bob hadn't mentioned how he would arrive. Was it by horse or by train?

If by train, then Ryder knew where to meet him. But if he came by horse, then which way would he come from? And where would he go first? Would he stop at a stable? Would he go to a hotel? Would he want lunch or dinner, or go directly to a saloon? And which saloon? Which restaurant? Which hotel? Which stable?

Too many possibilities, too few probabilities. Ryder pulled No Name's reins from the hitching rail and mounted her. Guiding her east, they meandered down to the end of town where he found a decent stable. Paying the stable hand for a stall, Ryder removed No Name's saddle and blanket and brushed her down, giving her the last of her grain and a drink of water from a bucket in the barn. He asked the stable hand to feed her, saying he would be back later when he knew whether he was staying or moving on.

The hand, a young man of sixteen, nodded. He promised to put Ryder's saddle bags and rifle in a safe place and keep an eye on them. Ryder nodded and walked back to the town's center.

He planned on finding someplace where he could eat a meal and maybe find a chair or bench outside where he could keep an eye out for Bob. His friend was a man of his word and if he meant to be in town today, he would be.

Bob had never let Ryder down, and he had never let Bob down. Unlike what he had done to Emily and his own family.

He frowned at that thought. More than two years as a Ranger and he still couldn't let go of the guilt and regret he felt for betraying the woman he loved. Would he ever be able to, he wondered? Would she ever forgive him? Would his ma ever forgive him? Did he deserve forgiveness?

As he couldn't forgive himself, he didn't see how anyone else could. He didn't deserve forgiveness. He was a terrible sinner and when he met God someday, he expected damnation.

The job was all that kept him going. He was helping to clean up the Territory and as long as there were banditos and desperados to capture or kill, he had a purpose and a mission.

Someday, though, it would be done, Arizona would become a state, and what would he do then? He didn't know if it would take five or ten years to clean things up, but it would happen and he'd help make it happen. Even if there wasn't anything for him to do afterwards.

He saw no future beyond the job. In fact, he couldn't imagine living beyond thirty. After the job, he'd go back to the wilderness. Someday, someone might find his bleached bones and wonder who he'd been.

He didn't care what people thought of him. He knew what he was. He had thought that he had done something valuable, defending his country in time of war. But now he knew that was just a fantasy. Reality was worse.

He entered a restaurant. There was no place to sit. It was crowded and full of cigar smoke, laughter, and loud people. After so many years on his own, it was a jungle to him. He felt crowded and confined.

He left.

Looking up and down the street, he spied a mercantile store a few doors down, with a pair of empty chairs out front. He walked over and went inside. Besides clothing and boots and shoes, there were shovels and saws and other tools, a small display of pistols and a couple of rifles, paper products, paper and writing instruments, jars of candy, and dried foods for cowboys on the go. He bought some dried jerky and some dried biscuits of the hardtack variety, then went outside and settled into a chair.

The biscuits were dry and hard, the jerky a bit more chewable.

While he struggled with his food, he watched the people moving up and down the street. There were many common folk moving about their daily business. Sometimes, rowdy cowboys rode in, yelping and whooping and chasing people out of the way. Some men leaned on the posts, which held up the small roofs over the wooden walkways. Occasional men who'd had too much to drink wandered about.

There were proper women walking with their menfolk. There were also women dressed provocatively who grabbed young and old cowboys alike and dragged them down to any of the several brothels.

While some men would have watched these scenes with amusement, Ryder's face was blank. Aside from keeping an eye out for Bob, he looked to see if any of these men, and a few of the women, were similar to any of the faces on the wanted posters on the walls of the Ranger Office in Flagstaff.

It was the job of every Ranger to study those posters until they could positively identify any one of them. And as Ryder had little life outside of being a Ranger, whenever in the Flagstaff office, or visiting any local postal and sheriff offices on his wide travels, he studied wanted posters whenever he could.

However, no one looked like any of the faces he had recently memorized. And he hadn't visited either Holbrook's post office or the sheriff's office, so he didn't know if there were any new wanted posters. It had taken him a few days to ride here and during that time new posters could have come out.

Besides, he wasn't here hunting banditos today but meeting an old friend.

The town was well protected, as far as he could tell. A pair of deputies patrolled the street together, wandering up and down the boardwalks, gathering up drunks and sending them on their way, stopping fights, greeting citizens and lovely women and talking to them for a bit. Even as the deputies did all this, they kept an eye on the town.

Ryder didn't know how many deputies the sheriff employed. When last here, a year before, besides the sheriff there were four deputies, two on during daytime and two for the night. The sheriff did paper work, attended city council meetings, met with ordinary citizens and business people and otherwise kept an eye on the town. A well-oiled machine, Holbrook was fast becoming less of a wild town and more of a safe town.

"You too poor to eat in a restaurant or too lazy?"

Ryder's head turned slowly to the left. He saw a pair of dirty cowboy boots, then brown slacks similar to the ones he wore. The pants were covered with dust. As his vision lifted, he saw a checkered shirt, blue with thin white lines, framed by an open long tan coat similar to the one he wore. Then a scruffy beard, a big grin, and Bob's face.

# CHAPTER FOUR

"**A**REN'T YOU DEAD?" RYDER asked, setting his food down and standing.

"Whaddya mean by that?"

"Heard they hanged you a few years back in Reno."

"Carson City, actually. An' I wasn't there. I was off in China then. Some little bastard had stolen my name an' was killin' people all over Nevada. The law caught up to him after he asked some poor feller in Carson City for directions an' didn't like the feller's response, so he shot him. There were plenty of witnesses, including the town sheriff. It was a short trial an' they hanged him a couple days later. I got back a few months after an' had to tell at least a dozen different lawmen that that wasn't me, an' I was still alive. But I don't have that problem anymore. Besides, if they hadn't hanged him, I woulda caught up with him an' shot him myself."

"China! What were you doin' there?"

Bob was amazed. "I tell you all that an' all you can ask is what was I doin' in China?"

Ryder shrugged, grinned, and stuck his hand out. "It was the only thing left to ask about."

Bob took his hand, shook it, and then pulled him into a tight bear hug. "You bum, I've missed you."

"I missed ya, too," Ryder grunted, hugging back and then stepping away.

"So I hear you're an Arizona Ranger. How's that workin' out for you?"

"It's somethin' to do. Beats cleanin' out spittoons."

Bob laughed. "I bet it does." Then his eyebrows twisted up in concern. "Did you do that?"

"Yep."

"What for?"

"Weren't no other jobs."

"What about home?"

Ryder stared at the board walk a bit before looking up. "They don't want me."

"Why the hell not?"

He told him. Told him about running out on Emily on their wedding day, about their little girl's birth and death, about the shame, about the town's hatred, and about his mother disowning him. And about leaving and never going back.

"Even your ma?"

"Even."

"That's tough. How'd you become a Ranger?"

He told him that, too.

Bob was silent for a long time.

Ryder sat back down and offered him a chunk of jerky.

Bob declined. "I'd rather go over to that restaurant an' have a beef steak, some tatters, bread, coffee or a beer, an' greens, if they got them."

"Me, too."

"Got any money?"

"Some. You?"

"Same."

Ryder stood and stuffed the remainder of the jerky in a coat pocket. Then he tossed the hardtack on the street. "Lead the way, cowboy."

"You first. I've always heard that Rangers lead the way."

"Do tell."

"I just did. 'Sides, there might be snipers over there."

"Snipers?" Ryder exclaimed. "I haven't thought about snipers since Cuba."

"Ain't you had to deal with them in the Rangers?"

"Nope."

"Lucky man."

"I sure hope so." Ryder crossed the street, Bob following him. The restaurant they entered was smaller and quieter than the one Ryder had visited earlier. They ordered steaks, bread, tatters, greens, and coffee. Ryder didn't want a beer and Bob decided against it, too.

As they drank their coffee, while waiting for their food, Bob said, regarding beer, "My pa an' grandpa always said it was better to be awake than sleep durin' the day. An' my ma would always reply, 'Darn tootin'.'"

Ryder laughed. "I think I'd've enjoyed knowin' your ma an' grandpa. Your pa still kickin'?"

"Darn tootin'," Bob replied, grinning. "But you shoulda seen his face when I returned home from China. Those bastard newspapermen sonsabitches in Carson City told him I was dead. He thought he saw a ghost when I came in."

"Bet he was happy to see you."

"He was. First thing he did the next day was write those sonsabitches to tell them that the real Bob McCorkle had come home. That the man they reported on as me was an imposter. A year after tellin' the world about all the bad things I never did, they had to tell the world I was alive an' that the man who did all that stuff was a fake and dead. It was an even bigger story than tellin' about the fake Cowboy Bob."

"Did they really call you Cowboy Bob?"

Bob shrugged. "Newspapermen. They're always writin' about stuff that no one ever did an' makin' up names for people who already have good ones."

"So they do."

# CHAPTER FIVE

"**W**HAT ABOUT CHINA?" RYDER asked. They were halfway through their steaks and taters. The greens were gone. The bread was gone. And a waiter had just refilled their coffee mugs.

"What about it?"

"Why'd you go?"

"I made friends with a Chinese. His name was Chiang Li. I met him in Hawaii."

"Hawaii? What were you doin' there?"

"I was headin' home. I spent almost a year in Australia."

"What were you doin' down there?"

Bob shrugged. "Tryin' to raise chickens an' pigs. Instead, I ended up raisin' lizards."

"Lizards! You're joshing me, ain't you? You've always been a helluva story teller."

"I ain't kiddin' you." Bob set his knife and fork down and spread his fingers wide, cupping his palms as he raised his hands, separating them by about two feet. "They have these really big lizards there that live in the rivers an' lakes. Those Australian guys call 'em crockasomethins."

"Crock of somethins? Sure you didn't drink a bottle or two of whiskey before comin' here?"

"I wouldn't do that. They call 'em crocodingoes, crocapillars, somethin' like that."

Ryder frowned.

"Crockadillows!" Bob exclaimed, dropping his hands to the table. "That's what they call 'em."

"You mean crockapillows? Somethin' to sleep on?" Ryder kidded, laughing. "Crockadillows?"

"I'm being' serious!" Bob growled. Then, after a moment, he laughed. "It's funny, though. We'll just call 'em crocs. These big lizards ate my chickens an' pigs. I'd bought a Henry while there, they ain't got no Winchesters, though that don't make no difference, since they're the same thing."

"Yep."

"I went huntin' them. They're dangerous things. Some of them are fourteen feet long. I bought a goat an' used it as bait. Tied it up to a tree by the river, then climbed that tree. Those big ones can almost climb up an' get at you. I killed four big ones before they could get to the goat. Hard to cut them up, but I did. Their backs and sides are leathery, like armor. I cut them up an' sold them in town. Told the merchants the meat was chicken an' pork.

"Funny thin' is, they didn't wonder about it. None of them had ever ate a croc."

"You fooled them."

"Sure did." Bob and Ryder laughed a while.

"What happened? Why'd you leave such good huntin'?"

"Ran outta big ones. Killed them all off. Were only little ones left, five or six feet long an' they kept outta rifle range."

"Learned good, didn't they?"

"Yep. There was one big one left, though, about sixteen or eighteen feet long. He ate my goat. I pumped sixteen forty-four slugs into him, but he got away. Found him a few days later, dead on the river bank, covered with flies an' smellin' bad. After that, I decided to leave.

"I was tired of killin' monsters an' outta farm critters. So I sold my Henry, packed up, an' took the first boat out, to Hawaii, where I met Chiang Li."

"An' from there you went to China?"

"Yep. An' I'll tell you about it some other time."

"Fair enough," Ryder said. "Don't think I can take too many more stories like that right away."

"It's a good one, ain't it?"

"Darn tootin'"

# CHAPTER SIX

THE WAITER CAME OVER and asked them if they wanted anything else. They asked if there was any pie and the waiter replied they had deep dish apple pie.

They both jumped at that opportunity and asked if they could get more coffee to go with it. The waiter brought two plates with apple pie five inches thick, then removed their dinner plates and returned with a pot of coffee and filled their mugs.

As they ate their pie, Bob asked, "How long d'you want to keep doin' this Ranger thing?"

"Whaddaya mean?"

"Do you like doin' it?"

"It's somethin' to do."

"Are you happy doin' it?"

Ryder shrugged. "I'm not starvin' in the wilderness, waitin' to die."

"Why'd you wanta do that?"

"Had no place to go, no one who wanted me. What else was there to do?"

"Live."

"How?"

"Find a place to go. Find people who want you."

"I did that. Sorta. The Rangers found me. Now I belong to somethin' again."

"An' you're happy with it?"

Ryder shrugged and sighed. "Killin' people ain't my first choice of a profession."

"D'you always have to kill them?"

"We bring them back dead or alive, an' most of them don't want to come back at all. They're used to killin' an' they don't want to do nothin' else. So they almost always try to kill me an' I end up killin' them. But once in a while I bring one back still breathin'. It ain't easy, but I always try."

"You don't sound happy."

"I ain't."

"Then why keep on doin' it?"

"Cause I ain't got nothin' else to do. But it doesn't make any difference. In a few years, maybe three, maybe five, maybe more, all the banditos an' desperados will be dead or chased outta the Territory an' then Arizona will be a state. An' it won't have any more need for the Rangers. Then, if I have enough money, I'll buy a little ranch. An' if I don't, then I'll wander the wilderness until I'm dead, I guess."

"You could come work with me," Bob suggested.

Ryder's face brightened. "Up on your Pa's ranch in Montana?"

"Nope."

Ryder's hope faded. "What d'you mean, then?"

Bob reached into his coat, fumbled for a bit, and then tossed a little metal circle with a star in it on the table. "I'm a U. S. Marshal. Well, a deputy marshal, actually. There's only one marshal an' the rest of us are his deputies."

"How's that different from what I'm doin'?"

"Well, I suppose there will never be an' end to desperados an' banditos in the country. You won't be limited to Arizona, though. There's never enough of us. Most of our time's spent bringin' in escaped prisoners or collectin' desperados who've managed to avoid gettin' caught."

"So, it ain't much different from what I'm doin' right now."

Bob shrugged. "You got me there. Though we don't always ride around alone all the time."

"Like you're doin' now?"

Bob grinned. "You got me again."

"What if I don't like bein' a marshall?"

"Then I'll see to it that you get up to Pa's ranch in Montana. I know he'll welcome you, even if your own pa doesn't."

"My Pa welcomes me. It's my Ma who don't."

"You'd still be welcomed."

"Thanks. Let me think about it."

"Just keep in mind, it's a one-time deal. I told my bosses about you an' they told me I could ask if you'd like to join up with us. We could serve together again."

"I'd like that. I just don't know if I wanta keep doin' this."

Bob nodded.

They finished their pie. Bob retrieved his badge and put it back on, under his left breast pocket, behind the lapel of his coat. Like Ryder, Bob didn't flash his badge. Too many gunslingers out there were happy to make any lawman's badge a target.

Done with their pie, they sat back and finished their coffee.

While they were relaxing and talking about old friends from the Rough Riders who they'd fought alongside, which ones they missed that had lost their lives in Cuba, and what they knew about any of the others, two men came into the restaurant.

They looked around until they spied Ryder and Bob. Then they marched right over to them.

Stopping at the edge of their table, one of them leaned over and growled, "Who are you an' what're you doin' here?"

# CHAPTER SEVEN

"I DON'T SEE HOW THAT'S any of your business," Bob said.

"We're makin' it our business." They pulled back their coats, revealing big pistols and their badges. "We decide who can stay an' who should go. We don't want no gunmen around here."

Bob laughed. "The toughest town in the West an' you don't want no gunmen? The place is full of gunmen. Probably a lot of banditos an' other nefarious people, too."

"Like you?" the second deputy said.

Ryder slowly lifted his hands. With his left hand, he carefully peeled back his coat's lapel, revealing his Ranger badge. "I'm one of you. An' my friend here's a lawman, too, though his badge has a lot more authority than either mine or yours does."

"How so?" snarled the first deputy.

Following Ryder's example, Bob drew back his left lapel. "I'm a deputy U. S. Marshal."

Both deputies relaxed.

"I'm Abe DeBois an' this here's my cousin, Gabe DeBois," the first deputy said. "You?"

"I'm Ryder Mann. This here's Bob McCorkle."

"Bob McCorkle's dead," Gabe said.

"Who told you that?" Bob asked.

"You callin' me a liar?" Gabe demanded.

"I'm sayin' that I ain't dead," Bob said.

"Maybe you ain't, but you ain't McCorkle."

"He's Bob McCorkle," Ryder said. "We fought our way together up San Juan Hill in Cuba."

"Says you."

Ryder let his voice grow cold. "So I do. You got a problem with that?"

"I do." Gabe's voice was cold now, too. He took a couple of steps back.

"You plannin' on causin' trouble?" Bob asked, standing.

Gabe said nothing, but stepped back again.

With careful motion, Ryder let his right hand drop into his lap. He gently moved it to the right, then even slower and more carefully drew his pistol. He aimed it under the table at Gabe's middle.

People in the café froze. They scurried away from their tables and over to the sides, out of the line of fire.

Abe stepped in front of Gabe, his hands up. "We don't want no trouble."

"What d'you want, then?" Bob asked.

"To know how you can be McCorkle."

"Simple. I was out of the country while some jackass was tearin' up the prairie pretendin' to be me."

"An' where were you?" Gabe demanded. He swept his long coat's lapels aside with his hands, keeping the lapels back with his wrists while his hands rested on the handles of his twin pistols, on either hip.

"In China."

"China?" Gabe exclaimed. His voice relaxed. "What were you doin' there?"

"Seein' the world, helpin' a friend, loosin' the woman I loved."

Without a word, Gabe's face softened. His hands moved from his pistols and he closed his coat.

"So you're the real Bob McCorkle, then?" Abe asked.

"I am."

"We're sorry about causin' you so much trouble. But Gabe an' me kinda worshiped you. When we heard you was dead, it kinda broke us."

"I ain't dead," Bob said.

"You ain't," Gabe agreed. He stepped forward and stuck out his hand. "An' I'm pleased to make your acquaintance."

Bob shook Gabe's hand.

Ryder holstered his pistol. "You boys busy? Wanta have a little coffee with us?"

"You sure, after havin' threated you with killin'?" Abe asked.

"Lawmen can't afford to be enemies. We got enough of those already," Bob said. "Join us, if you're a mind to."

"Thanks," Abe and Gabe said. They sat down.

The congregation in the restaurant returned to their tables and meals with a collective sigh, albeit a disturbed one. No one liked to find themselves caught up in violence. Even if their town was one of the most violent in the country.

"So, how'd you find yourself in China?" Abe asked.

The waiter interrupted as he came over. "What do you want, boys?"

"Coffee," Abe said.

"An' pie," Gabe said.

"Two coffees an' two pieces of pie?" the waiter asked.

"Yes, sir," they both said.

The waiter left.

Bob and Ryder drank some coffee.

"China?" Gabe asked.

Bob grunted. "I was seein' the world. I met this Chinese feller in Hawaii..."

"Hawaii?" Gabe asked.

"It's in the ocean west of California," Abe said.

"I know that!" Gabe snarled back.

"Who's story is this?" Ryder asked, "Yours or Bob's?"

"Sorry," both deputies said.

"Go on," Ryder said.

"You sure?" Bob asked. "I've bent your ear enough today."

"Bend it some more. You've heard my whole life story since we left the Rough Riders an' it ain't nowhere near as interestin' as yours."

Bob frowned a bit. "Okay, but I warned you."

"You met this fellow in Hawaii," Ryder reminded him.

"Yep. His name was Chiang Li. Some waterfront fellers were tryin' to beat him up for bein' Chinese."

"Why would they do that?" Abe asked.

"Why not?" Gabe said. "He's Chinese."

Bob glared at Gabe a moment.

"Go on," Ryder said.

"I was goin' to help him, but then I stopped."

"Why?" Gabe asked.

"There were four of them an' he was tearin' them up."

"How so?" Gabe asked.

"He was kickin' an' punchin' them, an' usin' the sides of his hands to hit them on their necks an' shoulders. One got him in a bear hug an' he hit the feller in the nose with his forehead. Blood splattered everywhere an' the feller let go of him. On his feet again, he grabbed the feller's right arm, spun around an' threw him over his shoulder."

"Threw the bloody-nosed feller over his own shoulder?" Abe gasped.

"No. Chiang Li threw the feller over his shoulder."

"I still don't understand."

"Chiang threw the bastard over his own shoulder," Gabe explained. "How can you not get that? Ain't you the smart one?"

"What happened then?" Ryder asked.

"It was over. The other three were on the ground, groanin' an' havin' trouble breathin'. An' Chiang Li seemed unharmed."

"What about the fourth guy?" Gabe asked.

"He was the same way," Bob explained.

"So?" Ryder said.

"So, I walked over an' said that was some fancy way of fightin' an' asked if he could teach me to fight like that. An' he asked me if it was so I could beat him. An' I said why would I want to do that. I had no beef with him.

"An' he said that I talked funny an' I said so did he. Then we laughed. I told him my name an' he told me his an' then we went to find somethin' to eat an' someplace to stay."

"An' you became friends," Ryder said. "Like we did."

"Yep."

Ryder listened as Bob talked. He was a natural storyteller and enjoyed the tale with as much enthusiasm as the two young deputies did. He continued drinking coffee and after a while, he began to wonder where the nearest outhouse was.

Holbrook was like many western towns in the earliest years of the Twentieth Century. It had a mixture of outhouses and fledgling sewer systems. Ryder had visited the town twice in the past two years. Many of the businesses had long, empty alleys behind them. Often, there was a narrow trench in the back with a ridge of dirt paralleling it. Men would go out and do their business, either standing or squatting depending upon their need. When they were done they'd take a nearby shovel and scoop soil onto their waste. It was less private than an outhouse, but more efficient and less obnoxious to the senses.

For women, there were always outhouses.

However, some businesses paid for the construction of sewer lines, consisting of adobe and lead pipes running underground out to cesspools which were open pits full of human waste and water. The towns tried to keep the pools far enough away not to affect well water or sicken residents on windy days.

When Ryder asked where the nearest outhouse was, he was directed to a shack behind the restaurant. In fact, there were two shacks, one for women and one for men. Inside the men's shack there were tubes to piss down and toilets with water pipes leading down from steel water tanks just above them. A beaded string reached up to the tank so that its water would flush the toilet's waste away.

For his need, Ryder chose one of the tubes. It reeked of urine, but Ryder was used to it. After he finished, he found a wash basin with soap and a pitcher beside it. Ever faithful to his upbringing, Ryder washed his hands after doing his deed.

Wiping his wet hands on his shirt, he returned to the restaurant.

When he had left, Bob was narrating his arrival with Chiang Li in the coastal city of Shanghai, in Southern China. He had told of ships' gangs scouring the docks for deckhands, kidnapping them, either by throwing a bag over their heads, getting them drunk, or hitting them with a belaying pin and knocking them out.

One such gang had kidnapped one of Chiang Li's cousins and Bob and Li had followed the men to a warehouse where they barged in and freed Li's cousin and several other men. It had been mostly a fist fight, with Li more than holding his own, until one of the kidnappers pulled a gun. The Shanghaiers, as Bob called them, hadn't know of Bob's love for fire arms. He always carried three pistols, arguing it was quicker to draw another gun than to reload one. He had a long-barreled pistol for distance shooting and two short-barreled ones for gunfights and close-up combat. He pulled one of the short-barreled pistols and winged the man with the gun.

And suddenly, the fight was over.

Ryder had heard all that when he left the table. Now, as he returned, he heard Bob explaining the advantages of different-length barrels for different situations.

Ryder sat back down. Picking up his half-empty coffee cup, he decided against it. He was done drinking coffee.

He stood and went to the door.

Bob was still talking and the deputies were still listening. Ryder didn't mind. Bob was his closest friend. They had gotten to know each other while training with the Rough Riders in Texas and then combat in Cuba had sealed their friendship. They had charged up Kettle Hill, the smaller hill next to San Juan Hill, together with their fellow Rough Riders, including some close friends who had been blown to bits by cannon shells or shot down dead by the barrage of rifle and machinegun fire.

While Ryder had held onto his rifle the whole time, Bob had tossed his aside in favor of his pistols. Having captured Kettle Hill, they charged across the saddle separating them to San Juan Hill.

Bob's pistols had come in handy, while Ryder mostly utilized his rifle as a club, bashing down Spaniards and the occasional German mercenary. It had been a bloody, wild, and dangerous fight, but they had both survived it.

The final assault had lasted just minutes, but after it was all over and the adrenalin had left their bodies, it felt like it had taken all day to overrun the hilltops.

There was such a stench of death, of blood, and urine, and excrement. The fallen soldiers, whether American, German, or Spaniard, groaned, prayed, cried, and died. And when it was over, those still standing stumbled around like drunks, barely able to move. They were exhausted. The shock of it all was in their eyes, on their faces.

All those feelings and memories flooded back, briefly, as Ryder stood at the door, looking back at his friend. He was glad to have him back. Life felt less empty, less lonely.

While Bob recounted his glories to the two deputies, Ryder went outside. He needed to move about. But mostly, he needed to be outside, where he felt safer.

Moving away from the restaurant's door, he watched the traffic in the street. For such a small town, there were a lot of people wandering about.

Though so many people often made him nervous, he was glad to be among humanity again. The wilderness was nice, if you wanted to run away, if you wanted to disappear, even die. But he had been raised in a family. He'd had friends growing up. He trained for war with almost a thousand men. He fought beside hundreds of Rough Riders against hundreds of the enemy. He loved people, though not many of them loved him.

He was glad to be a lawman, an Arizona Ranger. He protected these people, whether they knew it or not. Whether they wanted him to or not. It gave him purpose, a sense of value, a belonging.

There were two maxims that Rangers lived by: "the law was the law," and "justice must be done." And Ryder believed in them. He lived by them. He embodied them.

So there he stood, watching the people passing by, looking for trouble, keeping an eye out for villains. He did the job of the two young deputies inside, who held onto Bob's every word.

Bob was a legend and legends should be listened to.

# CHAPTER EIGHT

RYDER WATCHED THE PEOPLE pass by. Some seemed intent on where they went, while others just wandered about. Ryder knew there was an order to the world, yet from the outside it often seemed like chaos. But it wasn't.

Everyone had something to do, someplace to go. Some found it right away while others searched for a long time before finding it. And some never did, not really knowing where they were going or where they had been.

Knowing that everyone's life was ordered in some way allowed a lawman to spot those who seemed more intent than others. The ones who were so focused on their destination, on their goals, that they seemed out of step with everyone else.

Sometimes, these individuals were just lost. And sometimes, they radiated malice.

Ryder spied three men riding through town. They rode abreast, down the center of the street. From time to time, either the one on the left or the one on the right scanned the populace, the sidewalks, looking for something or someone.

Before the one on his side looked his way, Ryder stepped behind one of the posts holding up the roof over the boardwalk. He turned sideways, adopting a slack and relaxed posture. His left hand played with his lower lip, as if he twiddled a toothpick in his mouth. He kept his head down, but kept an eye on them.

The man on the left glanced briefly at Ryder, then his gaze wandered to the next person up the boardwalk. As the men road past, Ryder's instincts told him these men had no good in mind for the citizens of Holbrook.

Of the trio, the side men were about as big as either Ryder or Bob, neither leaner nor taller than the two deputies inside. But the center man, Ryder recognized him immediately.

The left side of his face was badly scarred from fire. His name was McAvoy and his poster referred to him as Mad McAvoy. He was a killer. He was fast on the draw and no man who stood up to him lived to tell the tale.

But his reputation came not from the number of men he had killed, somewhere around twenty, but from the women and children he had murdered. He enjoyed killing helpless people, and especially women and children. He enjoyed depriving innocent people of their most precious family members.

Ryder could believe that. When men, and sometimes women, turned to violence, escaping the law at every turn, they often let the devil devour their souls. Whatever hell they lived, they shared it with their victims.

Ryder turned and watched the trio ride down the street. They stopped before a bank. Dismounting, they tied up their horses. McAvoy and another went inside, while the third, the man who had sized up Ryder, fiddled with his saddle. He carefully glanced up and down the street.

With caution and a slowness of gait, so as not to give himself away, Ryder returned to the restaurant. He marched over to the deputies.

"Don't you boys have a job to do? Shouldn't you be out protectin' the people of this town?" he demanded.

Abe glanced up at Ryder, while Gabe glared at him for interrupting Bob's storytelling. Abe glanced at his watch and suddenly stood. "We've been here nearly an hour! Let's get goin', Gabe, before the sheriff finds out an' decides he doesn't need us anymore."

Gabe stood. As he turned, Ryder backed out of his way. "Thanks for speakin' up," Gabe said to him.

"Anytime."

As the deputies left, Bob said, "That was rude."

"Maybe," Ryder replied. "You ever hear of an outlaw called 'Mad McAvoy'?"

"Yep. In fact, that's one of the reasons I'm here. One of his friends ratted him out. Said he might be this way in a couple of days. Why d'you ask?"

"He an' two others just road down to the bank at the end of the street. McAvoy an' another dismounted an' went inside, while the third's standin' outside watching the street."

Bob stood up. "A lookout."

"Yep."

"Why didn't you tell the deputies?"

"I don't think they're a match for him."

"Why not?"

"Because they didn't know I had my gun on them while they confronted you."

"Good point."

"Yep."

Bob exited first, with Ryder close behind him. Bob was a couple of inches taller than Ryder and he hid behind him, hoping the lookout down the street wouldn't notice.

Bob stopped at the same post Ryder had leaned against earlier. A moment later, Ryder stepped to his right. He kept Bob between the lookout and himself.

"Wonder where the deputies are," Bob said.

"Don't know an' don't care."

"Why not?"

"They might get lucky."

"How so?"

"They might kill McAvoy."

"Most likely he'll kill them," Bob said.

"That's what I'm more afraid of."

"Me, too."

They watched as people rode and strode up and down the street. Several people, men and women, walked past the bank. Some of them glanced at the lookout standing by his horse. When he looked up, they glanced away. People were curious but didn't want to get caught prying into someone else's business. After all, frontier life was more boring than exciting. People worked hard, sometimes played hard, but mostly muddled through their days. Each day was a repeat of the day before. When one person asked another what was new, the most common reply was, "nothin'".

The lookout seemed oblivious to every person passing by but both men knew he was sizing them up, wondering which ones would run and which would put up a fight. He probably expected everyone to run. But both lawmen knew that if he was any good at all, he suspected some would stand and fight.

While killers and outlaws considered people sheep, as did some lawmen, many people were mountain lions, waiting for a chance to prove themselves.

There was nothing worse than when a local yokel waded into a gun fight between the law and desperados. Someone always got killed, and more often than not it was the law man who died trying to protect the damned fool who got involved when he should have stayed away.

"Too many people around," Bob said.

"Until the shootin' starts," Ryder said.

"Yep. An' we're too far away to help them."

"What do we do about it?" Ryder asked.

"Get closer."

"Yep."

"I'll go down this side an' you try an' get across the street."

"Gimme your hat," Ryder said.

"Why?"

"The lookout might've made me when he was riding by. If I button up my coat an' wear a different hat, he might think I'm a different person an' give me no never mind."

"Good point."

"So you keep sayin'."

"So I do." Bob traded hats with Ryder. Bob's hat was a little bigger and lighter colored than Ryder's dusty black hat. Ryder pulled his friend's hat down around his face, grasped his coat's collar, and hurried across the street.

Bob cocked Ryder's hat sideways on his head and staggered a little, giving a false impression of drunkenness. He made his way up the boardwalk.

The lookout spotted Ryder. While he looked familiar, the lookout noted the different hat and the slouched appearance and ignored him.

Bob, on the other hand, made the lookout uneasy. The jaunty black hat seemed out of character. But when Bob stumbled trying to get out of the way of two women walking down the boardwalk and then laughed a little too loud and a little too unevenly, the lookout wrote Bob off as some drunken cowboy.

So, Ryder and Bob's ploy worked. However, the real proof would be if they managed to get close enough to the lookout before the shooting started.

Ryder knew that when the bullets flew, men would be ducking, women would be screaming, and children would be wanting to watch what was going on. He couldn't think about them. He had to get to McAvoy and his men. Stopping the bank robbers would spare the citizens terrible tragedy. So he made his way as carefully and quickly as he could toward the bank without being too obvious.

Ryder wasn't afraid of death. He had nothing to lose, except his life, and he didn't value that very much.

Yet it was more than that. Ever since Cuba, he had let go of his fear of death. He'd either survive or he wouldn't. And if he didn't, he wouldn't know about it because he'd be dead.

Ryder knew that the best way to survive was to be determined. Determination allowed you to reach the end, regardless of the consequences. Determination got you where you needed to be and as a lawman, it also helped you to do what needed to be done.

Stopping McAvoy and his men was what needed to be done.

# CHAPTER NINE

McAvoy AND HIS MEN had picked the right time for robbing the bank. Just after lunch, the streets and boardwalks were filled with people. They were everywhere, slowing movement down.

When the shooting started, people would be running every which way, screaming, knocking each other down. Panic would reign. The sheriff and his deputies would be unable to get through the mess. Meanwhile, he and his henchmen would escape. They'd shoot at the panicked populace. A man murdered here, a woman killed there, children stomped dead by horses, the terror would protect their getaway.

McAvoy hated everyone, even his own men. He hated them because he hated himself. In his thirty years as an outlaw he had enjoyed killing people of each sex and every age. Killing others kept his own self-loathing at bay. He was more feared in the territories than any other desperado. He was even more feared than the Apaches and the Comanches combined. And he was proud people feared him.

After a slow ride through town, trying not to attract attention, they stopped at the bank. McAvoy and one of his men went inside, determined to kill and steal. The third man, outside, would alert them if any law dog came their way.

They saw five people inside, two male tellers and three women. The men stood behind a waist-high counter. They waited on the women.

Glancing about, seeing no one else, McAvoy eyed the women. One of them was attractive and young. He planned on taking her hostage. The law would think twice before following him.

The other four he planned on killing.

He had learned from the Indians that violence kept your enemies away. The crueler you were, the more feared you were, the less likely anyone would bother with you.

It was a lesson he lived by.

While McAvoy prepared to strike, he had no idea that two lawmen, both experienced killers themselves, closed in on him. But even if he had known, it wouldn't have mattered to him. Half the men he had killed were law dogs. They were as weak as children. Soft. More concerned at stopping violence than creating it.

Pistols drawn, hammers pulled back, sharp commands issued, and the bank clerks and their visitors were as bugs in a spider's web. A teller opened the safe. The other teller knelt in a corner with the women, their hands clasped behind their bowed heads, praying.

# CHAPTER TEN

RYDER WAS FRUSTRATED AS he pushed through the crowd. How to get to the bank without creating a scene, without alerting the lookout?

He noticed that Bob had already crossed the street further up and was making his way down behind the lookout. The crowd was thinner up past the bank. There were less shops and only one saloon, which was closed.

But even though the lookout didn't pay any attention behind him, Bob still had to close with him. He had to find a way to take the man down without alarming the robbers inside.

Two women popped out of a store and collided with Ryder. One went down. The other, a bit frightened, scolded him on his carelessness.

Having been raised as a gentleman, Ryder bent over and helped the fallen woman up. He even gathered up her dropped packages and handed them to her, apologizing for the mishap.

But as he handed back the packages, the woman who scolded him saw his pistol hidden by the loose lapels of his coat. She started to cry out when Ryder covered her mouth and hissed for her and her friend to keep quiet and stay in the store, if they knew what was good for them.

After he was gone, the women hurried back inside to the store's owner and told him a man with a gun had just threatened them. When the owner asked where he went, they replied he headed towards the bank.

The owner immediately sent one of his clerks out the back door, instructing him to run down to sheriff's office and let him know that a man was planning on robbing the bank.

Meanwhile, Ryder wended his way through the crowd.

The lookout had seen the collision between the women and Ryder, half a dozen doors away. He slipped a pistol out of a saddle bag. He recognized Ryder as the man he'd seen crossing the street earlier and realized he had spotted him leaning against a post when riding into town.

He also realized Ryder was wearing a different hat than before, one lighter and bigger. He might be a law dog, and there might be another sneaking up behind him.

Cocking his pistol, he glanced to his left and behind. There wasn't anyone there. He turned to his right just as Bob reached out and struck him.

Bob had always been a fighter and was as good with his fists as he was with his guns. But in China, he had discovered that men fought differently, kicking and striking as well as punching. Whomever he managed to strike with either fist always went down. But sometimes his punches were blocked.

So his friend, Li, had taught him a new way of fighting, which included not only punching and kicking but also twisting wrists and arms and sweeping a man's feet from beneath him, as well as throwing an opponent over one's hip or shoulder. This new way of fighting also included other targets than just a man's face or stomach, such as the throat, the chest, the ribs, and the groin. Bob knew the last one. He had kicked a couple of Spaniards there while fighting for his life on San Juan Hill.

So when the lookout turned and saw him, Bob struck him across the chest with the edge of his hand. Though he didn't quite understand what the purpose of the blow was, he used it. The blow knocked the man's breath out of him and he lost consciousness.

Bob quickly removed the fallen lookout's pistol from his hand. He carefully uncocked it and stuffed it inside one of his coat's pockets. Then he dragged the lookout into a side alley beside the bank. Pulling a bandana from the pocket where he put the pistol, he stuffed it inside the lookout's mouth, tying it behind his head. Removing a piece of leather string from another pocket, he tied the man's hands behind his back.

By the time he returned to the front, Ryder was only twenty feet away, pistol ready. In response, Bob drew both pistols from his gun belt.

Down the street, the sheriff yelled at Ryder to put his hands up. At the same time, shots rang out from the bank as McAvoy killed the tellers and one of the women. A screaming woman ran from the bank.

Another shot and the woman fell.

Most of the people on the street turned around to see what was going on. Those closest sought cover or flattened on the ground. Several nearby kids stretched their necks to watch.

The sheriff raised his shotgun and aimed at Ryder's back. Deputy Abe knocked the sheriff's gun up. It went off with a loud bang. Without looking back, Ryder pancaked on the boardwalk.

Deputy Gabe shouted, "Don't shoot, he's a Ranger!"

McAvoy came out of the bank, holding his female hostage around the waist, a pistol aimed at her head. "Git back, if'n yew don't want her dead!"

McAvoy's other man stepped out behind him, two saddle bags over his shoulders. When he didn't see the lookout, he turned around. He saw Bob. Bob saw him. He aimed his pistol at Bob. With his left pistol, Bob shot the man in the foot.

All this happened in seconds.

Ryder, on his stomach, saw Bob shoot McAvoy's man in the foot, heard the man scream in pain, watched him collapse on the boardwalk.

Ryder aimed at McAvoy's foot, just inches away, and shot it.

McAvoy also screamed in agony and anger. He shoved the woman from him and turned toward Ryder. Ryder shot him in the chest.

Simultaneously, Bob blazed away at him with both pistols.

Deputies Abe and Gabe also shot at McAvoy. And the sheriff, dropping his shotgun, drew his pistol with amazing speed and emptied it into McAvoy. In less than ten seconds, nearly thirty bullets penetrated Mad McAvoy.

He dropped dead.

The young woman ran away.

# CHAPTER ELEVEN

RYDER GOT TO HIS feet. He holstered his pistol and looked at the bloody mess that was McAvoy. He glanced in the bank and was sorry he had. He glanced at the wounded bank robber. Reaching down he took the robber's weapon away from him.

Then he looked at Bob, who holstered his pistols. Blood stained his left shoulder.

"You okay?" Ryder asked.

"Just a nick. The bullet's in the bank's wall. Let's just say someone around here needs to learn how to aim."

"It wasn't me."

"I know that. What's it like in the bank?"

"Like a slaughterhouse."

"We weren't quick enough."

"Who the hell are yew?" the sheriff asked as he came over.

"He's a U. S. Marshall," Gabe said. "An' this here's Ranger Mann."

"I recognize yew," the sheriff said to Ryder. "Why didn't yew tell me yew were in town?"

"I came to see my friend. I didn't plan on getting' in a gunfight."

"No one never does," the sheriff said. "I almost blew a hole through yer back."

"Glad you didn't."

"Me, too. Who's that?" The sheriff pointed at McAvoy's remains.

"Mad McAvoy," Bob said.

"Yer kidding!" the sheriff said. Then pointed at Bob's bloodied shoulder. "Yew okay?"

"Yep. Just a nick. Got a doctor in this tiny town?"

"We ain't so tiny," Deputy Gabe said.

"Don't yew have somethin' to do?" the sheriff growled. Gabe gathered up the wounded outlaw while his cousin Abe looked inside the bank.

Another deputy, wearing flannel long underwear, boots, and a gun belt around his hips, raced out of a hotel across from the bank. He carried his pistol in his left hand. His badge hung crookedly from his long johns. Sleeping, he'd been awaked by the shooting.

He knelt by the woman McAvoy had shot running away. Examining her, he shook his head. Rising, he joined the sheriff and the others at the bank. "What happened?"

"Mad McAvoy robbed the bank. This Ranger and that U. S. Marshall just happened to be around and stopped him." The sheriff jerked a thumb at Ryder and then pointed at Bob. Then he asked, "How many dead?"

"Karen White," the long johns deputy said, pointing back at the street.

"Three more in the bank," Abe said.

"There's another robber down the alley here," Bob said. "I trussed him up. He was their lookout. When he wakes up, he's gonna have a helluva headache."

"We'll cure that with a rope," long johns said.

The sheriff assigned his deputies and some onlookers to clean up the bodies and sent the crowd on their way. The bank president, who'd been at lunch, hurried down, glanced in his bank, and sat down on the boardwalk where Ryder had lain moments before.

"You okay, sir?" Ryder asked.

"That's my family in there."

Ryder said nothing. Things like this happened all the time in the territories. Selfish men and women took what they wanted, regardless of whether it belonged to them or not. And the innocent always suffered.

"Abe," the sheriff called out, pointing to the young woman who had been McAvoy's hostage. She sat by a watering trough up the street from the bank, shaking. "See to Alice. Take her to Doctor Wallaby. Then send Wallaby down to my office."

"Yes, sir," Deputy Abe responded.

"A lot of excitement today," the sheriff said.

"Don't you always have a lot of excitement here?" Bob asked.

"It's known as the town too tough for women," Ryder said.

"We're tryin' to change that. There's a lot of families movin' in here. Used to have a lot of Mormons, too, but they all moved south. Yew boys need anythin'?"

Ryder shook his head.

Bob said, "Had a good meal an' good gun fight. Don't need nothin' else, except maybe a doctor."

"He'll be in my office directly," said the sheriff.

"I could use a couple of forty-five shells to replace the one's I fired," Ryder said.

The sheriff nodded. "Forgot the Territory don't pay you as well as Holbrook pays us." He took two shells from his gun belt and handed them to Ryder.

"Whadda 'bout you?" Ryder asked Bob. "How many times did you shoot? Twenty? Forty?"

Bob shook his head derisively. "Five times. My right shootin' finger's a might faster than my left."

"Bet the women say that, too," Ryder replied.

"Shut up." It was something the two friends had learned to do in Cuba, using humor to release their tension after a battle. Some men cussed. Some drank alcohol. Some threw objects. Some said nothing, did nothing. And some wept.

There was no shame in weeping. Combat was exhausting, terrifying, shattering. When it was done, you did what you had to do to release the pressure and adrenalin.

The sheriff gave Bob five shells. "Yew two look like good friends."

"We fought side by side in Cuba," Bob said.

"Rough Riders?"

"Yep," Ryder replied.

The sheriff nodded. "Anythin' else?"

"Well, my job was to capture McAvoy and return him to Colorado," Bob said. "But there ain't enough to take back. Could you telegraph the marshal office in Durango an' let them know what happened?"

"Sure will. But won't yew be doin' that?"

"Yep. We federal marshals are peculiar that way, though. We want to make sure someone we say is dead, is dead. Helps if someone else can say so, too."

The sheriff grinned and nodded. He turned to Ryder. "And yew?"

Ryder stood. "Telegraph down at the train station?"

"Sure is," the sheriff said.

"I'll go down there an' see if there's anythin' they want me to do while I'm here. I'll let them know McAvoy's dead."

"Before yew go, there's a thousand-dollar reward for McAvoy. Yew two want to split it fifty-fifty?" the sheriff said.

"Nope," Ryder said. "We're not supposed to, though some Rangers do. It ain't against the law, though. Just unprofessional."

"Unprofessional?" the sheriff exclaimed. "What's that got to do with anythin'? What're yew gonna do when yew can't lawman anymore, clean out spittoons?"

"Already done that," Ryder said. "Never gonna do it again."

"Oh."

"He was raised as a gentleman by his parents," Bob quipped. "But not me."

"So you want it?"

"Nope."

"Why the hell not?"

"Like he said. It's unprofessional."

"Don't that beat all?" the sheriff said. "What's the modern age comin' to?"

"Less violence, I hope," Ryder said.

# CHAPTER TWELVE

**A**FTER THE TOWN'S DOCTOR cleaned Bob's wound, the bullet having scratched his skin just enough for it to bleed profusely before clotting, Bob and Ryder went down to the telegraph office. They sent off messages to their respective headquaters. Then they went in search of accommodations for the night.

The best hotel in town was the Cattlemen's. They couldn't afford it. But when deputies Abe and Gabe found out that it had turned them away, they went and told the hotel's owner about them being the two lawmen who stopped the slaughter at the bank. Likewise, when the father of the young woman whom McAvoy had taken hostage found out, he offered to pay for their stay, no matter the cost.

So, deputies Abe and Gabe searched the town until they found Bob and Ryder and then dragged them back to the Cattleman's Hotel.

"Why you doin' this?" Ryder asked. "We just did our jobs."

The hotel owner replied, "You did good for us and we just want to pay you back."

"Sometimes it's good to be a lawman," Bob said, grinning.

"Guess so," Ryder said, frowning.

The hotel had two floors. One side of the first floor contained bathing rooms for men and women. A man could rent a room, hop into a copper tub full of hot water and soak as long as he wanted. There was a rope near the tub that connected to a bell in the servant's area, letting an attendant know when the tub's occupant wanted food, drink, or just more hot water. There was even fragrant soap for washing. Not far from the tubs was a barber's shop where a man could get a shave or a haircut. Beside it was a salon for women.

On the other side of the first floor was a fine restaurant. It included a bar, but it wasn't a saloon. The bar was only open to guests and their friends.

Best of all, for a quarter, the hotel would have your clothes washed and even pressed, if you so desired.

Ryder spent the better part of the afternoon in a tub of hot water. He let the heat, the steam, and the water comfort him. It wash away the guilt and sorrow he felt, which was always with him.

In the evening, they had dinner with deputies Abe and Gabe. The young men spent hours listening to Bob talk about his adventures.

Unlike Ryder, who wandered the west seeking to hide from himself and the sin he had committed against his almost bride, Emily, Bob wandered the world in search of adventure. His stories seemed endless, full of danger and excitement. Bob always wanted to know what was over the next hill, or what was at the end of each road he took. But for Ryder, all he wanted was to go home.

However, he had neither a home, nor a family anymore.

Yes, the Rangers were his family now, but it wasn't the same. He knew they had his back, but at the same time he knew most of these men were only a dollar away from being desperados themselves. These were men who fought alongside you but not men that you would take home to meet your family.

Ryder wondered if the marshal service was any different. But what did it matter? He didn't have a family. He doubted he ever would. In fact, he couldn't even see any future beyond the next bandit he had to chase down.

It wasn't that he looked for death, or even expected it. It was that he simply didn't see any reason for living after he was done as a lawman. So whether he died now or next week or next year, even though he didn't want to die, what did it matter? Except for Bob, what real family had he left?

The next morning dawned bright and sunny, with blue skies almost too painful to look at. The air was crisp, with a little chill. In a few weeks, winter would be whistling down from the mountains.

Ryder dressed and went downstairs, carrying his hat in his hands.

When he entered the restaurant, he glanced around. It was as much a habit as anything else. Since joining the Rangers, he had learned to look for danger whenever entering any building or room. But mostly, he as looking for Bob.

He had expected to find his friend waiting at a table for him. Bob had promised to meet him for breakfast at eight, but he was nowhere to be seen.

He hadn't found Bob in his room. The door was open, the bed stripped, a cleaning woman already tiding up. Bob's belongings, his saddle bags, and blankets, were gone.

Bob carried some clothes in one bag, and, as far as Ryder knew, a small arsenal in the other. Bob liked guns, especially pistols. Besides the long pistol he carried in the holster under his left armpit hidden away from the world, which was the famous Colt Peacemaker, the so-called gun that won the American West, though both Bob and Ryder knew the West was still being won, he also carried two Colt Gunfighter Specials, so-called because of their four and three-quarter inch barrels, which made them the quickest and easiest to draw. He carried them on his hip. Behind his belt buckle Bob also carried a derringer. Likewise, in his bag full of guns and shells were three other pistols, four now that he had taken another Gunfighter Special from the lookout at the bank. Ryder didn't know what kind and size the other three were. However, all his pistols were the same forty-five caliber, with the exception of the derringer.

Ryder also carried a Colt Peacemaker. He found the forty-five- caliber ammunition had the best stopping power. He knew that Bob felt the same way. Stopping power was important when someone was trying to kill you and the only way to stop them was to shoot them.

Yet everything was gone from Bob's room. If his hat and guns and saddle bags were gone, Bob was gone. And since he didn't seem to be downstairs, Ryder didn't have a clue as to where his friend had gone.

The only thing Ryder knew was that neither Bob, nor he, were the kind of men to run out on each other. Bob was somewhere about, but where, Ryder didn't know.

Ryder raised a hand to the waiter. The waiter nodded and indicated that Ryder could take any table he wanted. There were a dozen empty tables, but only one in a corner with windowless walls behind it. Tossing his hat on the table,

Ryder sat with his back to the corner. From there, he could see every window and door, every table, and even the street beyond the great bay window in front. It wasn't paranoia but common sense that made him sit there. No experienced lawman would ever sit with his back exposed when alone.

Those who did, didn't live long.

Ryder glanced around the dining area. Two older men sat at a table, drinking coffee. Both men sported big grey mustaches and wore weather-beaten hats. They looked like cattlemen. Maybe they were a couple of ranchers meeting for breakfast or visiting town for some unknown reason. They wore gun belts with older model pistols and seemed harmless enough.

Over by the windows sat a well-dressed couple, a young man and a young woman. The young man wore black, had a thin, little mustache over his lip, and sported a small pistol, just under his left arm pit, in a cross-body holster like Bob's, partially hidden by his coat. His black hat rested on the side of the table by one of the windows.

The young woman wore a beautiful blue dress and a bluish hat, from which protruded purple-colored paper flowers. There was something about her lips, thin, with a hint of red lipstick, that stirred him. When they talked, in whispers so as to maintain their privacy, they frequently smiled at each other.

Her smiles, the liveliness of her eyes, and her clothing, made Ryder think of Emily Walker, the love he lost.

He tried not to stare at her, at them, but he couldn't help himself. From the way the young woman glanced his way, he knew it disturbed her. She reached across the table to her companion. He glanced at Ryder. His eyes were cold and hard.

Getting up, the young man in black came over to Ryder. His jacket was open just enough for Ryder to see the pistol.

"You got a problem, mister, with my wife? You're makin' her nervous." There was iron in his words.

Ryder leaned back against the wall and tried to make himself seem as unintimidating as possible. "She reminds me of someone I used to know."

"You don't know her and she doesn't know you."

"Nope." Ryder tried to make himself look smaller and less threatening. He didn't want to get into a fight with this man, nor for his wife to watch her husband die.

Leaning back a bit more, but not too much that he couldn't draw his gun or jump up and punch the man before the other could draw his pistol, Ryder shrugged a bit so that his left jacket lapel slipped open ever so slightly, revealing the Arizona Ranger badge pinned to his shirt.

The young man snorted. "You think you're a lawman? You're just playin' at it. You're a wanna be. We're the real deal."

The young man reached up with his left hand and opened his lapel, revealing the Texas Ranger badge pinned on his black vest, which covered a white shirt.

"Billy," the young woman called over.

Billy ignored his wife, continuing to glare into Ryder's eyes.

"Billy," she called again, ever so softly. "Please come back."

"You better do as she says, Billy, because he's as much a lawman as you are," Bob said, standing in a doorway not far away.

"Who the hell are you?" Billy demanded.

Ryder could see that the Texas Ranger was sizing them both up, wondering which one he would have to kill first. Of a sudden, Ryder felt a chill. Maybe he wasn't better than this young man.

"Bob McCorkle, deputy U.S. Marshall."

"He's dead."

"Not hardly," Bob said. "You got a right pretty wife over there. You on your honeymoon? You don't want to be killin' anyone in front her today, do you?"

Billy took a step back, turning slightly so he could keep an eye on both Ryder and Bob. "I don't believe you're McCorkle. They hanged him in Nevada back in Nineteen Hundred."

"That guy stole my name. If they hadn't hanged him, I would've killed him myself. Listen, Billy, your wife doesn't need to see you kill anyone today and she sure doesn't need to see you die in front of her. Why don't you just ease off a bit and leave things be. My friend isn't worth dyin' for." By now Bob had brushed his jacket lapels back, revealing his arsenal of weapons, the two pistols in his belt and the one under his arm.

Taking a deep breath, the young Texan let it out slowly. He let his gun hand drop and with his left hand, he pulled his lapel back over his badge and his gun. He turned to Ryder. "You keep your eyes to yourself and your legs closed, too. She ain't your woman and she ain't gonna be. Got that?"

"Yep," Ryder said.

The Texan glared at Bob and returned to his table. As he sat down, he cast a cold look at Ryder.

Ryder leaned forward and turned away from the young ranger. Without looking at the couple at the window,

Bob sat down across from him. "So, what d'you want for breakfast?"

"All of a sudden, I ain't hungry," Ryder said.

"Shake it off," Bob said.

"Who is that kid?"

"William J. Dodd, Texas Ranger. Billy, for short. Some say the J stands for justice, but that's just bullshit. He's only twenty-one and already he's killed ten men. An' every one of them thought they were better than him."

"I thought I was better than him until I saw the way he was lookin' at both of us, like the way a grizzly bear looks at its next meal."

Bob nodded. "He's a cold one. You shouldn't have been sizin' up his woman."

"Do tell."

"Come on, have some breakfast with me, anyways. We got a couple of hours before our train leaves."

"Train? Where we goin'?"

"You're goin' home. I'm just comin' along for the ride."

# CHAPTER THIRTEEN

"**W**HAT D'YOU MEAN, I'M goin' home? I haven't been home in years an' I ain't plannin' on it anytime soon."

Bob smirked at him. "Well, you're goin' now. You got yourself a telegram."

"From whom?"

"From your Ma. She wants you to come home, an' fast. So we're takin' the train over to Santa Fe an' from there we'll ride east until wherever home is."

"The railroad goes all the way to Las Vegas, which is a day's hard ride from Brannan. It's a bit east of where Fort Union was, out towards the Canadian River," Ryder said. "It'll take a couple days by train to get there and another by horse."

"I was plannin' on taking my horse anyways. I've had Teddy for the last couple of years and I'm not givin' him up," Bob said.

"You named your horse after the President of the United States?" Ryder exclaimed. Heads turned their way.

"Shush," Bob hissed. "There's no need for a ruckus."

"My question stands."

"You know we'd follow him anywhere."

Ryder nodded.

"What about your horse?" Bob asked.

"Her name's No Name."

Bob stared at him. "No Name? What kinda name's that for a horse? A horse is your best friend. She should have a better name."

"I thought you were my best friend."

"Your horse is your best friend when I'm not around."

"I see."

"You get along with her? She a good horse?"

"Yep."

"Why 'No Name'?"

"Well, I was gonna call her Emily, but after returning home after the war, I decided against it."

"Good thinkin'."

"I called her 'Horse' when I bought her an' after home for a while, an' then I started callin' her No Name. She seemed to like it, so I kept callin' her that."

"Makes sense. Horses are people, too. They like a name, they keep it. We'll just book passage for them. Other people do it. The railroad takes good care of them. They make more money that way an' it keeps their passengers happy. We better buy some food an' water for the trip. An' get some grain for the horses."

"Good idea. I ain't got much money, though."

"I ain't, either." After a moment of silence, Bob added, "You know, Mister Texas Ranger over there's a lucky man. Texas pays its Rangers well. That's why he's got a wife while we ain't got no one."

"What woman's gonna marry us? We have so much blood on our hands," Ryder said. "It's a wonder he's got a wife, with all the blood his soul's soaked up already."

"Too bad it didn't work out with your girl. The way you talked about her in Cuba, it sounded like she woulda waited for you."

Ryder looked sad for a moment, his gaze shifting to the young woman in blue by the window, then out into the street.

After a few moments, Ryder turned back to Bob. "What about you? Any prospects?"

"Naw. I like to wander too much. A woman wants a man who will stay around, help keep the house standin', bring home money, an' occasionally scratch her back. I ain't good at any of that."

Ryder nodded. Looking up, he said, "Here comes the waiter. I think I feel like eatin'."

When the waiter arrived, Ryder ordered first. Then while Bob ordered, Ryder watched as the Texas Ranger and his wife walked out the door and down the street. He dropped his eyes and thought about what he could never have with Emily Walker and what a fool he had been leaving her at the altar.

# CHAPTER FOURTEEN

THE TRAIN LEFT TEN minutes late, which was considered almost on time for anywhere in the territories. Bob and Ryder got passage for their horses in a car that had previously carried cattle and would again someday soon.

They climbed into one of the four passenger cars. The seats were well kept, though a bit lumpy from all the passengers that had come before. The car was mostly full. There was a pot-bellied stove at one end and doors that connected to the other cars, including the caboose, but not the cattle car. A conductor came through for their tickets. A little afterwards, the train shook and clattered, huffed and puffed, and rolled out.

Being a coal-powered train, it was capable of greater speed than wood-powered trains. Soon it sailed along at forty miles an hour, dazzling its passengers. But it didn't go far before it slowed for the next town and the next station. What could have been a fast trip was slowed down for every station in every town along the way.

Gallup, New Mexico was about a hundred miles from Holbrook, Arizona. The train had left at noon and arrived in Gallup around five o'clock. The sun was setting as the conductor announced that the train wouldn't be leaving until ten that night. It had to take on water and coal and the crew needed dinner and a rest.

Ryder and Bob took the stop as an opportunity to stretch their legs. First, though, they checked on their horses and made certain they had water and food. Brushing their horses down, they patted them and talked to them and let the horses know they were still important.

There were four other horses in the car as well.

"This place stinks," Ryder said. "I wonder who mucks it out?"

"Well, I doubt the conductor does," Bob said. "See if you can open the door. I see a shovel over there in the corner."

Ryder tried the door from the inside, but it was locked. So he went outside. A bolt with a nut on the end secured the door handle. He unthreaded the nut and pulled the bolt out, then slid the door open.

Ryder moved back while Bob slung shovelfuls of manure out. Soon the train yard was littered with hay and horse droppings.

"Hey! What are yew two doin' makin' a mess here?" A train yard guard came over carrying a big shotgun. "Yew ain't got no right to do that."

Bob put the shovel down and drew back his lapel, revealing his badge. "I say we do. My partner and I have horses in here."

The guard's attitude quickly changed. "Sorry, marshal, I dint know."

"That's all right. Know of any places we can eat around here?" Bob asked. "And some place to clean up now that we're dirty?"

"The station has a wash room," the guard said, his shotgun pointing downward. "Yew can use that. Calico's is the best place to eat. It's on Main Street, jist back a couple blocks from the station."

"Thanks," Bob said.

The guard touched his cap and returned to the station.

"Sheesh," Ryder said. "Everyone wants to shoot everyone anymore."

"So they do," Bob said.

"Even so, the territories ain't goin' to be states anytime soon when everyone's first choice is killin' off the population."

Bob nodded. "Yep."

"So much for the brave new century," Ryder said.

"Hell, it's probably goin' to be that way always," Bob said. "Scared people always turn to violence first, while violence comes natural to the mean-spirited."

"Seems so. You done?"

Bob looked around inside. "Guess so. Hope we don't have to do this too often. Next time, it's your turn."

Ryder nodded. "Guess we should've ridden to begin with."

"It would've taken us weeks to get you home. This way, it's just days."

"At this rate, it'll probably be weeks," Ryder said.

After cleaning up in the station, they made their way up the street to Calico's. They had been amazed that the station's wash room had indoor running water and even an indoor toilet. They had both experienced indoor toilets in hotels in the East, but with the exception of a few places like Denver, Flagstaff, and Phoenix, much of the rest of the West seemed devoid of modern eases.

As they walked up the street, they saw young men lighting the street lights. When they reached Calico's, they found the restaurant painted a bright white, with blue trim around the windows and doors. Lights blazed inside. Somebody played a piano, and not the usually rowdy tunes of saloons, but something sweeter, softer, and more genteel.

"We dressed good enough for a place like this?" Bob asked.

"Don't know. But it'd be nice to eat somewhere where I don't have to worry about someone wantin' to put a bullet in my back," Ryder said, referring to saloons.

"Looks civilized," Bob said. "Let's give it a try."

It was a cool night and the glass and wooden doors of the entrance were closed. But a man with slicked-down hair and a big handlebar mustache, and wearing black pants and shoes, and a black vest over a white shirt, stood just inside. As Bob and Ryder approached, he opened one of the double doors.

To either side of the entrance were boot scrapers, thin metal strips bolted into the board walk. Ryder used the scraper on the left while Bob used the one on the right. Done, they entered.

It was warm and pleasant inside. But it was the smells, of beef, chicken, pork, fish, and lamb cooking that caught their attention. They smelled coffee. They smelled whiskey. They smelled fruit pies, and cakes. They smelled garlic, basil, and oregano, and a variety of other spices.

Their tired eyes widened. Little smiles appeared on their faces, spreading the whiskered shadows they wore.

"Any tables?" Ryder asked the door man.

"It will be a twenty-minute wait. Please, have a seat." The doorman motioned toward a plush-looking bench covered with red velvet. They nodded, removed their hats, and sat down.

"Hope it won't be too long," Ryder said. "This place is makin' me hungry."

"I see your friend's here," Bob said

Ryder looked where Bob nodded. There sat Billy Dodd and his lovely bride. "What're they doin' here? For that matter, what're they doin' so far from Texas?"

"Back in Durango, I heard that young Mister Dodd, the pride of the Texas Rangers, was marryin' a young woman whose daddy was a railroad baron. Or somethin' like that. Heard tell he lives in Flagstaff."

"Geez, am I goin' to have to worry about runnin' into him every time I visit the Ranger office there?" Ryder said.

"You sound worried. You could take him."

"With what?"

"A repeating rifle at three hundred yards."

"Some friend you are."

Bob grinned.

"Oh, no, he's seen me," Ryder said.

"Here he comes."

Ryder closed his eyes and leaned back, bending his head down, feigning sleep.

"Coward," Bob whispered.

"Just tryin' to avoid confrontation."

"Sure."

"What are you two doin' here?" Billy demanded.

"Hopin' to eat dinner," Bob said, cheerfully.

"What's with your friend? He too chicken to look at me?"

Ryder opened his eyes and sat up. "I ain't chicken. I was just hopin' to avoid fightin' with you."

"Too late. You started it this mornin'."

"Look, I'm sorry for this mornin'. We're headin' east an' it looks like you are, too. We're probably on the same train. We didn't know you were goin' this way. So, I'll stay away from you an' your bride, an' you stay away from me. Good enough?"

"Not hardly." Billy grabbed Ryder's lapels with both hands and lifted him up. Before Bob could do anything, Billy hauled Ryder out onto the boardwalk. "I'm makin' sure you stop followin' us."

"So now you're killin' lawmen?" Ryder said.

"I ain't gonna kill you." Billy punched Ryder. Ryder stumbled off the boardwalk and fell into the dirty street. "Get up."

"Texas," Bob, his voice cold, said behind Billy. "You ain't home. This ain't your jurisdiction."

"It ain't his, either," Billy said. He didn't turn around but continued watching Ryder.

"But it is mine. If you don't calm down, I'm goin' to put a hole the size of Texas through your kidney."

Billy stiffened. His hand crept toward the gun holster under his left armpit.

"That how they taught you in Texas? To try to out-draw a man when he's holdin' a Colt only inches from your back?"

Billy said nothing. But his hand dropped away.

"What's goin' on out here?" a new voice said.

Without turning around, Bob said, "You the town sheriff?"

"I am. An' I'm aimin' a Colt Thirty-eight at your back."

"Well, I've got three Colt .45s an' I'm a deputy U.S. Marshall."

"Your name?" the sheriff asked.

"Bob McCorkle."

"I've heard of you. What's your beef with him?"

"He's a hothead Texas Ranger who wants to hurt my friend out there in the street, who's an Arizona Ranger."

"This some sort of lawman fight?"

"Yep."

"I've seen it all now, I guess," the sheriff said. "I don't cotton to back shooters. I'd be obliged if you'd lower your gun. I don't want to kill you."

"An' I don't want you to kill me," Bob said. "It'd ruin your life somethin' fierce."

"How so?"

"Killin' a federal marshal's a federal crime. There wouldn't be a place in the whole country where a poster wouldn't be up for you. An' they wouldn't stop until you were in prison or dead."

"I see." The sheriff holstered his pistol. "My gun's been put away. I'd like you to do the same."

"With pleasure." Bob holstered his pistol.

Billy spun around, driving his right elbow into Bob's face. When Bob dodged back, Billy tried kicking him. But Bob scooped up Billy's leg and flung him out onto the street.

Dust rose as Billy hit the dirt. His hand went to his gun. He had just cleared leather when he saw both of Bob's hands aiming pistols at him. The sheriff, slower than Bob, had his pistol out and aimed at Billy, too.

"You got too much temper, boy," the sheriff said. "I think you need to spend the night in the hoosegow."

"Don't do it," Ryder said. "I'm the villain here. I was sizin' up his bride this mornin' in Holbrook. She reminded me of someone I used to know. He's tryin' to protect her honor."

"And his pride," Bob said. "You're fast, Texas, but before you could've pulled your trigger, I'd have put two slugs into your gut. Think about that for a while."

"What you boys want me to do?" the sheriff asked.

"Let him finish his dinner," Ryder said. "I'll stay away."

"How can I trust you?" Billy asked, getting up.

"Well, we know we can't trust you," Bob said. "You stay in the forward car an' we'll stay in the rear car."

"That sound good?" the sheriff asked Billy.

"It'll do."

"Good," the sheriff said. "I'll take your pistol, boy. You can pick it up before your train leaves. Got that?"

Billy flipped his pistol around and handed it to the sheriff, handle first. The sheriff holstered his own pistol and took Billy's gun.

"Where you goin' to?" Bob asked Billy as he climbed the boardwalk.

"Home," Billy hissed, "You?"

"Las Vegas."

"You stay there." Billy turned to Ryder. "You ever come into Texas and I'll kill you. We call it justified homicide there."

Billy went inside.

Bob walked over and helped Ryder to his feet. "You used to be a better fighter."

"Gettin' old, I guess."

"Cowshit."

"Guess we better get back to the train and dig into some of that stuff we brought to eat."

"Guess so."

"So, you think I'm not a very good fighter?"

"You're as good as me. You just don't know all the tricks I learned in China."

"One of these days, I'd like you to show me some."

"One of these days, I will."

# CHAPTER FIFTEEN

T HEY SPENT THE NIGHT sleeping in their seats while the train clunked along on the tracks. They made Albuquerque by morning, where Ryder and Bob, and their horses, changed trains, leaving Billy Dodd and his wife to continue east on the other train. By noon, they were in Santa Fe, and by mid-afternoon, they were in Las Vegas, New Mexico.

"What now?" Bob asked.

"Now we get outta town. It's safer that way." Ryder gave him a friendly backhanded slap across the chest. "Come on."

After Ryder and Bob had unloaded their horses, they walked them for a while until they limbered up. Their horses had been standing in the cattle car for days and needed light exercise before they could ride them. When the horses felt frisky, excited at going somewhere, the two men saddled them. They made certain the saddle straps were tight, but not too tight to hurt the horses. Then they attached their saddle bags, canteens, rifle boots, rifles, blankets, and their packs. Each man carried a pack for supplies and camping gear that didn't fit in their saddle bags.

Double-checking everything, especially the saddles, they mounted up.

"Ready?" Ryder asked. The sun was low in the sky, but they still had a couple hours of daylight left, just enough to ride through the town's outskirts and set out across the prairie.

"Not quite." Bob pointed at the telegraph office by the train station. "Gotta check in, see if they need me to do anythin' while I'm here in New Mexico."

"Okay." They rode over to the station and Ryder waited outside while Bob went inside.

Bob was gone five minutes. When he returned, he mounted his horse. "Anything happen while I was inside?"

"Nothin'," Ryder said. "Why?"

"Just wonderin'."

"Learn anyhin' while you were in there?"

"Yep. Got a reply almost immediately."

"About what?"

"I've been asked to go up to some town called Springer an' after that, northwest to Cimarron."

"How come? Don't they have U.S. Marshals in this territory?"

"Not at the moment. The service is a little strained in this territory, with not enough deputies around. Those that are here are busy down in Las Cruces, near the borders of Texas and Mexico, dealin' with a bunch of banditos raidin' north of the border. So I've been asked to look into a couple of things up here."

"Such as?"

"Some bounty hunter brought in the body of a killer an' the sheriff in Springer wants me to identify him. An' over in Cimarron, some gun-happy kid's been shootin' people.

He's already killed a deputy. They want me to go take care of him."

"Want me to come along? I can always visit home another time."

"Nope. Your mom sent for you. She must want to see you pretty badly. Three years is a long time for a mother not to see her son, especially when he's still alive."

Ryder nodded.

"Besides, we survived McAvoy. I can handle some kid."

"Don't get too full of yourself," Ryder retorted. "He might be faster than you."

"It's not speed that matters, it's accuracy. We both know that at three feet apart, anythin' can happen. But at twenty feet, the slightest shakiness in your gun hand can send a bullet right past your opponent without even grazin' him. So, unless this is Billy the Kid's ghost, I've a reasonable chance of beatin' him."

Ryder nodded.

"But I can still ride with you for a day or two, until we go our separate ways."

The two men skirted around Las Vegas. The town was one of the reasons New Mexico still hadn't become a state, being full of killers and bandits that kept good people from settling the territory. It took voters, not guns, to become a state.

By late afternoon, they were northeast of the town, following the old Santa Fe Trail. The trail was full of history and stories, with military invasions, banditos attacking stage coaches and travelers, and countless Indian attacks on wagon trains and anyone weaker than them. The Comanches and Kiowa, up from Texas, the Cheyennes, down from Colorado and Kansas, the Apaches, the Navajo, even the Utes from Utah, had all raided along this trail. However, the last raiders had left the trail a decade back.

"It's a good thing the Indians are all on the reservations nowadays," Ryder said, as they rode along.

"Not so good for them, though. Whites want everything anyone else has. An' the Indians have always been in the way," Bob said.

"We're not all that way," Ryder reminded him.

"No, we're not," Bob agreed. "When my grandfather first settled in Montana, there were Sioux, Nez Perce, Blackfoot, an' a slew of other tribes up there. But he made peace with them all. He didn't want to spend all his days killin' Indians an' watchin' them kill his family an' friends."

"What'd he do?"

"Well, if cattle went missin' an' all signs indicated an Indian raidin' party, he let it go. He was tough on rustlers, but Indians were another matter."

"An' they didn't take advantage of that?"

"Nope. He told their chiefs that the world was big enough for everyone, an' if they were willin' to get along with him, he was willin' to get along with them. He gave them beef in hard times. He also made sure that none of his cowhands were trigger happy with any young bucks whoopin' it up. An' he let them get away with the occasional raid to steal horses. 'Course, when a chief found out about it, he made sure the horses were returned or the bucks brought a gift to make things better.

"We still have a fine blanket hangin' on a wall at home that a young buck named Crazy Wolf gave gramps as a gift."

"Your grandfather sounds like quite the man."

"Well, all those things you told me in Cuba about your granddaddy tells me he was quite the man, too."

"Guess we got a lot to live up to," Ryder said.

"We do. But our dads are as good as their dads."

"They are."

They camped that night near a little grove of trees whose leaves were yellowing.

They noticed the woods were full of birds. And they saw squirrels and rabbits and even a rat or two, which told them that if there was still game about then there were rattlesnakes about, too. And probably coyotes.

They made sure their horses were close by and that the fire burned bright and hot. The day had been mild but as the sun set the air grew crisp, with the promise of a cold night. But the sky was clear, full of stars, so they doubted there'd be any rain or snow. Even though it was late October, it was still early for winter weather to set in.

When the train had stopped in Santa Fe, they had visited a store where they bought coffee, beans, bacon, and hard tack. Ryder did the cooking.

"Where'd you learn to cook like that?" Bob asked.

"Ma made sure that I could take care of myself. So did Pa."

"They did a good job. Smells good. When will it be ready?"

"Soon."

Bob grinned and rubbed his hands together, brushing the dust from them. They had a limited water supply and washing was out of the question, except for emergencies. He got out their metal plates and big soup spoons.

Cowboys carried knives for cutting food, forks, and spoons for eating everything else. But some riders dispensed with forks since spoons could do everything a fork could do. Space was limited on a horse and getting rid of non-essential items meant more beans, bacon, or bullets, whichever was most needed.

While they ate, they talked. "You still readin' them weird books?" Bob asked.

"What do you mean weird?"

"Well, back in Cuba, you were readin' one about some guy buildin' some sort of thing that drove him to the future."

"You mean, 'The Time Machine'?"

"Yeah, that one. By some English feller. He must have been stoned out of his head with opium."

Ryder laughed. "He may have been, but it was a great book."

"So you said. Many times."

"Did I?"

"Yep. I liked the one about the people climbin' down into the earth an' comin' out in China."

"Italy. They came out in Italy."

"Same difference. One's as far away as the other."

"You've been to China. What's it like?"

"Same as any other place. Mountains, trees, rivers, cities, towns. They dress differently, smell differently, talk differently, but they're just like us. There are mean ones, greedy ones, funny ones, drunk ones, nice ones. The men tend to be a bit shorter than us but they fight better. More rules, less guns. The women are beautiful an' sometimes wonderful..." Bob grew silent and lay back, setting his empty plate down beside him. He stared up at the stars.

"The stars are the same there as here," he said.

"Did you meet a woman there?" Ryder asked.

"Remember I told you about Chiang Li? The Chinese say their last names first. Don't ask me why. He was almost as good a friend as you. We had some bizarre adventures."

"But you met a woman. An' she was beautiful."

"She was beautiful. Mei, was her name an' it meant beautiful."

"May? Like the month?"

"Maybe. Spelled a different way, but said the same way."

"Oh."

"Mei. Chiang Mei. Beautiful, pleasant, sweet, patient, kind, gentle."

"Was she Chiang Li's sister?"

"Nope. It's one of those names, like Johnson or Taylor, Jones or Smith. You can have fifty people all with the same name in a room an' none of them are related."

"Who was she, then?"

"The woman that Li loved."

"An' you, too?"

"For a while."

"So, that's why you left China?" Ryder asked.

"Not quite. She was engaged to some fat old fart, must've been a thousand years old. Her family had arranged it. He wanted her, but she wanted Li. An' Li wanted her."

"An' so did you."

"Yep."

"What happened?"

"She married that goddammed bastard, that's what happened!"

"How could she?"

"Because family means even more in China than it does here. You do what your parents an' grandparents tell you to do. The law's behind it, society's behind it, your family's behind it. You do what you have to do. Even if it breaks your heart."

"Like yours?"

"Yep."

Ryder got up, gathered up the plates and spoons, threw dust on them and rubbed them down as good as he could, then wiped the dirt off with a clean cloth.

"Check the horses, while I finish cleanin' up," Ryder said.

"Will do."

# CHAPTER SIXTEEN

MORNING CAME, CRISP AND cold, with a little frost. Ryder dug out some cloth filled with six strips of cold bacon cooked the night before, which they ate. Bob fed and watered the horses, then saddled them up. Ryder rolled their blankets up. He took his own things, including his blankets, saddle bags, and other things and tied them to his horse. Bob did the same with his things.

When they were ready to go, they started out by walking alongside their horses. It was as much to get the kinks and stiffness out of their own legs as to do the same for their horses.

"You never said what book you're readin' now," Bob said.

"It's called 'War of the Worlds' by the same guy that wrote about the Time Machine."

"War of what worlds?"

"Mars and Earth."

"Mars is a world? I always thought it was a star."

"It's a planet, just like Earth," Ryder explained.

Bob grunted. "Never too late to find out about other places. How'd we get there?"

"We didn't. They came here. The Martians, that's what people from Mars are called, have these big cannons that shoot giant shells full of Martians an' their machines."

Bob laughed. "Not much of a war. Them Martians blow themselves an' all their stuff up when they get here."

"They don't blow themselves up. Somehow, they survive. They build these big, tall machines that walk on legs an' they start shootin' people an' blowin' everything up."

"Really? How do they power 'em? With steam, maybe?"

"Maybe. I never really thought about it."

"Why not?"

"Because it's not important to the story."

"Oh," Bob said. After a pause, he said, "Why do they come here?"

"Because their world's dryin' up an' they're out of water an' food, I guess."

"Well, we have plenty of water here. I'm not too sure about the food, though."

"They eat people."

"That's just crazy. Who eats people?"

"The Martians do."

"Now I'm sure that writer-feller does opium."

Ryder glanced at his friend and grinned. They walked on in silence for a while. The trail followed mostly flat terrain, though there were draws and creek beds. Most of the creeks were dry by October, but some still had little trickles of water in them. The prairie grasses were dry, some blond-colored and some just brown.

Finally, they mounted up. When they began riding, Ryder broke the silence. "You like bein' a U. S. Marshall?"

"It's okay, I guess. I like bein' useful an' people need protectin'. Besides, it's a good job for someone like me, who likes to move around."

"Don't you want to settle down someday?"

"I wanted to in China."

"You ever think of goin' back?"

"Nope."

"Why not?"

"There ain't nothin' there for me now."

"Just like me."

Bob turned and looked at his friend. "Guess I never really thought about it that way. Guess we're two peas in a pod."

"Yep."

They road on.

The blue sky was partly filled with white, wispy clouds. The air was cool, comfortable. Late October could be a comfortable time along the eastern side of the Sangre de Cristos Mountains, in north-eastern New Mexico.

By mid-afternoon, they came to a fork in the trail. The historic Santa Fe trail continued to the north, while a wider, more used wagon trail led east.

"Time for me to leave you," Bob said.

"Where to first?"

"Follow the trail west to Cimarron, about half a week's ride, I suppose. Take care of that gun-happy kid who thinks he's the new Billy the Kid, an' then back down to Springer to find out who the bounty hunter brought in. I sure hope they've kept that body in a nice cool place or its gonna stink."

"An' after that?"

"If the Marshall Service don't have much more need for me, I'll come back your way. How far is it from here?"

"Some hours. I'll be gettin' home well after dark."

"What's the town called, again?"

"Brannan. It's out near the Mora River. East of it is The Island."

"The Island?"

"A big hill that sticks outta the prairie."

Bob nodded. "How long you stayin'?"

"Don't know. If things haven't changed, not long. I'll see how much I can take before I can't take it anymore."

"You mean with that girl?"

"With everything an' everyone."

"Good luck."

"You too."

Ryder watched as Bob rode away. Then he turned to the right, entered the wagon trail, and rode on.

# CHAPTER SEVENTEEN

THE RIDE WAS LONG, lonely, tiresome, quiet. Mile after mile crept by. Ryder thought of nothing but the road. Sometimes, he glanced at the countryside. But mostly, he stared straight ahead.

He wasn't afraid of going home, not exactly. He just remembered his disappointed parents. And how angry the Walker family was, for leaving their daughter, their Emily, unmarried and with child. He remembered the shame he felt as the cold, judging eyes of the people of Brannan glared at him when he rode through town the last time. Some spit on him, others threw rocks.

And Emily. Sweet, beautiful, precious Emily. Heartbroken and despising Emily. Emily, the mother, crying out while giving birth to their daughter, while he charged up San Juan Heights with the other Rough Riders. And imagined her tears, her intense, unrelenting sorrow as their little girl died in her arms just months later.

He remembered the hate in her eyes, the anger. How she slapped him. Her cruel words, like knives in his chest. And her cold eyes, hard and vindictive.

He remembered her Pa and Ma ordering him away. Her brothers, older and younger, running out with shotguns in their hands, ready to punish Ryder for the shame he had brought them all.

How intolerable the shame must've been, being abandoned at the altar. And then, many months later, the unbelievable pain of losing your child, of holding her limp, lifeless form in your arms?

And all this happening while Ryder was away.

He couldn't take the hate, the shame, the anger directed at him, so he left. But not before breaking one more heart.

His little brother, Riley, was the only one who had welcomed him home. He had greeted him with smiles and laughter and joy. He had planned all sorts of adventures with his older brother, the hero, the Rough Rider who had brought honor and pride to the family's name!

Riley was too young to understand all the pain and shame Ryder had brought to his family, to the Walkers, to Emily.

But he wasn't too young to understand the sorrow Ryder felt at having lost a little girl he never knew. Riley had taken him to where his daughter was buried, on a little hillside not far from their farm. Their mother, Rowena, had asked Emily if they could bury little Hannah in their family cemetery. Emily had agreed.

That night, while his parents and brother slept, Ryder rode away. It was a cowardly thing to do, but he did it.

And, now, Ryder was coming back to it all. After three long, lonely years, how much pain remained? How much sorrow? How much hatred?

Ryder reached Brannan well after night fall. Kerosene lanterns lit the streets. At eight hundred people, even by

1903 standards, in the New Mexico Territory Brannan was a moderately-sized town. It had its share of saloons, but it also boasted two churches, a school, a library, several stores, smiths, boarding houses, even two hotels. And a sheriff's office and jail.

Even a doctor's office.

He saw a deputy on the street, walking his patrol. The deputy stared at Ryder, but Ryder kept staring at the street, avoiding eye contact, avoiding trouble.

Less than fifteen minutes later, Ryder had traversed the town. He continued east, down the road as it wound its way through draws and gullies. Soon, he reached the turnoff for their ranch.

He stopped his horse at the entrance. He looked back down the road to see if anyone had followed him. He felt more like the kind of men he hunted in the Arizona Territory than he did like the lawman who travelled all this way home at his mother's behest. With a sigh, he continued down the trail.

He rode into the barn yard. Lights were on in the house. It was late and he should have found everyone asleep. He felt like sleeping. Like sleeping for a thousand-million years.

He road over to the house, where a small hitching rail stood a few feet from the front porch and front door. He dismounted and tied No Name up.

In the cool late evening air, he could smell the lavender his mother had planted around the house. Lavender kept the scorpions from sneaking inside. He didn't know why it worked, but it did.

He heard muted voices inside.

Ryder removed his gun belt and hung it from his saddle's horn. There was a small metal boot-scraper by the porch. He used it.

He stepped onto the porch. He took his hat off. He took a deep breath, sighed. He took another deep breath. Then, gently, he rapped on the door.

There was silence inside.

He heard footsteps come to the door. The bolt was dragged back. The door swung open. For a moment, the light from within blinded him.

Then, as his eyes grew accustomed to the light, he looked down and saw Emily's face.

Before he could say or do anything, his mother rushed out and struck him hard, across the face. "Where were you? Where were you? You could've saved him! You could've saved him!"

He stepped back, shocked by his mother's attack. She followed him, beating his chest and face with her fists.

"You could've saved him!" she screeched, over and over.

Ryder was aware of his father stepping out, wrapping his arms around his mother and escorting her back inside.

Ryder reached up and wiped blood from his nose and mouth. His mother had never before struck him.

What had happened?

Emily came out with a wet cloth and began wiping the blood from his face. "Where have you been?" she asked, her voice ice.

"In Arizona. I came as fast as I could."

"Not fast enough."

"What happened?"

Emily looked up at him. The light from the house illuminated her angry eyes. "They hanged Riley yesterday."

His father called out for her and she returned inside, leaving the door open.

# CHAPTER EIGHTEEN

RYDER STOOD ON THE front porch, stunned, staring inside. He saw the fire place, full of flames and wood. He saw the table, the chairs, the cooking stove, the couch, the rugs, the dog. He saw his mother, overwhelmed with anguish and agony and anger. He saw his father, also anguished, unsuccessfully trying to comfort her. And he saw Emily Walker, the woman he still loved, doing her best to comfort his mother, but failing.

He felt like a stranger, an intruder, spying on a foreign family, listening to a language he couldn't quite hear, nor quite understand.

Inside was a world both familiar and alien all at once. A world he had once belonged to but now couldn't comprehend.

He had come home because his mother had telegraphed him to come home. And he had come, against his better judgement, because he wanted to see his mother, father, and especially, his brother, again. And because he still loved Emily, though she didn't love him anymore.

But he had arrived too late.

What could Riley have done that someone, anyone, could have hanged him for it? And why had his mother assumed he could have saved his brother?

Emily returned to the porch, closing the door behind her. "What are you doing here?" she demanded.

"Ma sent me a message to come home."

"And it took you a week to get here?"

"I just got it a couple of days ago."

"What were you doing that it took so long to find you?"

"My job."

"Murdering people?"

"Bringing killers to justice."

"Then why weren't you here to bring justice to your brother? To bring justice to your mother?" She wanted to ask him where was her justice. She was still so angry with him. But now, his absence had crushed one of the finest women she had ever known, a woman she might once have had the right to call mother, except for the actions of the selfish man standing before her.

Ryder didn't know how to respond to her attack. So he did the only thing he could, he asked, "What happened?"

"Riley shot Mr. Gleason in the back."

"When? Why?"

"The morning after his birthday. Sunday morning, though little difference that would make to you."

He stared at her. "Where did this happen?"

"Out by the road, where it drops down into the deep gully."

"What was he doing out there?"

"Hunting. Your parents gave him your grandfather's rifle the night before. He said he shot at a coyote, but missed it. The shot went into Mr. Gleason's back just as he came up out of the gully. He was driving his buggy."

"But how did anyone know that Riley shot him?"

"Riley dropped the rifle and ran off, out towards The Island."

"That's miles away."

"It is," Emily said. "Apparently, he ran all day. He didn't have any food or water. He slept among the rocks out there."

"Then what?"

"Then Deputy Rixx found him the next day. Riley was all blistered and sun-burned. He didn't have enough moisture for tears or spit. He apparently babbled all the way to town. Said he'd been hunting and that he wanted to kill something with his new rifle. Said he didn't mean to kill Mr. Gleason."

"They bring him home?"

"They took him to jail and arrested him for murder. Mr. Gleason's horse had brought the buggy into town. The sheriff had raised a posse. Your Pa joined it, until word from your Ma came that Riley was missing. Then he split off to find Riley, along with some of the posse."

"An' he didn't find him?"

"I told you Rixx found him."

"Oh. Then what?"

"They sent for the circuit judge from Las Vegas. He has one of those fancy new cars. Would have taken him two days to get here by horse but he got here in a few hours. He convened a jury. There was no one to defend Riley, so retired Judge McHugh volunteered."

"Who was the circuit judge?"

"Harland Garson."

"Was he a fair-minded judge?"

Emily wrapped her arms around her shoulders. Her teeth chattered, just a little, as she said, "No."

Ryder offered Emily his coat.

"I don't want anything from you." She turned and went back inside, closing the door after her.

Ryder stared at the door. He thought of knocking, but all of a sudden, it seemed rude. It was as if his family wasn't his anymore.

He left the porch again and tended to his horse, digging out of a saddle bag a handful of grain and offering it to No Name.

Done, he walked back to the house to ask if he could spend the night. Just as he stepped onto the porch, as the boards squeaked, the lights inside went out.

His head dropped down. He returned to his horse and mounted up. He was only a few miles from town. Maybe, even as late as it was, he might find a place to spend the night.

# CHAPTER NINETEEN

A KNOCK AT THE DOOR woke Ryder up.

The room he was in was cold. He had opened a window last night, before stripping and climbing into bed. He'd seen no reason to wear his long johns, what with how warm the room was. So, now, as he kicked the cover back, he quickly found his long underwear and climbed into it.

The knocking occurred again.

"Give me a moment," he hollered at the door. There was no reply.

He had found a room at Guzman's Hotel. Brannan wasn't much of a town, being a steadfast community of cattle ranchers, farmers, and sheep herders. The train didn't come here, the nearest station two days' ride away. Close enough to deliver grain, cattle, sheep, even hay.

He put a shirt on. It smelled of a week of riding a horse and so he found his spare shirt, folded in a saddle bag, smelling of leather, a bit of horse, and a bit of dust. He pulled that shirt on and folded the other up. He was certain Mrs. Guzman would wash it for him.

The Guzmans were a hard-working New Mexico couple. All three of their sons were dead, the youngest, Diego, dying of chicken pox in 1898, a mere five years before. Ernesto, the eldest, had been gunned down by a drunken cowboy in 1900. He'd been unarmed. The middle son had died just a couple of years back in Arizona, trying to rob a bank in Tucson. Ryder had been one of the Rangers who had chased down the gang he belonged to. He hadn't known Emilio had been among the banditos that were killed that day. He only found out later.

When he knocked on the front door last night, Merced Guzman had come a few minutes later with a kerosene lamp. His night shirt was tucked into his pants, his boots pulled onto the wrong feet. When Merced saw it was Ryder, he called to his wife.

Coming out in her night gown, seeing who it was, she wrapped her arms around Ryder and wept, saying, "I am so sorry for your lost, Mister Ryder. Your brother was a good boy, just like my sons. Come in. Come in."

They didn't ask why he wasn't at home. They just welcomed him in. He signed the register. They guided him to a room. They were quiet and gloomy, but as supportive as they could be.

The knocking began again.

"All right, all right, I'm coming," Ryder said, pulling his pants on. Out of habit, he grabbed his pistol from where it rested on the dresser top.

At the door, he growled, "Who is it?"

"Me."

Ryder opened the door. Before him stood his father. "Pa!"

Roger Mann peered at his son. "I'm sorry about last night. May I come in?"

"Yes," Ryder said, stepping back. His bare feet felt the coldness of the waxed wooden floor.

Roger entered. He glanced at the clothes on the floor, at the uncovered bed, at the pistol on the dresser near the door. He saw the saddle bags by the bed.

"I was feedin' the livestock when Merced Guzman road up this morning. He told me where you were. As soon as I finished my chores, I cleaned up and came into town. I was gonna ask you to breakfast, but seein' as it's almost lunch time, how 'bout that instead?"

"Sounds good to me," Ryder replied. "Just let me get a little cleaned up."

"Sure. Don't forget your socks and boots."

"Yep."

Ten minutes later, they were descending the stairs from the second story. Delores Guzman saw them and came over with a big smile.

"So good to see you up, Mister Ryder. You slept a long time. Is there anything I can do for you?"

Ryder handed her his shirt as he stepped off the stairs. "It needs cleanin'. It smells."

"I imagine all of your clothes do," Delores said. "Do you have any spare pants?"

"No."

"Well, I still have some of Ernesto's things. You look like his size. I will see if I have any pants for you."

Ryder fidgeted. Delores noticed.

"Don't worry," she said. "Ernesto didn't believe in fanciness. His pants were as plain as yours. Emilio was the fancy one. Everything had to have red in it."

She stopped and stared at the floor. After an awkward moment, she glanced up at Ryder again. "I never got a chance to thank you for catching the ones who led my Emilio astray."

"I was only one of three Rangers, Mrs. Guzman."

"Delores. Call me Delores. You have my permission. You are family to us. And whether you caught them all by yourself or with help, Merced and I thank you. We wish you could have been here to save Ernesto. He was one of your friends."

"I was elsewhere."

"We know. How I wish Merced hadn't listened to me. How I wish he had ignored me and let Emilio go with you to join those Rough Riders. But I wanted Emilio safe and Merced forbade him to go. A few months later, he ran off with those banditos, those skunks. They killed many people. They robbed banks. And my poor Emilio. This world is filled with so much sorrow."

Ryder's father, Roger, tugged at his son's shirt sleeve. They left her weeping for her son, the lost soul, Emilio.

Exiting the hotel, they walked down the boardwalk toward an intersection where two cafes stood diagonally opposite each other.

When they stopped, Ryder asked his father, "Why didn't you speak with Mrs. Guzman?"

"I spoke with her when I arrived. She consoled me over Riley's death. I'm in enough pain as it is, son. I don't feel the need to talk with her more about it. Neither did I want to cry with her over the deaths of our separate sons."

Ryder nodded.

After a moment's silence, Roger asked, "Would it have been better if Emilio had joined the Rough Riders?"

Ryder shrugged and shook his head. "Who knows? We lost so many men and so few came back. Many died of malaria. Many more died at the hands of the Spaniards. They would have turned him down because of his age. No boys allowed, one sign said."

"No boys allowed," Roger repeated. "That should be the name of this town."

Ryder stopped and turned to his father. "What happened? How could they convict and hang a boy for an accidental killing?"

"Judge McHugh couldn't keep Riley from testifying. Riley said he felt the power of god in his rifle, the power of life and death. And he wanted to kill something."

"That's it? That's all it took?"

"No. Mrs. Gleason convinced the jury to convict Riley. The prosecuting attorney let her speak. McHugh tried to stop her, but the circuit judge, Garson, overrode him.

"Brenda Gleason's usually a quiet woman, but she spoke with urgency and such sorrow that the jury listened to her. They took ten minutes to convict him. Garson ruled that he be hanged.

"The prosecuting attorney, Herman Fields, asked for leniency. He asked that Riley serve ten years in prison. Even Brenda pleaded with the judge. But the judge overruled them. Said he wanted to make an example of Riley for all the other delinquent youth in the territory. So he ordered Sheriff Carlson to hang him immediately."

"He was just a boy."

Roger looked away, as if he staring into infinity. Looking back, he said, "Harland said it was the law. That if you murdered someone you had to pay the penalty and the penalty was hanging. He said justice must be done."

Ryder blinked. Justice must be done. It was one the maxims he lived by and now it bit back at him.

# CHAPTER TWENTY

RYDER'S FATHER LOOKED AT him. There was pain in his eyes, in the wrinkles on his face, in the way his neck bent and his head hung down. His shoulders sagged and his spine went limp. When his father spoke next, the words caught in his throat, straggling him.

"I don't know how they did it, Ryder. There were men on that jury who have teenage sons, sons no older than Riley. But there were others on that jury, too, who were out for blood and they didn't care how young Riley was. They wanted him dead."

Roger Mann straightened his back, stood taller, pulled his hat down to hide his face from the late morning sun. Ryder saw the glint in his eyes, the tears, the tears.

Roger coughed and wiped his eyes with a hanky. "Dammed dirt, always gettin' in my eyes," he said. "Let's get somethin' to eat." They crossed the street to the further cafe.

"Why not the other?" Ryder asked. "It's closer."

"This one's better."

Just as they climbed onto the next boardwalk, Roger pointed toward a thick-necked man in a red and gray plaid shirt approaching them. A sheriff's deputy, he had a bowlegged walk, a sure sign of more time riding a horse than walking anywhere in particular.

The deputy was fat, though from the way he moved, Ryder felt the weight didn't slow him down. He had cold eyes, serious and stern. Not the eyes of a killer, but definitely somebody who could kill, if need be.

"Where ya goin', Mister Mann? An' who's that with ya?"

"My son," Roger said.

"The runner, right?"

Ryder stared at the deputy. The deputy stared back. Neither looked away.

"This is my eldest son, Ryder. Ryder, this is Jeff Rixx, Sheriff Carlson's deputy."

Ryder nodded at Rixx. Rixx grunted back.

"Ya mean yer only son," Rixx said, smirking. Even though he talked to Ryder's father, he never took his eyes off of Ryder.

Deputy Rixx wore two pistols, both the shorter barreled gunfighter specials. Ryder didn't have any guns on at the moment. Neither did his father.

"We don't want any trouble, Rixx," Roger Mann said.

"An' yer not gonna get any, either. I know yer hurtin', Mister Mann an' I won't bother ya. I jist wanted to know who ya were with. My job, ya see? In case, jist in case, ya was thinkin' of causin' some trouble."

"I'm not."

"Good. What about the runner? Ya gonna cause any trouble?"

"Nope."

"That's good. We got 'nuff hotheads runnin' 'round here. We don't need no more."

Rixx took two steps back and let Ryder and his father enter the cafe. From the beginning of the encounter, the deputy had held his gun belt with both hands, just forward of his pistols, in a manner intended to intimidate any trouble makers. Ryder knew that Rixx could swiftly draw his twin pistols with little wasted effort.

Once inside the cafe, Ryder glanced back out through one of the windows. Rixx looked in at him. After a moment, the deputy tipped his hat toward Ryder and stepped into the street.

"A wannabe tough guy," Ryder said to his father.

"Maybe. He found Riley an' brought him in. I don't know which way Rixx stood with Riley's execution. But I tell you one thing, his brother, Tony, is a cold-blooded killer. He's got six notches on one of his pistols an' he isn't afraid to kill."

"Tony a two-pistol shooter, too?" Ryder asked.

"Yep," Roger said. "Watch out for him. He's a mean one. He doesn't' start gunfights, but he does like beatin' people up."

"I'll be careful, Pa."

A young, pretty waitress waved them to a table. As they sat down, she came over with utensils, cloth napkins, and menus.

"What will it be today, Mister Mann?" the waitress asked.

"Coffee. An' whatever you have for lunch."

"Well, we have chicken stew with dumplings. But you can also get ham sandwiches. Or roast beef, with gravy. We have fresh biscuits and fresh apple pie. And, as always, the coffee's fresh, too."

"I know, Becky." Roger smiled at her. Then he sighed. "I don't really care. Bring me whatever you think is good."

Becky looked at Roger a moment. Then she leaned toward him and gently squeezed his shoulder. "You know we're sorry, Mister Mann. We care for you and Misses Mann. We don't know why God let this awful thing happen to you. But we know that God wishes you well and is ready to comfort you whenever you choose to turn to Him."

"Thank you, Becky. You an' your father have been very helpful an' comfortin'."

She smiled. Turning to Ryder, she said, "And you, sir? What do you want for lunch?"

"Whatever Pa's havin'."

"Pa?" She looked from Ryder to Roger.

"Becky, I'd like you to meet my son, Ryder. Ryder, this is Becky Jarrett, Dell's daughter."

Becky turned back to Ryder. She stuck her hand out, smiling warmly. "You were one of the Rough Riders? And you're an Arizona Ranger, right?"

"Yep." He shook her hand, its softness surprising him.

Dropping her hand, she smiled again, then hurried off to get their orders filled.

"That's Pastor Jarrett's daughter?" Ryder stammered at his father.

"Yep," Roger said, grinning. It was the first joyful expression he'd seen from his father since coming home. How many dark days were ahead of him, though?

"She seems like a good girl," he said.

"She is."

Ryder folded his hands on the table in front of him. "I don't deserve good, Pa."

"Why not?"

"You know why."

Roger nodded. "Emily's found a new man, a good man. His name's Barry Farrell. He loves her and she loves him."

"My penitence, then."

"Maybe so."

"I should have come home sooner."

"Could you have?" Roger asked.

"I don't know. I should have."

"What were you doin' on Riley's birthday?"

"I don't know. Just a few days ago, I was savin' innocent people from bein' killed by a mad man."

"Then you came home as soon as you could."

"That's not what Ma said last night."

"Son, a terrible thing has happened to us. Your ma's sufferin' a great deal. Her baby's dead, before he could even become a man. An' she knows he couldn't have killed anyone. She's both angry an' sad, horrified over seein' her baby swing at the end of a rope. She doesn't know what she's sayin' an' may never know. Her grievin' is great. I hafta be strong for her. But who's gonna be strong for me?"

"I'll be strong for you, Pa."

"Then help me find out who really killed Vern Gleason. Help me clear my boy's name."

"I'll help you."

"Good." Roger reached out and grasped his son's hands. "You've always been a good son. Here's our food. Dig in."

"Yes, sir."

# CHAPTER TWENTY-ONE

**S**ELF-DOUBT IS THE GREATEST enemy of any human being and as Ryder sat with his father, eating roast beef with gravy and sliced potatoes and fresh biscuits, and drinking coffee, he doubted that he could help his father. He doubted that anyone would talk to him. He doubted that there was any good that he could do.

When he had last come home, everyone had turned their backs on him. He left one of the loveliest and nicest women God had ever created at the altar while he ran off to play soldier in Cuba. And while he was gone, Emily had their baby and that baby had died before he returned home. The shame he had brought on Emily, on her family, on his family, and especially on himself, was unforgiveable. And now, here he was, being asked to help find Mr. Gleason's real killer, for it wasn't just the town that hanged Riley, or the sheriff or the judge from Las Vegas, somebody wanted his brother dead. Somebody wanted Riley to take the blame for Gleason's murder.

But the real question was, how was Ryder going to solve this murder?

"What are you thinkin' about, son?" Ryder's father asked him.

"How to do what you ask."

"It's simple, ask around, stick your nose into other people's business, an' keep pryin' until somethin' gives or someone snaps. It's what you do as a lawman."

"It's not what I do, Pa."

"What do you mean?"

"I mean I don't know any of that detectin' stuff."

"But you're a lawman," his father protested.

"I am," Ryder replied. "But my job is bringin' in killers, rapists, robbers, and other desperados already known by the law who have escaped for one reason or another. My job is to serve the law, to make sure justice is done."

Roger Mann put his mug down. "I don't understand."

"Arizona hired me to bring these people in, dead or alive. Preferably alive. I'm only a glorified bounty hunter, only I don't get any of the reward money. I have to buy everythin' but my own bullets. I don't make good money, but I'm helpin' to pacify the Arizona Territory, so it can become a state someday. I'm contributin' to the future."

"I still don't understand," his father replied. "Didn't they teach you nothin' about bein' a lawman?"

"Only how to track people down. They hired me because I wasn't afraid to fight for my life. Because I was willin' to kill people, if I had to. I know how to be a killer, Pa. I know how to track a man down an' bring him to justice, but I sure don't know how to solve any puzzles."

His father sighed and shook his head. "And Riley thought you were a hero."

"Riley was wrong, Pa."

"So it seems." Roger Mann stared out a window.

"I'm sorry, Pa. Maybe I'm just not the man for this job."

His father turned back to him and stared into Ryder's eyes. "You're my son. You're smart and educated. I told you what you need to do: keep stickin' your nose into other people's business. Keep pushin' and proddin' until someone cracks. You remember your Bible?"

"I do."

"What did Jesus say about the truth?"

"He said to know it an' it will set you free."

"Then find it, know it. It's the only way you're gonna set your brother's soul free an' give your mother peace."

Frowning, Ryder nodded.

# CHAPTER TWENTY-TWO

AFTER THEY FINISHED EATING, and after they said goodbye to Becky Jarrett, who said to Ryder as they left, "I'll be seeing you soon," which left Ryder wondering what she meant, they exited the restaurant and walked down the opposite side of the street from the Guzman's Hotel. Ryder said to his father, "Pa, why aren't you doin' what you're askin' me to do?"

"You've seen your ma," he said. "She's all busted up. Emily Walker's comin' regularly to help out, but she can't be there all the time. So I have to be there. I'm tendin' to the ranch and to your ma.

"You, on the other hand, are free to look into things. You ain't got any other chores except that."

"I can come out an' help on the ranch."

"I don't want you to. Somebody needs to figure out if Riley was really guilty or just framed for somethin' he didn't do."

As they walked, as the boards beneath their feet creaked with each step, Ryder removed his hat and ran his fingers through his hair. It was greasy and filthy and he realized he needed a haircut. "What makes you certain he was framed?"

Roger swung around in front of him, stopping his forward movement. "Do you really think your brother could've felt the 'power of God' in his rifle and killed somebody just because he wanted to kill somethin'?" Roger demanded, sharp and cold.

Ryder returned his father's stare for a moment. Then he glanced at the boardwalk. He noticed how dull the thick boards were. How fibers and splinters stuck out of them. How in some spots they were so worn and smooth that if on some cold winter day or night ice or snow clung to them a grown man could lose his footing, slip, maybe seriously hurt himself.

"I don't know what to think about Riley," Ryder said, still staring at the boardwalk. "I hardly knew him."

"An' whose fault was that? You hardly visited. Maybe, if you'd come home more often, you'd have known him better."

"I was plannin' on comin' home for his birthday."

"If you had, if you'd been here for that night an' that next mornin', maybe your brother would still be alive!"

Ryder's head snapped back up. His face was red with anger. He glared at his father, who glared back at him. Then the anger slipped from him.

"I'm sorry, Pa," Ryder said. "But I am who I am. I don't know if Riley could've done it or not. But I had hoped that he would've grown-up to be a better man than me."

"So did we all." After a moment, Roger's voice cooled. "I'm sorry, too, son. You were doin' what you had to do. I can't fault you for that. I can't fault you for anythin'."

"Except for runnin' out on Emily."

"You were young. We all make mistakes when we're young."

"Even Riley?"

"I pray that his mistake was feelin' guilty for somethin' he didn't do. I pray that Riley didn't kill Gleason, that someone else did an' Riley mistook what he saw for his own action when it wasn't his. That's what I want you to find out."

"I'll do what I can. But what if it's not anyone else's fault? What if Riley really killed him?"

"Then why did the people of Brannan hang my son? Last year, two different people were killed accidentally. Once when a loaded pistol went off while it was bein' cleaned an' another time when some friends were out huntin' an' one of them tripped an' fell. His rifle went off an' he killed his best friend. No one was hanged for that. No one even went to jail. Why hang my son for an accident? Why?"

"I don't know. But I'll do my darnest to find out."

They continued down the boardwalk. Soon they were opposite the hotel. After glancing both ways, they crossed the street. Roger walked over to a brown horse with a white spot on its forehead.

"You're still ridin' Toby?" Ryder exclaimed.

"This ain't Toby. This is Charley, Riley's horse. I had to put Toby down last winter."

"Oh."

"I noticed you were ridin' a nice brown mare last night. What's her name?"

"No Name."

"You haven't named here yet? How long have you had her?"

"Two years, come December. An' that is her name."

"What is?"

"No Name is her name. She seems to like it."

Roger laughed. "She probably likes it because it rhymes. It probably sounds musical to her. Horses like a little music."

"I know."

After inspecting his saddle and gear, Roger untied Charley and holding onto the reins, swung up into his saddle. He extended his left hand down to Ryder. Ryder placed his right hand in his father's and they squeezed.

"When can I come see Ma?" Ryder asked, dropping his hand.

"I don't know. She's so broken right now. Not today."

"What about Riley? Where'd you bury him? In the town cemetery?"

"No. Your ma wanted him buried in that plot on the ridge over behind the barn."

"Where grandma and grandpa are?"

"Yep."

"Any problem if I visit him?"

"Just make sure your ma's not around."

"I'll be careful. I don't suppose I can come out to the ranch an' stay? I can live in the barn."

"Not now. Maybe in a few days."

Ryder nodded.

"I'll see you soon, son," Roger said. Then he rode away.

# CHAPTER TWENTY-THREE

RYDER WATCHED HIS FATHER disappear down the street. Then he entered the hotel. He didn't see either of the Guzmans so he went upstairs to his room.

There were twelve rooms in the hotel, but few guests. Maybe three others besides himself. It was late October and few people travelled out here this time of the year. Spring and Summer months were the heavy months, with visitors wishing to buy horses or cattle or land. Lots of drummers and other salesmen, came through here in the good months.

Who the other occupants were, he didn't know. Nor did he care. It wasn't his business. He was a lawman in the Arizona Territory, but not here. Here he was a civilian. If he shot someone here, even in self-defense, he could be thrown into jail. And seeing what had happened to Riley, he could even be hanged for it.

He entered his room. His pistol was in its holster, where he'd left it. His pistol belt still contained fifteen forty-five caliber bullets, enough for three reloads.

Glancing around the room, everything was as he left it.

Except for the clothes on his bed. Mrs. Guzman had brought two pairs of pants that had belonged to her ill-fated son, Ernesto. She had also brought some of his socks and two shirts. One shirt was a faded blue work shirt, of the kind favored by just about every man who worked out on the range. The other was a dark blue shirt, more of the kind one wore when courting young women. And beneath that, to Ryder's surprise was a third shirt, a deep, dark purple one, definitely for celebrating and enticing the ladies.

As Ryder looked at the dark blue and dark purple shirts, he frowned slightly. "Now, who am I gonna wear these for?" he muttered.

There was a note by the pants informing Ryder to remove his pants, shirt, and socks and then either fold them nicely or roll them up tight and leave them for Mrs. Guzman. If nothing fit, she suggested he go out and buy some new clothing. Certainly underwear, she wrote. Men might share shirts, pants and socks, but they never shared long underwear. "So, please buy some underwear. And bathe again. Women will like you more if you are clean," she had written.

Ryder snorted. His own mother might be incapacitated at the moment, but Mrs. Guzman was ready to play the doting aunt, if not the mother substitute.

So he went to scout out the bath room in the middle of the hall. He found two tubs there, one full of hot water, with a note that said: RESERVED FOR RYDER MANN.

Ryder shook his head in wonder. While he was in his room just now, Dolores and her husband must have brought the water up.

There were fresh towels on a nearby table and a bottle of flowery-smelling cologne. On a smaller table by the tub sat a dish with a large bar of white soap. Beside it was a neatly folded white washing cloth.

He hurried back to his room, carrying a large folded towel. He stripped to his underpants, intending to wash them in the tub when he washed himself. Rolling his clothes up and leaving them on the bed, he grabbed the faded blue shirt, both pairs of pants, in case one pair didn't fit, and returned to the tub before the hot water cooled.

Stacking the clothes on the dressing table, he removed his underwear and tossed it into the water. Then he eased into the tub. The water was indeed hot and he repeatedly winced as he lowered himself in. Yet once he was used to the water, it felt fantastic.

With the soap from the dish, he scrubbed his long johns. After rinsing several times, he draped them on the side of the tub. Then he leaned his head against the back of the tub and sighed.

While his life was horribly depressing, a hot bath was a small miracle that lifted his spirits.

He dozed for a while, until he heard the door creak open. Then he dropped an arm over the right side of the tub, groping the floor for his pistol. But he had left it in his room.

"Do not worry, it is just me," Mr. Guzman said. "My wife, she wanted me to make sure you were washing and not just sleeping."

Ryder sheepishly smiled. "I was sleepin'."

"So I noticed," Mr. Guzman said, with a small smile. "It must be difficult."

"What must be difficult?" Ryder asked.

"Relaxing, when you live by the gun."

"I don't live by the gun," Ryder retorted.

"But you do," Merced Guzman said. There was a chair by the dressing table. He pulled it out and turned it around, sitting down and folding his hands in his lap. "You searched the floor for it when you heard the door creak open. How could you know that it was me and not someone come to kill you? Lawman or gunman, all are the same. Without the gun, you are vulnerable."

"I suppose so."

"But we are all vulnerable, whether we live with the gun or without it. The Heavenly Father did not make this world easy for us. Look at Adam and his wife. They lived in paradise. But there was no challenge there and so life meant nothing to them.

"So they went looking for a challenge and The Heavenly Father cast them out. But casting them out was a greater gift from Him than letting them spend eternity without anything to do except grow fat and dull."

Ryder sat up. "So you're sayin' that a hard life is a gift from God?"

"It seems so."

"How can all this pain an' sufferin' be a gift from God? Can Riley's death be a blessing to my mother?" Ryder demanded.

"I'm saying that challenges keep us alive. They give us a reason for living. Marriage is a challenge. Fatherhood is a challenge."

"But what about Riley? How was his dyin' good for him? How was it good for my mother or my father? How was it good for me?"

"In the Bible, Our Father says that He takes no pleasure in the death of any man. Or woman. Or child. But without death, life has no meaning. Without suffering, how do we learn to love?"

"Merced, I don't understand a word you're sayin'."

"I can tell."

"Did the deaths of your sons make you learn to love better?"

"It taught me to be more compassionate for my wife. It taught us to love everyone's sons and daughters like our own. Before, we only loved our own sons and hated and feared anyone that might take them away from us. But now we know that love is not limited to just us or our children, but it is for us to share with everyone."

"And what about the gun?"

"Christ tells us that if we live by the sword, we will die by the sword."

"But what about the gun? The gun is mightier than the sword."

"The gun is the sword. The sword is violence. The sword is death."

"I know that," Ryder said. "How can you condemn me for protecting others from evil and death?"

"I don't condemn you at all. The gun isn't always the answer. I have heard that you don't always kill. That you often bring in dangerous men without killing them. But I wonder, if you had been here a few days earlier, would you have killed to save your brother?"

"Would you have killed to save your sons?"

Merced shook his head. "I do not know. But if I had, I would not be the same man. I would not be a better man."

Ryder leaned back in the tub. The water was cooler now. "I don't know if I would have killed to save him, either. I've taken an oath to protect the innocent an' to bring the guilty to justice, which is to bring in the killers that plague Arizona."

"Would you have killed to protect Riley?" Merced reiterated.

"Was Riley innocent?" Ryder asked, in desperation.

"He was. But so is almost everyone else."

"I don't know what I would've done."

"Then that is the question you must find the answer to. I am sure your father has asked you to find his real killers. But what if there aren't any? Will you kill even if no one is guilty?"

Ryder looked away. Light gray wall paper, covered with vertical blue stripes and dotted here and there with white or yellow flowers, covered the walls. "I don't know. I hope not."

"You should bathe. Is the water still warm?"

"No."

"I will bring you more hot water."

"Thanks."

After Merced was gone, Ryder stared at the wall. Never in his life, not in Cuba, not after returning home to find Emily full of hatred for him, not in the short gun battle he had recently fought in, not ever had he faced such a dilemma and such sorrow as he did now.

Merced was right. The gun was no answer to this situation. But it was a tool, the tool of his trade. What was a lawman without a gun? Especially, when surrounded by gunmen?

So, he must carry a gun. But when to use it and when to avoid it, those were the real questions.

His parents had raised him to be a good man. But he had forgotten that when he ran off to war, leaving Emily behind. What shame he had brought on himself and her. And where was he when their baby died?

He didn't know.

But was the war with the Spaniards really a great adventure? In some respects, yes. He had seen new lands and experienced the comradery of the military and combat. And he had fought alongside some of the best men he would ever know, including and especially Bob McCorkle and Colonel Roosevelt. But as Merced had just pointed out, wasn't marriage more important than the comradery of war? Wasn't mercy more important than violence?

He had ruined so much for so many. And now, because he was hesitant to return home, because of all the shame and anger and hatred of these past years, he hadn't been present to defend his brother when he most needed it. And so his brother had died, in the most horrible manner possible, by hanging, with a hood over his face and darkness in his eyes, maybe hearing people laughing and cheering, jeering and screaming at his death, while Ryder was far away. What kind of man was he? What kind of brother? What kind of son?

# CHAPTER TWENTY-FOUR

ASHED AND DRIED, HE dressed. Both pairs of pants fit, though one was tighter than the other. But he hooked his thumbs inside the waist and ran them around, pulling it outward. The action loosened the pants just enough. He put his belt on. His underwear was damp, but comfortable beneath his new pants. Returning to his room, he put socks and boots on.

Before leaving, he put his gun belt on. He slid his pistol up and down a couple of times, making certain it moved smoothly in the holster.

It did.

He thought about what Merced Guzman said to him. But a man in the West without his gun was a fool. Just its presence was more of a deterrent than actually using it.

Now he was ready to go.

He had a destination in mind and it didn't include interviewing anyone. In fact, it didn't include seeing anyone.

Except Riley.

He wanted to visit Riley's grave.

He went down to the stable where he kept No Name. After saddling her up, making certain he had water, a little grain and a carrot for her, he mounted up and rode out of town. His destination wasn't too far away.

He enjoyed the countryside he rode through. It was like every other piece of the West, quiet, open, rugged, often dry, peaceful and beautiful. But there was something about the eastern New Mexico Territory that made all the rest of the world seem small, empty, and lonely. It was where Ryder grew up. It was home.

The sun was lower in the sky when he reached the ridge where the family plot was. He approached it from the opposite side, guiding his horse slowly, keeping the skyline between him and the other side. His father had said to make certain his mother wasn't around when he visited his brother's grave. He stopped at an oak tree a hundred feet downrange. Dismounting, he tied No Name up.

He walked the last little bit. The grasses were dry, even brittle. There was no sneaking up while wearing boots. Nonetheless, he moved as silently as he could. Three small oaks separated him from the plot as he crested the ridge. He pushed through them and there she was.

Emily.

He watched her. She hadn't heard him approach. She poured a little water from a canteen into a jar in front of the wooden marker bearing Riley's name. She then carefully fitted four yellow flowers in the jar. Standing, she screwed the cap back on the canteen. She starred at the grave and flowers.

Ryder loved her still, even though he knew her love for him was as dead as Riley was.

She sighed and wiped the back of a hand beneath one of her eyes. Then she turned and spied Ryder.

"What are you doing here?" she demanded.

"I came to visit Riley."

"By sneaking up on me?"

"No."

"But you did, didn't you?"

"I did."

"Why?"

"Pa told me not to visit if Ma was around. Where is she?"

"Sleeping. I hope."

"How long has she been like this?"

"Ever since you failed to arrive in time to save Riley."

"I did the best I could."

"Your best is never good enough." Emily kneeled down and gathered up the paper she had wrapped the flowers in. She neatly folded it into quarters and then stuffed it inside a little bag she carried. Then she gathered up the canteen, looping its strap around her neck and shoulder.

Ryder noticed that she wore sturdy shoes and a faded blue dress with faded white flowers.

"I have to get back to my home," she said.

"Why?"

"Because my parents will miss me."

"I see. Thank you for takin' care of Ma."

She started to leave the miniature cemetery, but stopped and glared up at Ryder. "I didn't do it for you."

"I didn't think you did."

"I did it for your mother. She was almost my mother. I wanted her to be my mother. I love her as much as I love my own mother. My mother's a good woman. She loves me. But your mother's a good woman, too. And she also loves me, I think, even a bit more than my mother does. If not for you, she would've been my mother!"

Ryder was aware that Emily, sweet Emily, had found a kinship with his mother, one she didn't have with her own mother. Emily's mother, Martha Walker, was more of a cool and private person. She loved her husband, two sons, and daughter as much as she could. But she couldn't be friends with them, not even with her husband. The relationships were always husband-wife, mother-son, or mother-daughter. Deeper and closer relationships eluded Martha's abilities. And in the case of her daughter, crushed her heart until she got to know Rowena Mann.

Rowena was warm, while Martha was cold. Rowena laughed, while Martha never laughed. Rowena was artistic, painting and singing and making up songs and stories. Martha was good at cooking, good at sowing, could read and write and knew the Bible. But Martha knew little else.

To Rowena, cooking and sowing were arts. She read and studied and understood the Bible, but she read other books, including poetry. And when Ryder was very little, his mother was his best friend, telling him stories and making even the most mundane chores adventures.

When Ryder's and Emily's love had reached for marriage, Rowena's heart had glowed like the sun. She was all smiles and laughter and song.

Then, war with Spain broke out. And when the day of their wedding came, when Emily and Ryder, best friends always, lovers forever, were to be married, Ryder left his parents a note saying he had gone to see what war was like.

Emily was left at the altar, alone, embarrassed, ashamed. Heartbroken and abandoned. And the dream that Emily had dreamed, the same dream Rowena had dreamed, was shattered.

"I don't know what to say."

"There's nothing to say! You left me. You left me alone, with a child on the way. Laughed at, jeered at, treated like a slut. Men came after me like I was common dirt. Some tried to have their way with me. And Bennett, what a good brother. At sixteen, he killed his first man. This filthy giant who wanted his way with me, even though I was six months with child.

"Sixteen! He defended me because you weren't there. Now he's a killer, like you. He let the town know what would happen if anyone harmed me, if anyone spoke poorly of me. And he let everyone know that it was your fault.

"Oh, why couldn't you have stayed? Did the war need one more man to fight it? I needed you more than Teddy Roosevelt did. Couldn't you have seen that?"

Ryder said nothing. She was right. Just as she had been three years before, when he returned home.

"And you still have nothing to say?" she spat at him. "The big law man? The killer. The coward. It's easier for you to kill people than it is to stand by your woman at the altar! Maybe Hannah would've lived if you had stayed.

"But you didn't stay. You never held her in your arms. You never kissed her, never smiled at her, never saw her smile! You never felt her hold onto one of your fingers. You never heard her laugh. You never comforted her when she cried. All because war was a grander adventure than being a father and a husband.

"I have no love for you anymore. All I feel for you is contempt. But, I still love your mother. And I pray to Holy God that she doesn't end up hating you as I hate you."

All Ryder could do was look down at the ground. He still loved her. Yet there was no future there. Only loneliness and shame.

"Still nothing to say?"

Ryder carefully stepped around her. He entered the family plot. He stared at the carved pine plank at the head of the grave. RILEY.

"Is this all there is?" he asked.

"What did you expect? He's only been..." her voice caught. "He's only been in the ground a couple of days. Your father has ordered a granite stone from Denver. It will take a few weeks. It will say more. But not enough. It won't say how sweet your brother was to me. How he kept hoping you would return and things would change between us. How he hoped I would become his sister.

"When he was eleven, he told me he wished he could have been old enough to marry me. To keep me from being shamed. To keep my heart from breaking."

"He was a good kid."

"He was a better man than you'll ever be." She turned and started down the ridge, along the path that led to the barnyard and the ranch house.

He watched her go.

But she stopped. She stomped her way back up to him. "I want to show you something!"

She shoved her way past him, to a small corner where a large oak tree stood just outside. There, shaded from the late October sun by the oak, was a small granite marker.

"That's your daughter," Emily exclaimed, her voice choked with emotion. "You never stayed long enough last time to say hello to her. Spend a little time with her. Maybe someone in Heaven will tell her that you're her father. You'll never know her other than what you see of that stone. May you always remember that. That you could have been her father. That you could have had a child that loved you."

"I know."

"You know nothing!"

"I know what I could have been. Riley brought me up here before I left last time. He told me about her, about Hannah. I wish I could have known her."

Tears of rage filled her eyes. "He was more of a man than you'll ever be."

"I know that, too."

This time, Emily did leave.

Ryder made his way over to the little marker. HANNAH WALKER MANN.

He didn't know what to feel, other than regret.

After a moment, he made his way over to Riley's grave.

Ryder knew how to be a lawman. He never knew how to be a brother.

Nor did he know how to solve his brother's slaying, if there was even a way to solve it. But though he had failed his brother in life, he wouldn't fail him in death. He would find out the truth, whatever it was.

Standing straight, he put his hat back on. He looked down at his family's ranch, at the house, at the barnyard.

He rode No Name back to town.

# CHAPTER TWENTY-FIVE

WHEN HE RETURNED TO town, it was late. Dismounting, he walked No Name back to the stable where he unsaddled her, brushed her down, watered her, petted her, gave her the carrot he carried and a handful of oats from a nearby bucket, and tied her into her pen. Then he walked back to the Guzmans' Hotel. With what had happened to Riley, he had no idea of the town folks' regards toward him or his family, though they had found it easy to hang his brother.

At the hotel, he found the front door locked, so he went around back door, which was also locked. However, the kitchen was lit. He knocked and, after a moment, the door's window shade was pulled back. Merced Guzman looked out. Smiling, he opened the door.

"Did we not give you a key to the front door?"

"No, sir."

"I am sorry. I will get you one. Come on in. Have you eaten anything? Dolores was just fixing fajitas with refried beans. You may have some."

Ryder scraped his boots on the metal scraper by the door, stomped twice to loosen any remaining dirt, and entered the kitchen. He smelled onions, peppers, and beef frying. He also smelled corn tortillas.

"I don't wish to be a bother," he said.

"No bother," Merced replied.

"You are family, Ryder," Dolores exclaimed, from over by the stove. "Merced, set a place for him. Would you like some beer or something stronger?"

"Water, if you don't mind."

Merced set another plate, along with a cloth napkin and some utensils, on the kitchen table.

"Just water?" Dolores replied. "We have good beer."

"It's been a long day. I just want to eat and sleep. Thank-you, though."

"Well, then, water, and a beer chaser, perhaps?" Dolores said.

Surrendering, Ryder nodded.

Merced pulled up another chair. "Sit. Rest yourself."

Ryder sat down.

Dolores brought over a frying pan and scooped a generous portion of fajitas onto his plate. She took a more modest amount for herself and then also gave her husband a generous serving.

"Don't you want more?" Ryder asked her.

She laughed. "More has led to the body I now have. Less might make me look more like the woman I was when I married Merced."

"You are the woman I married," Merced replied.

"Shameless. But thank you."

Merced remained standing when his wife walked away. Ryder glanced at him and quietly cursed himself. He stood.

"Forgive my manners," Ryder said.

"You are just like my boys. They never stood for me, either," Dolores said.

"Ernesto always stood," Merced said.

"Only after you reminded him," Dolores countered.

"He always stood. So did the others."

"Only after you swatted their backsides."

"They needed to learn respect. But Ernesto understood it."

"So I remember," Dolores replied.

As Dolores moved toward her chair, Ryder stepped over to pull it back for her. But Merced placed a gentle hand on his shoulder, so Ryder moved back and let Merced attend to his wife.

After they had sat down, Dolores smiled at Ryder and said, "Merced shows his love for me through his kindness and respect."

"And with flowers," Merced said.

"Si, with flowers," Dolores replied. "He always has beautiful flowers on my bedside table, morning and evening. He grows them out back, beyond the oaks."

Ryder smiled.

"It is nice to see your smile, Ryder," Dolores said. "I see the clothes fit. Good, no?"

"Good, yes," Ryder replied.

"Why didn't you wear one of the lovelier shirts?" she asked.

"I have no one to wear them for," he said.

"Not even Emily?"

"Especially not Emily."

"Have you spoken to her since you came home?"

Ryder nodded.

"When?"

"Dolores, you are being rude," Merced suggested.

"I spoke with her last night and again today," Ryder said.

"Where?"

"Last night, at the ranch. At the house. The same today, at the family cemetery."

"No hope?" Merced asked.

"None."

"Ai-yeee. Women hate forever."

"Including me?" Dolores asked.

Merced smiled. "Never, mi corazon."

# CHAPTER TWENTY-SIX

THE NEXT MORNING, RYDER began his investigation. The night before, Merced and Dolores agreed that he should start by either talking to Doc Welsh, who had examined Vernon Gleason's body or Sheriff Carlson, who had been forced to lock Riley up. He decided he'd talk to the sheriff first.

He was up early. He dressed, putting on the purple shirt Dolores had given him. She said it was a strong color and would give him a strong appearance, even while presenting a less aggressive demeanor.

He also made certain he had his pistol with him. Brennan was a tough town, and after Merced startled him in the bath yesterday, he didn't want to take the chance of meeting someone who wished him harm without his pistol handy.

However, since there was a chill in the late October air, he wore his long tan coat.

Descending the stairs as quietly as possible, the key Merced had given him safely tucked away in his shirt pocket, he exited the hotel. His first goal was the cafe where his father had taken him for breakfast the day before.

As he walked the boardwalk, he noticed the sun still stood low behind the buildings. The air was more than crisp, it was cold. The sky looked frosted, but cloudless. No rain or snow today.

Nary a person walked the streets.

Nearing the café, he was pleased to see that it was open. As he opened the door to go in, three young men pushed their way out, laughing and jostling one another. All three wore long coats similar to Ryder's.

Ryder stepped aside to let them pass.

One of the young men, younger than Ryder, stopped and turned toward him. "Don't I know ya?"

"Nope." Ryder noticed his eyes were cold and mean.

"Yer wrong," the young man said.

"Careful, Tony, he looks tough," said a second young man. He and the third kept back while their friend, Tony, talked to Ryder. They blocked the café's doors, keeping anyone from entering or exiting.

"Nope."

"But I know ya!"

Ryder shook his head and started to push past him.

The young man thrust out his right arm, blocking the way. "Where ya think yer goin'?"

"To breakfast."

When Tony had thrust him arm out to block Ryder, Ryder noticed the short-barreled pistol he carried as his long coat opened up. Ryder thought about reaching out and grabbing Tony's pistol, but he knew it would make the young man angry and he didn't feel like starting any trouble this early in the day, so he kept his hands to himself.

However, Tony stepped close to Ryder, just inches from him. When he spoke, spittle spewed onto Ryder's face. "Yer that low life that failed to save his baby brother. Another loser in a family of losers. How can ya claim to call yerselves 'Man' when yer not even man enough to fight for yer own? Yer old man wouldn't fight. Yer brother shot another man in the back. Yer probably a back shooter, too."

"When I have to be," Ryder said.

"Listen to that, Tony, he admits to it, said it right to yer face," the third man said. He was large and rough looking.

Tony lowered his voice to a whisper, which only Ryder could hear. "Ya an' me are a lot more alike than ya think. We're both renegades an' killers. Nobody wants us an' nobody loves us. Who's gonna miss us when we're dead? We're unwanted, ya an' me. No one loves me. Who's gonna love ya?"

"My pa loves me," Ryder whispered back. "I don't know who's gonna love you an' I don't care."

Tony dropped his arm and with both hands swept his coat's lapels back, revealing two pistols on either hip, the handles reversed. "I'll give ya a chance to clear away yer coat. Then I'm gonna kill ya!"

"Get him, Tony," said the second man.

"Kill 'im," said the third.

"You gonna kill me because my pa loves me?" Ryder whispered.

In a loud voice, Tony said, "I'm gonna kill ya cause yer a law dog an' a liar."

"I don't have to out-draw you. You'll be down before you can clear leather," Ryder said.

Tony laughed. "Listen to him, boys. Dead man talkin'. Thinks he's faster'n me when what he's really doin' is probably pissing his pants right now!"

"You're too close," Ryder replied. "Before you can get your guns out, I'll have driven my fist into your chest. Your wind will leave you, maybe even your life."

Tony moved for his pistols.

Ryder punched him in the chest. Tony's face twisted in pain and he stumbled backward, his hands dropping away. His friends caught him before he fell.

Gasping for air, Tony hissed, "I'm gonna kill ya!"

"Not taday ya ain't, little brother," a voice said from down the boardwalk. Deputy Rixx stepped over. "He got ya good. Now even an old blind grandma could cut ya down."

"We can cut him down," said the third man.

"No ya won't," said Rixx. "That'd be murder. Ya don't even know if he's packin'. An' his coat's buttoned up. Even if he's packin', ya ain't got no right to kill 'im for hittin' my little brother."

"Ya wouldn't throw us in jail for that," the second man said.

"I would. I may not like Mister Mann here anymore'n ya, but I take being a deputy seriously. It could only end for ya in two ways, jail for murder, or gunned down for stupidity."

"You wouldn't do that to us. We're Tony's friends."

"I'd do it, all right."

"Tony wouldn't let ya."

"I would," Tony gasped. "He's my brother. I wouldn't hurt him anymore'n he'd hurt me."

"That's right, little brother. Button up yer coat, ya ain't killin' anybody taday."

Standing, swaying just a little, Tony stared at Ryder. "This ain't over between us yet. Yer a dead man."

"Everybody keeps sayin' that to me," Ryder said.

"I mean it."

"Not in this town ya ain't, Tony," Rixx said. "I ain't stringin' ya up fer murder."

Tony muttered something no one could hear and started to walk away. But he spun around, aiming a left hook at Ryder. Ryder moved into the punch, blocking it. Planting both hands on the gunslinger's chest, Ryder shoved him backwards. Tony stumbled off the boardwalk, falling into the dusty street. His hands darted for his guns, but his coat was in the way.

"Tony!" a stern voice bellowed.

Tony looked up. Sheriff Carlson stood in front of him.

"I can kill both ya an' him before ya could draw!"

"I doubt it," Carlson said. "For one thing, I wore a short jacket today rather than a long coat. For another, I'm not afraid of you an' I'll kill you before you can get your coat open."

"Jeff wouldn't let yew," Tony said.

"I would," Deputy Rixx said. "Yer my brother, but he's mah boss."

"Get out of here, Tony," the sheriff said.

Tony's friends rushed to help him up. He shoved them away and got up on his own. "This ain't the last of it!" Tony growled.

"It is for today, Tony," Carlson said.

"Jeff?" Tony whined.

"Ya heard him," Deputy Rixx said.

Tony, wiping dust from himself, stomped off.

"One of these days, he's gonna get me," Carlson said.

"He is," Rixx replied. "He's gettin' faster every day."

"I know."

Ryder watched the gunslinger go.

Sheriff Carlson turned to him. "What're you here for?"

"Breakfast. With you, maybe."

"Why?"

"To talk about my brother."

"I knew you'd get around to it, sooner or later. Seems like its sooner."

"It is."

"Rixx?"

"Sheriff?"

"Keep an eye on Tony. I don't want no murders today."

"I will, sheriff. Can I get somethin' to eat first?"

"Somethin' you can take with you."

"Yep."

Ryder and Sheriff Carlson kept an eye on Tony and his companions while Deputy Rixx entered the restaurant and ordered food to go. A few minutes later, Rixx emerged from the café. He had a handful of sausage and a bagful of goodies.

"Which way?" Rixx asked.

"They turned left before the saloon. Make sure they don't get into trouble."

"Will do, sheriff."

As Rixx left, Carlson said to Ryder, "I'll buy you breakfast. Just this once. An' I'll tell you whatever I can about your brother. I'm sorry what happened to him."

Ryder said nothing.

"You handled yourself well."

Ignoring him, Ryder entered the café. Carlson followed him inside.

They found a table in a corner, away from the other guests. A different waitress, not Becky Jarrett, to Ryder's disappointment, brought them plates and flatware, took their orders, and left. She was back moments later with coffee. Then she was gone again.

Ryder was uneasy. He wanted to know what had happened to his brother, but his emotions were all jumbled. He wanted to demand that the sheriff apologize for hanging his brother. He wanted to hit him. He almost wanted to kill him. He hated the man and wished he could take revenge for his brother's death.

Yet, at the same time, he was ashamed he hadn't arrived in time to save his brother, just as he was ashamed at running off to war rather than marrying Emily. He was even more ashamed at running away again rather than facing his family's wrath after returning from the war.

The flood of emotions overwhelmed Ryder.

"I can see how hard this is for you, Ryder. It would be hard for me, too. What with the history you have around here an' with your brother's death. I can't say I'm happy with the part I played. However, I had a job to do and I did it."

"And how good of a job did you do?"

"I understand the anger you feel. I sent out searchers for Riley. We didn't know when we began looking for him, what he had done. Your parents were afraid that he was hurt somewhere. All through the day an' night, while we looked for him we were afraid he had been captured or killed by whoever had killed Vernon Gleason. We had no idea he was responsible."

"An' how did you know he was responsible?" Ryder demanded. "Were there witnesses?"

"None that we know of."

"Did you look for any?"

"Of course we did. But no one came forward."

"Then how could you know it was him?"

"He told us he did it."

"He told you?" Ryder exclaimed. "Who found him?"

"Rixx did."

"Where?"

"Out by The Island."

"What was he doin' out there?"

"He'd spent the night out there. When Rixx found him he was half crazy from exhaustion and fear. Rixx said when Riley talked his voice was dry and harsh, worn out like an old man's voice."

"Did Rixx give him water?"

"Of course. But he found that Riley couldn't hold it down. He was too parched to drink much so Rixx had him sip some an' swallow it. Then he had him swish some around in his mouth an' let it trickle down his throat."

"Did he talk to him like he was the killer?" Ryder growled.

"He arrived that way. Rixx said that for twenty miles Riley bawled about shooting Gleason in the back. Rixx couldn't take a chance with him getting away or attacking him from behind."

"Then how'd they get back?"

"Rixx only had the one horse. It was tired out, so Rixx let the boy ride while he walked. After a few miles, Rixx mounted up. By then Riley had told him what he had done an' why an' Rixx had tied the boy's hands behind his back so he couldn't choke him while they rode."

"What made Rixx think my little brother would do that?"

"Because he was plain loco, Ryder. Rixx said he was babbling an' bawling for God to kill him for the horrible thing he'd just done. He bawled how he had shamed his family an' how could his brother, The Hero, ever respect him after this. After runnin' all the previous day, he was so exhausted he could hardly walk."

Ryder continued glaring at the sheriff.

"At some point, Riley fell off the horse. He had fallen asleep an' even after the fall, he seemed too tired to get back on. So Rixx lifted him up an' tied him to the saddle. He climbed up after him.

"Their progress was so slow that they didn't get in until after dark. Your parents had to wait two whole days before they knew he was safe."

"Did he say why he killed Gleason?" Ryder asked.

"He said he was shooting at a coyote. Said he might've nicked it. But we didn't find any dried blood around."

"How'd you know where to look?"

"We found your granddad's Henry repeater. Rixx an' I combed the area. We only found one shell casing."

"There could have been two casings, maybe more?"

"Could've been. But we never found any sign of a coyote. All we found was the casing an' some blood down in the road where the forty-four slug tore into Gleason's back."

"Maybe he was shot before then?"

"Maybe. But we backtracked the buggy's trail all the way to Gleason's ranch. His wife said the kids had left earlier an' that Vernon had left afterward. We didn't find any indications of anyone attacking him there.

"She said she wasn't feeling too good that day, but she went out to say goodbye. She also said she woulda heard a gunshot if somebody had been shootin' at him."

"When did you see her?"

"An hour or so after Gleason's horse pulled the buggy into town."

"So," Ryder began, his voice hoarse with emotion, "you organized a search for Riley an' then you had time to investigate Gleason's murder?"

"No. I got the posse out right away. Rixx took care of the body while I went out to backtrack the road. I ran into your parents out scoutin' for Riley a few hours later."

"An' when an' where did you find the blood?"

The sheriff leaned forward. He took a sip of his coffee, then frowned. It was already cold. He waved the waitress over and had her refresh his coffee and asked about their breakfast.

The waitress told him it would be out soon.

Turning back to Ryder, he asked, "What was your question again?"

Ryder frowned at him. "Where did you find the blood?"

"Couple miles from town. About where the road dips down between the bluffs on either side. It was just below where we found the Henry an' the shell casing, though I didn't know that at the time because I wasn't lookin' for your family's Henry then. It wasn't until Riley told us about where he'd been that Rixx an' I went out an' found the rifle and the casin'."

"When was that?"

"Two days later."

"An' you're sure he did it? Not someone else?"

"He admitted to it."

"Couldn't the blood have been from the coyote?"

"Could be. But the way the wound was, it looked like the slug had come in from an angle. The wound was all torn open an' Gleason's buggy was covered in blood. There was plenty of fresh blood covering the ground when I went by less than an hour later."

"An' you didn't do any other investigatin' that day?"

"We were out lookin' for your brother. We didn't know he was Gleason's killer. We thought he might've been captured by the killer. Your mother was frantic. I organized a posse an' we searched day an' night for him. Most of us returned after dark, but Rixx kept lookin'. That boy was outta water, all dried up, an' without food or strength when Rixx found him. If Rixx hadn't found him, he couldna died out there."

Ryder said nothing.

The food arrived. Two plates with steaks, with two sunny side up eggs each, boiled spinach, and taters.

After the waitress left, Sheriff Carlson said, "Maybe he should've died out there. Hangin's a dirty way to die."

Ryder stood. He looked at his food. He fished in his pocket for some money and tossed a couple of coins on the table. "Thanks for breakfast. I've lost my appetite."

"You needn't go. I told you I'd buy you breakfast."

"Another time, sheriff," Ryder said.

He left.

# CHAPTER TWENTY-SEVEN

OUTSIDE THE CAFÉ, RYDER struggled with his emotions. Resentment and regret ripped him apart. How could his brother be a killer, at thirteen? And why, why had he hesitated to come back? His parents needed him. His brother needed him. But, like a coward, he stayed away.

The fact that he hadn't known of his brother's peril when he received the telegram from his mother seemed irrelevant. He should've come immediately. After all, when had his mother made such a request to him, for any reason, ever?

Then why had he resisted coming? Because the shame he felt overwhelmed him. All he wanted to do the rest of his life was hide from it, leave it far behind.

It was Bob who forced him to come back. He had wanted to stay away. Yet here he was and now he had to deal with the shame, the regret, the self-contempt. More, he had to deal with the knowledge that his little brother was dead, at the hands of not just one person or a few people, but an entire town, and a judge who wanted to make an example of him.

Anger burned through him. He knew his father wouldn't lie to him about what happened, so since the sheriff's tale was different, he must be lying. But in his short career as an Arizona Ranger, he had discovered that no one truly had the same opinion about events. The task before him hadn't changed. He had to gain as much information as he could, listen to as many different accounts as he could, and then figure out as nearly as possible what the actual truth was.

But Riley was dead, hanged as a murderer. How could that be? How could Riley have been guilty? And how could a whole town full of supposedly decent and honorable people let this happen?

Of course, from his view point they weren't decent or honorable. They had shown him a lack of compassion when he came back, having fought for his country. To him, they were as guilty as he was, as dirty, as dishonorable.

However, rage wouldn't help him find out the truth about Riley's hanging. Taking a deep breath, he calmed himself down. He needed all his wits to solve this puzzle.

Ryder started down the boardwalk. Walking helped him think.

Sheriff Carlson had said they found a lot of blood near where Riley had fired their grandfather's repeating rifle. That they had found the rifle there a couple of days later, but found only one shell casing. But Riley had stated that he had been shooting at a coyote. His claim was that he'd nicked it and as it bounded away, he shot a second time. Unlike pistols, repeating rifles ejected spent shell casings. Where was that second casing?

Had somebody removed it? Had either the sheriff or his deputy stuffed it in a pocket, to make it look like Riley was lying about the coyote, suggesting he had only fired one shot?

But the sheriff had said Riley had claimed to have fired twice. And why had there been so much blood on the road, if Riley had shot Gleason in the back? Even as nasty as rifle wounds were, they seldom bled that much. In fact, if Gleason hadn't died right away, if he had continued to bleed, that was the only way there could have been so much at the scene. Gleason would have had to remain there for a bit before urging his horse into town. And if the blood wasn't Gleason's, if his horse hadn't bolted forward, dragging the buggy all the way into town, then the excess blood had another source. Which could have been the mortally wounded coyote. Yet they had found neither a coyote, nor it's remains.

Either somebody was lying here, or Gleason had been shot sooner. But where, and by whom?

There were too many unanswered questions for Ryder to accept the story Sheriff Carlson had told him. Somebody was either confused or lying about the facts. Someone else must know more.

Where to begin, or more correctly, continue, was what rattled around inside Ryder's head. He suddenly wondered if Riley had had any visitors while in jail. Well, his parents were obvious visitors. And retired Judge McHugh had defended him. He must have visited, too. And probably Pastor Jarrett. Dell Jarrett was a friend of the family, as well as their pastor. He would've been among the first to visit, to help Riley calm down, to comfort him.

He now knew of at least two more people to talk to.

Ryder changed directions, cutting across the street. He didn't know where Judge McHugh's office was, or if he even had one. But he knew where Dell's church was. And he knew the Jarretts had a house behind the church.

For the first time in years, Ryder was off to church again. Not for redemption, nor salvation, but for enlightenment.

Dell Jarrett's church was like so many fronteir churches Ryder had seen, designed for economy more than beauty. It was a long and narrow building, with a high roof making for a high ceiling inside. In the summer, while it broiled outside, the high ceiling collected the heat, making the interior more tolerable. In the winter, its various woodstoves kept the church toasty.

Additionally, the tall ceiling allowed for tall windows. These windows, along the long walls, were covered with screens which kept the flies and mosquitos out yet allowed breezes to blow crosswise through the church. When opened in the warmer months, a slight cross breeze flowed through the church.

The church was designed for two hundred people, though it rarely held more than one hundred, and usually only fifty or sixty souls. By frontier standards, it was a large congregation.

In the winter, and sometimes in the summer, dances and parties were held within the church. The many pews could be pushed against the walls, creating a large space for fancy stepping and twirling, for church bazaars, for games, for anything and everything that brought the congregation together socially and spiritually.

Two steps climbed to the altar in the front, where a painting of Christ's crucifixion covered the wall. On one side stood Pastor Jarrett's podium. He'd been pastor of the church for three decades and everyone seemed more or less pleased with his sermons. Some said he was too soft on sinners and some said he was too hard on the righteous, but all agreed he was an exceptionally kind and strong man. A fair man, filled with love for his congregation and for visitors alike. He tried not to judge others, rarely scolding or condemning anyone.

His church and congregation weren't Baptist, or Lutheran, Methodist, Congregationalist, nor any other denomination. In fact, it was the typical frontier church, with pastor and congregation attached to no particular Christian sect, just following the teachings of the gospels as best they could.

However, Pastor Jarrett was one thing that most frontier preachers were not, he was a seminary school graduate. He had studied the Bible and learned its lessons from some of the best religious leaders of the day. He was a legitimate pastor, with a diploma to prove it.

After walking several blocks, Ryder found Jarrett's church where he remembered it being. It stood on the far side of town, on the road leading out to the Gleason and Mann ranches, as well as a dozen or more others, all members of Jarrett's congregation.

It had taken Ryder almost fifteen minutes to reach the church. The front door was unlocked. In fact, it was never locked. Ryder went inside. Except for the light shining through the windows, it was dark inside.

So Ryder went back outside and started walking around the church. Once he was in the back, he knocked on the door leading to the pastor's office, behind the altar. He twisted the door knob. It was locked.

And why not? It led to Jarrett's private study, where he worked on sermons and spent much of the day in prayer and study.

Ryder turned and started toward Jarrett's house.

"Excuse me, son," a voice said from above. "I'll be down as soon as I can. Sooner, if you be a mind to hold the ladder while I descend."

Ryder turned around and glanced upward. Jarrett knelt on the roof of the church.

Walking around to the other side of the church, Ryder saw a tall ladder resting against the side of the almost as tall church. Grasping the ladder with both hands, he placed a foot on the bottom rung and leaned into it.

"Thanks, son," Pastor Jarrett said. "Mind your head."

A dangling rope lowered a bucket of nails, a claw hammer resting atop them, down from above. After the bucket clattered to the ground, another bucket filled with broken wooden shingles was lowered down beside the first bucket.

Then the ladder jiggled.

Ryder looked up and saw Jarrett carefully climb onto the ladder far above. Then, in what seemed like an eternity of ladder wiggling and jiggling, the pastor made his slow, careful way to the ground.

Safely down, the pastor bent over to stretch his back out, then mopped his face with a dusty handkerchief. After a moment, he waved Ryder away from the ladder. He walked a few steps while Ryder trailed behind him.

Finally, Pastor Jarrett stopped and turned around. "What can I do for you, son?"

"I wonder if I might have a word with you, sir," Ryder said.

Jarrett's eyes widened and his mouth opened, but no sound came out. With two steps, he closed with Ryder. Big arms, arms impossibly strong for such an old man, wrapped around Ryder's shoulders. He found himself pulled into Jarrett's hug.

"Ryder. Ryder. Oh, God, full of mercy and kindness, thank-you, thank-you. Thank-you for bringing Ryder home and safe and to your house. Ryder, I am so glad that you've at last come home!"

# CHAPTER TWENTY-EIGHT

P ASTOR JARRETT LET GO of Ryder. Stepping back, he said,
"Let me look at you, Ryder. You look as big and strong
and healthy as ever. But there's age in your face, age a
man as young as you should never know."

Ryder nodded.

"We make many mistakes when we're selfish, when we're
afraid. Those mistakes bring us such sorrow, such pain."

"How can you talk about sorrow, pastor? I ran out on
Emily. I was too cowardly to return after the last time an'
now my brother's dead, before he even had a chance to
be a man. An' he paid for a crime I doubt he committed.
How can you imagine you know about sorrow?"

"The Bible teaches us about regret and sorrow. Consider
all who suffered for their sins. There was Jacob, who stole
his older brother's birthright. Then came his son, Joseph,
whose brothers sold him into slavery, because they were
jealous of him. All suffered for their sins.

"God didn't punish them, they punished themselves,
with guilt and regret. Just as I suspect you're doing,
too. You've condemning yourself, when you should be
forgiving yourself."

"How can you know what I'm feelin'?" Ryder retorted.

"Because I'm a man, too. And it's how I'd feel if I were you. Years ago, you ran away from here after I tried to console you. You ran because you felt guilty. And you ran because you didn't want to be comforted, but only to forget. But there's no real forgetting until you forgive yourself. You were young and you made mistakes. But everyone makes mistakes when they're young."

"You might be a man, pastor, an' you might know sufferin' from the Bible, but until you've lived it, you don't know nothin' about it. When you've lived it close up, then you can lecture me on it!"

"But I do know it, Ryder, just as I know you know it."

"An' how's that?" Ryder demanded, his face reddening. "Just because you were goin' to marry Emily an' me? Just because you saw how the town treated me after the war?"

"Not because of any of those reasons. I know it because sixteen years ago, my wife was murdered."

"What?" Ryder asked, stunned. "How?"

"Some drunken men broke into our house one night, while I was out comforting the Larkins' after their son died of injuries from being gored by a steer. But you probably don't remember that. You would have been nine then. Some things, God bless them for their innocence, escape children."

Ryder was afraid to ask what happened next. He knew what the violent men in the territories were like. How they thought they could do anything they wanted, hurt anyone they fancied. He had caught quite a few such men in his brief time as a lawman. Every criminal he caught felt justified in what he had done. And every single one had paid the final price for wanton aggression.

"Lucy, that was my wife's name. Lucy put Rebecca out the window and told her to run to the neighbors for help. Which were the Walkers, I believe. When they arrived, Lucy was dead. She lay on the floor in a pool of blood. The men had shot her and then run off with some silverware we had. The town was searched and then the countryside. A posse, led by the sheriff, then Bill Waller, found them outside of town a few miles. They bragged about how this ghostlike figure came out of the darkness, a broomstick in its hand. Two of them bolted out the door and the other two shot at it. Then they grabbed the silverware and ran. They forgot their horses and just ran for their camp, about two miles away."

"They didn't hurt your wife?" So many attacks on women started with rape and ended with murder.

"No."

Ryder was somewhat relieved. "What happened?"

"There was a trial. They were hanged."

"It seems like the only penalty this town knows."

"It's not always like that," Jarrett said.

"How would I know? They hung a thirteen-year-old boy for an accident."

"Those men who killed my wife were proud of what they did. And only showed remorse when they knew it was a pastor's wife they had killed and not some old ghost."

"Did you visit them in jail?"

"No. We have another church in town, if you remember. Father Timothy from the Catholic Church gave them last rites, bless his soul."

"What happened afterward?"

"I went to a dark place afterward. So dark, I almost didn't recognize Rebecca. But I had a little girl to care for, and a congregation to attend to. One Sunday, as I gave a sermon, as I just flipped through the pages, not really interested in being a pastor any more, not even interested in life, I came across our Lord on the cross. And I read these words, 'Father, forgive them, for they know not what they do.' And that's when I started thinking about forgiveness and moving on."

"How long did that take?"

Jarrett rubbed his forehead with a sleeve. "Let's go inside. Rebecca's home and she can give us some tea or coffee. Have you eaten anything yet?"

"No."

"Well, then, come on. Let's get you fed." Jarrett started toward his house.

As they walked, Ryder said, "You haven't answered my question."

"There's a saying about the truth being a two-edged sword."

"How does that relate to my question?"

"Repentance doesn't end with just forgiving others. You have to forgive yourself, too."

"I don't understand."

"I blamed myself for not being there. A husband's supposed to care for and defend his wife. And I was out tending to others rather than tending to my family."

"Didn't you think it was God's will that your wife died? That my brother died?" Ryder demanded.

"God doesn't work that way."

Ryder stopped and stared at Jarrett. "Every preacher I've ever met says that God punishes you for your sins. Often they tell you that the innocent in your life are punished for what you've done. Even you've told me that."

"I never told you that. And I never read anything from the Bible that claims God will kill your loved ones for your sins."

"What about David an' Bathsheba's illegitimate baby? It died. Wasn't that to punish David for murdering Bathsheba's husband while sleeping with her, a married woman?"

Jarrett smiled. "I'm glad to know that you were listening to some of my sermons."

"But God punished him."

"He did. But the Prophet Samuel told David that he and Bathsheba would have more babies. Solomon was their son."

"I forgot that. Why did God give him more children?"
"Because God loved David."

"I don't understand."

"That's because the Jews felt everyone needed to be punished. Their enemies needed punishing. Sinners needed punishing. Heroes and kings needed punishing. Even prophets needed punishing. They not only thought of God as a vengeful god, but wanted him to be so. Fear the Lord, for the Lord will punish you if you don't. But then Jesus came along and challenged all that. He preached God's love and forgiveness. Everything we know about forgiveness comes from the New Testament. In the Gospel of John it says, 'The Law came by Moses, but grace and truth came by Jesus Christ.' God doesn't punish us for others' sins."

"Then how come my brother's dead?"

"That's the sin of others."

"And mine."

"No. Others."

"What others?"

"The ones that condemned your brother. They were too quick to judge, too quick to send a boy to the gallows."

"Do you know that for sure?"

"I do," Jarrett replied.

"Then they're the guilty ones."

"Not necessarily," Jarrett said. "They voted as they saw fit, from the evidence they had. But there was so little evidence. It was your brother who convinced them he was guilty."

"Why would he do that?"

"Because he felt responsible. He felt guilty and felt he needed to be punished for murdering Vernon Gleason. He was just like you, believing in guilt instead reasoning things out. He should have looked for the truth, rather than condemn himself."

"How?"

"On the witness stand, in front of the judge and jury, he proclaimed that he was guilty. That he wanted to kill someone or something to prove his manhood and he shot at a coyote when he should have waited until he crossed the road. He felt guilty for widowing Mrs. Gleason and taking her children's father away from them and claimed, no, demanded that he be punished for it. And the jury was happy to oblige him."

Ryder bowed his head. He whispered, "Riley, you shouldn't have done that."

"Sometimes, Ryder, I think the greatest sin is guilt. It puts everyone in hell."

"Aren't we there already?"

Jarrett nodded. "Often, I think that the only Hell isn't deep in the Earth, but here where we live. We all suffer so much before death. That suffering is the only true hell."

"Seems so."

They reached the house.

Jarrett gently grasped Ryder's arm. "Come on, son, have breakfast with me. With Rebecca and me. And I'll try to tell you everything else that I know about your brother's time in jail, little that I know, though."

"I came here today for information," Ryder said. "I doubted you when I should have trusted you. I didn't come for salvation or repentance."

"Well, I hope you found some salvation and redemption, son. We all need as much of it was we can get."

They went inside.

# CHAPTER TWENTY-NINE

HERE WAS A HAT rack beside the door and Ryder put his hat there.

It was a typical house, with a living room in front, a woodstove off to one side. On the far side of the room a hallway led deep into the house. There were two closed doors, one on either side of the hall, probably bedrooms, Ryder thought.

Off to the right, past the closed doors, was a bathing room, it's door open. As Ryder followed Jarrett down the hallway, he glanced inside. A claw tub dominated the room. There was also a dresser with three large drawers. Sitting on top of the dresser, in front of a large mirror, was a white washing bowl, with a large white pitcher next to it. There was also a tall chair and some sort of large cabinet, its doors closed.

Opposite the bathing room was a small dining room. In the back was the kitchen, with a large wood-burning stove. Across from the stove was an open pantry. Beside it was a large, metal icebox.

As Jarrett led Ryder into the kitchen, he saw behind it a closed-in porch, with wire screens mounted to let the air in but keep the bugs out.

Jarrett called his daughter's name, but there wasn't any reply.

"She was here just a little while back," Jarrett said.

"Maybe she went to the outhouse."

"We don't have an outhouse. That's what the little room built into the bathroom is for. It's called a water closet."

"Does it store water?" Ryder asked.

"In fact, it does. There's a tank outside that we fill once a day. The water flows down pipes which lead to the toilet. When you pull a string, the water empties the toilet and the refuse flows through more pipes into a cesspool outside of town."

"Where do you think your daughter went?"

Jarrett shook his head. "She was just here before you came around the church. She told me the coffee was ready and that she had made a little cake. I was on the roof of the church and called out that I had one more shingle to replace and I'd be down. Then you arrived."

"She has to be close by."

"One would suppose so."

At that moment, down the hall, the door opened to the bedroom beside the bathroom. Becky Jarrett exited. Her hair was neat and tidy, combed back from her face and fluffed up a bit. She wore a bright violet and white plaid dress, which reached to her bright and shiny black shoes. A beautiful, big bow, a darker purple than her dress, bounced up and down as she walked down the hallway.

"Becky, for goodness sake, why are you all gussied up?" Jarrett asked.

"We have company, poppa. A young woman should always look her best when a man comes a-calling."

Jarrett turned to Ryder. He winked at him, who squirmed just a bit. Jarrett turned back to his daughter. "Is that what he's doing, darling daughter, coming a-courting?"

"Oh, Poppa, I never said he was coming courting. He's just visiting and a woman should be clean when company comes."

She motioned for the two men to leave the kitchen and enter the dining room. Then she stepped back so they could pass. Jarrett led the way, followed by Ryder. As he passed her, he noticed that she smelled of lavender.

Around the dining table, large enough to seat at least eight, stood three chairs. Becky had stretched across the table a light blue cloth adorned with yellow flowers. She had set fine pink plates in front of each chair. Dark blue napkins rested beside the plates, silver cake forks on top of each napkin. A small breakfast cake occupied a medium white plate, a silver serving spatula beside it. Pink cups on pink saucers stood in front of the plates.

A steaming coffee pot sat on a silver tray, a small pitcher of milk and a bowl of sugar guarding the pot.

"My goodness, Becky, is President Roosevelt coming for breakfast?" her father asked.

"Poppa, be polite. I'm just trying to make the meal special."

"Of course," Jarrett replied, a twinkle in his eye.

Becky glared at her father. When his face became contrite, she turned to Ryder. "Will cake and coffee do?"

"It'll be just fine, ma'am," Ryder said.

"Ma'am?" she said, ice in her voice.

Jarrett turned away, covering his mouth with a hand to hide his grin.

"I—I mean, ah, ah, Becky. Becky, right?" Ryder stuttered.

"Becky," she said, staring at him a moment. She turned away, like her father, to hide her smile.

Jarrett went over and sat down at the end of the table. Ryder approached his chair and stood beside it. His parents had taught him that good manners were good manners.

"Sit," Pastor Jarrett said. "You are our guest, Ryder. Sit."

"I'll stand, sir."

"As you wish," Pastor Jarrett said.

"Don't be mean, Poppa," Becky snapped.

"What? I'm not being mean."

"Suit yourself," she said. She poured the coffee into the cups, first for her father, then into Ryder's cup. Then she poured some into her own cup. "Milk and sugar?" she offered Ryder.

"I prefer it black," Ryder said.

Becky looked disappointed, but politely nodded. She turned to her father, her eyebrows raised.

"Milk and sugar, Becky, as usual," he replied. She mixed both into her father's cup. Then she did the same for herself.

Next, she served the cake, a large slice for her father, a much larger slice for Ryder, and a dainty slice for herself.

When she started to sit down, Ryder quickly stepped over and held her chair while she sat. Then he helped her scoot forward. Afterwards, Ryder sat himself down.

Ryder started to dig into the cake when he saw that Pastor Jarrett and Becky were unfolding their napkins and placing them in their laps. He followed their example.

While unfolding his napkin, he noticed them bowing their heads. How could he forget to give thanks for his food? He wasn't in a church, but wherever Pastor Jarrett was, it was a house of God. So Ryder bowed his head in silence.

"Dear Father," Pastor Jarrett began, "we thank thee for this wonderful day and this blessed moment and blessed food. And we thank thee for Ryder's return to us, in this time of trouble for his family. We thank thee for all thy blessings and for thy eternal guidance. Guide Ryder in his quest for the truth. And guide him home to you. Grace him with enlightenment and show him the way. Amen."

"Amen," Becky said.

"Amen," Ryder muttered.

"Let's eat," Jarrett said.

Ryder cut into his cake. He started to place it in his mouth, but then he put it down. He stared at Jarrett.

Becky noticed Ryder wasn't eating. Then she saw him looking at her father. "Oh, poppa, stop embarrassing him."

Jarrett looked up from his food. "What did I do?"

"You know, poppa."

Jarrett said to Ryder, "Have I offended you, my son?"

Ryder shook his head. "No one has blessed me for a long time. I've forgotten what a kindness it is. But I don't deserve it. I'm a sinner. I shouldn't even be sitting here with you."

"We're all sinners, son," Pastor Jarrett replied. "Every bit of anger, every selfish thought, every lust, fear, hateful thing we think or say or do, makes us sinners. But God is the loving father of us all. He forgives us and shows us the path to redemption."

"And what is redemption?" Ryder demanded. "Most people think of revenge rather than redemption. They think of hurting others. Those are the people I hunt down.

For every ten good men or women, there's at least one who believes in hurtin' or killin' others.

"An' how am I different than them? Look how I hurt Emily. I left her at the altar. I left her with child. An' for what, to run off to war, to kill men who didn't want to die anymore than I did. All that killin', what good did it do? An' now I'm too late to save my brother. I'm not a good man, just a selfish sinner."

"Oh, Ryder," Becky said, "there's good in you. I see it. I'm sure Emily sees it, too. She just can't get past her pride."

"Is it pride, or disgust?" he said, standing.

"Don't go," Becky pleaded.

"I've lost my appetite."

"Poppa, please stop him."

"I can't keep him if he doesn't want to stay."

"What good would it be to stay?" Ryder demanded. "Can you heal my sorrow? Can you release me from my guilt, my shame, the pain? The only thing I'm good for is hurtin' others."

"Is that what you want, Ryder, to give up?" Jarrett asked.

"What else is there? All I've learned since gettin' here is how much Emily hates me, how much my ma hates me, how much this town hates me."

"I don't hate you, Ryder," Becky said.

"I hate me. You should, too."

"So you're just gonna run away, without solving your brother's murder?" Jarrett said.

"What makes you think it was murder?" Ryder demanded.

"What make you think it wasn't?" Jarrett countered.

Ryder stared at Jarrett. He glanced at Becky. He saw the tears in her eyes, rolling down her cheeks. He had hurt her, too. Just like he hurt everyone else. What a jackass he was.

He sat back down. Again, he asked, "What makes you think it was murder?"

"Because I cannot believe that such a fine young man as Riley was, could have killed anyone."

"The jury felt differently."

"I knew him for all his life," Pastor Jarrett replied. "He was a good lad, a kind person, full of honor, love and respect."

"All good words, pastor. But nothin' that I don't already know about my brother. Yet I've seen brave men run in battle. I've seen good men murder for money or women. Everyone has that one moment when they behave badly an' suffer for it. Most become outlaws."

"Riley wasn't an outlaw."

"Then why'd they hang him?" Ryder paused and glanced at Becky's sad face. "Sorry, ma'am."

"I'm not a ma'am, I'm Becky."

"Yes, Miss Jarrett."

"Becky."

"Miss Becky."

"Stop being the lawman for a moment, Ryder. Just call me Becky."

"Becky."

"Thank you."

Ryder nodded toward her. She smiled. He turned back to Jarrett. "I've seen how men can change. I'm an expert on it. Look what I did to Emily."

"You were young," Pastor Jarrett replied.

"I was selfish."

"You were. But I think you went to war because you were afraid of being trapped in a marriage, your whole life written for you, without any kind of future for yourself."

"What makes you think that?"

"Every man and woman feels doubts about getting married. Many of them run away when the moment of truth comes upon them."

"Why didn't you run?"

"Because I trusted in God. And I'm glad I did. The greatest adventure isn't out there, it's right here at home, beside your wife, loving her, working beside her, sharing life's burdens together. And when children come, caring for them, being young again when they're little, letting go when they leave home, hoping you'll see them again. You squandered one chance, Ryder, but other chances are waiting for you. You just have to have the courage to take them."

"And what about Riley? He'll never have that chance, to fall in love, to marry, to have children. Why do I deserve a second chance when he'll never have one?" Ryder demanded.

"His second chance is you."

"I don't understand."

"You do. You know you do. You're his second chance. He ignored his chance to prove his innocence. Now you can do it for him."

"And what makes you think he was innocent?"

"What makes you think he wasn't?" Jarrett replied.

"Because he said he wanted to kill somethin' to prove that he was a man. He knew that our ma an' pa wouldn't like that kinda thinkin'."

"Who told you that?"

"Sheriff Carlson."

"That was the guilt Riley felt," Jarrett retorted.

"How would you know?"

"I was visiting him when Carlson interviewed him. Rixx probably kept after him, declaring again and again that Riley wanted to prove something, anything, even proving that he was a man. Rixx is that way. Insidious. Making innocent people believe they're guilty when they aren't."

"Why would Rixx do that, poppa?" Becky asked.

"To get a confession out of Riley. It's how he is. He keeps pushing and pushing and pushing until he gets what he wants."

"Even if it's untrue?" she asked.

"Even if it's untrue," Jarrett said.

"How could he? He seems like a nice man."

"He may be. But he thinks it's the right thing to do. Sheriff Carlson lets him work at a prisoner until the man confesses. Once you have a confession, especially if the confessor believes it's the truth, then the confessor will admit to the crime in court and its easier than finding witnesses or evidence to convict a man."

"But poppa, you didn't believe Riley was guilty. Why would Riley believe so?

"Because he was young," Ryder interjected. "I've seen lawmen do this before. They keep after someone. They don't let them sleep. They withhold food an' water. They beat them. Whatever it takes to break a man."

"And do all men break?" she inquired.

"No," Ryder replied. "Some men are too strong. They laugh at their accusers. They smile. They spit at them. The strongest don't fold, even after brutal beatings."

"Do you know any such men?" Becky asked.

"A few. I'm not one of them. I'm not that strong."

"I think you're strong," Becky said.

"So do I," Jarrett concurred.

"You're just being kind. I know what kind of a man I am."

"Then you're wrong," Becky said.

Ryder wanted to correct her, but he saw her eyes. There was conviction in her eyes.

Turning back to Jarrett, he said, "These are all fine words, but I need proof. Physical proof, not just opinions."

"Then you should interview Doc Welch."

"Why?"

"He said there was too much blood in the surrey. That there was something wrong about the wound."

"What was wrong about it?" Ryder demanded.

Jarrett shook his head. "I wasn't really paying attention. I was more concerned about Riley's emotional state. However, though Doc Welch told the sheriff, once Carlson had Riley's confession, he didn't care about anything else."

Ryder leaned back in his chair. "Seems like there's more to this than I thought. Anythin' else I should know?"

"That's about all I have to tell you."

"There's more to it, poppa," Becky said. "Tell him what Riley told you the morning they hanged him."

Ryder sat straight up. He glanced from Jarrett to Becky.

"It's not important," Jarrett replied.

"I think it is," Becky countered.

"What is it?" Ryder demanded. "What did he tell you?"

Jarrett shook his head.

"Tell me."

"Tell him, poppa."

Jarrett sighed. "He said he'd seen a tall man riding into town that morning. A man coming to save him. I thought he meant you."

"I wasn't here yet."

"I know."

"Who was it?"

Jarrett said nothing.

"Tell him, poppa."

"He said it was an angel coming to take him to heaven."

Ryder sat back in his chair. He had nothing to say.

# CHAPTER THIRTY

**T**HEY ATE THEIR CAKE in silence. After they were done, while Becky cleaned the table off and took the dishes into the kitchen, Ryder said to Jarrett, "Why didn't you want to tell me what Riley said? You're a believer, a preacher, why would you hesitate to mention to me what Riley thought he saw?"

"You just said why."

"I don't follow you."

"You said, 'What Riley thought he saw'. I didn't want you to think your brother was crazy."

"He just admitted to being guilty of a crime he didn't commit," Ryder said. "What's more crazy than that?"

"We both know that Rixx put that idea into his head. But most people don't want to believe in is angels, even when they go to church. They're afraid of being called out as stupid or Holy Joes, or any number of things. It takes courage to publicly believe."

"And even more courage to behave the way God wants you to," Becky said, back in the dining room. "Most people laugh at you because they're embarrassed that you're behaving the way they're afraid to behave. It takes courage to be a Christian."

"It takes more than that," Pastor Jarrett said. "It takes strength of character."

"An' Riley had that?" Ryder asked.

"Don't you think he did?" Pastor Jarrett wondered.

Ryder shook his head. "I didn't know him. I went to war when he was eight. He grew up a lot while I was away."

"He did," Jarrett said. "Perhaps you should find out a little more about your brother before you judge him anymore."

"I'm not judging him," Ryder retorted. "I'm the guilty one. I didn't get here in time to save him an' my ma is right."

"About what?" Becky asked.

"About being guilty. If I'd come a few days earlier, like I was told ta do, I might've been able ta save him."

"How?" Jarrett said. "With guns and bullets? Would that have saved him or would it have sentenced both of you to running until a lawman like yourself tracked the two of you down? And then what, more killing or the noose together?"

"What am I supposed to do now?" Ryder asked.

"Prove his innocence. Save his soul."

"And yours," Becky said.

"An' what good will that do me? Emily will never love me again. What good is having a soul when you're not loved? Who's gonna love me?"

"Me."

Jarrett turned to his daughter. "Becky!"

But Becky ignored her father. "I love you."

"You don't even know me!" Ryder said.

"That's what the future's for," Becky replied.

"I've done a lot of bad things. I'm a sinner."

"I forgive your sins. Just as my father does."

Jarrett stared at his daughter a moment longer, then he turned to Ryder. "If my daughter forgives you, then so do I. I forgive you, my son."

"And God forgives you," Becky said. "Just like He loves you. As I love you."

"An' what kinda love is that? Romantic love, brotherly love, friendy love? I'm six years older than you. I've been to war. I've killed men an' watched them die. How can you know anythin' about love? You're just a baby by comparison. A child."

"Do I look like a child?"

"No."

She turned to her father. "Poppa, how much older were you than momma when you married her?"

"Ten years older."

Becky turned back to Ryder. "See?"

"You've only known me a couple of days. How can you love me?"

"Love is not limited to time."

"But, why? Why do you love me?"

"Does it matter? I do."

"It matters to me. I want real love, not little girl pretend love. Why do you love me?"

"I just do," she said. "I don't know why I do. No one knows why a man or woman loves someone. You just do or don't, and I do love you."

"I have nothing to offer you."

"You're all I want."

Ryder shook his head. "I don't know you. How can I love you? What will people say?"

"Why should that matter?" Becky asked.

Ryder pushed his chair back and stood up. "Until I find out what really happened to Riley, there's nothing else that matters to me. Not my parents. Not Emily. Not you."

He started for the hallway. He stopped and turned to Becky and Dell Jarrett. "Thank you for breakfast."

Turning, he proceeded down the hallway and out the front door, collecting his hat on the way. He stopped on the front porch to put on his hat. He wasn't surprised that Jarrett followed him out.

"Where are you going, Ryder?" Jarrett asked.

He looked up at the cool and blue sky. Then he looked at Jarrett. "I don't know. I'm learnin' stuff, but I ain't learnin' the right stuff."

"You just need more information."

"An' where would I get that?"

"Well, you could start by talking to Doc Welsh."

"Where would I find him?"

"He could be just about anywhere. However, if he's in town, he will be at his clinic."

"Where's that at?"

"On First Street. You see, the space between my house and church is part of First Street. It runs beside Main Street. Keep looking down the side streets until you see the sheriff's office. The next building on First is Doc Welsh's place."

"An' if'n he's not there?"

Jarrett shrugged. "Try another day."

Stepping from the porch, Ryder nodded to Jarrett and left.

# CHAPTER THIRTY-ONE

As Ryder strolled down Main Street, he thought of how small Brannan really was. He'd spent so little time in it. The school he had attended was on the southeast side of town, about a hundred feet beyond the last houses and buildings. The school house, Jarrett's church, the feed store, the mercantile store, Joad's black smith shop and stable, the Walker's house, that was about the sum of what he'd seen of Brannan as a boy and as a young man. He had visited the post office only occasionally to mail a letter or to collect the family's mail. He had visited Imhoff's Gun Shop when he was seventeen, when his pa bought him his first pistol. He bought ammunition for it and for his grandfather's Henry rifle, but spent little other time in town.

Except for courting Emily Walker, all the rest of his life had been spent on the ranch, riding and hunting the plains, the gullies, the draws, and hills of eastern New Mexico. That had seemed enough.

He found all the adventure he needed in the grasslands, the thin woodlands, the streams and rivers of the territory. And in Emily's eyes, her sweet smile, and her even sweeter kisses.

Ryder proposed to Emily when he was twenty. He was old enough to be a man, but was still a kid at heart. He had planned on living his life with her, raising a family, living on the ranch, maybe even stretching it into a greater spread.

Then the Spanish had blown up the battleship Maine in Havana's harbor and the country went to war with Spain. The newspapers proclaimed that the duty of every young man was to defend his country, to run to the war with Spain. William Randolph Hearst's newspapers told stories of women and children being beaten and killed in Cuba. Of how if the Spanish weren't stopped, they'd come to America, where they would kill all the men and enslave all the women and children.

And after a while, Ryder started having nightmares of Spanish soldiers invading New Mexico. Of killing his family and all the men in town, of abusing Emily and then murdering her.

When he was awake, he laughed the dreams off. But he began to doubt whether he wanted to be married at all. Twenty was too young for marriage. Would he be able to take care of Emily and any children? Was he enough of a man to settle down?

Until the war with Spain, he hadn't doubted the future he had planned. But was his first responsibility to family or to his country?

The wedding plans were made. They had been sleeping together, away in the woods and along quite stream banks, for sometime. Then Emily was with child.

And Ryder was afraid.

In Texas, Roosevelt was gathering men into a volunteer regiment.

Hearst's papers proclaimed glory and victory in the war with Spain. Commodore Dewey had defeated the Spanish Fleet in Manila Bay, a world away in the Philippines.

The papers were full of drawings of Spanish soldiers bayoneting old men and children and dragging young girls, their clothes in rags, into buildings. The girls' faces showed horror and terror, while the soldiers laughed and leered.

The day of the wedding came. His parents had bought him a new suit. His mother was so proud of him, she couldn't stop talking to everyone who would listen about how her son had found love and was going to tie the knot, to marry the most beautiful girl in town.

But Ryder had spent the night wide-awake, sweating, wondering what he was getting into. Dawn came. He went to the creek to bathe. While his parents and brother performed their chores, he returned to the house, dressed not in his new suit but in travelling clothes. He grabbed his pistol and some ammunition, filled his canteen with water, stole some food. When his parents and brother returned to the house, he climbed out a back window. In the barn, he saddled one of the horses, opened the doors wide, left a note nailed to a post which read "Gone to fight for my country" and rode away. It was Texas for him; for Roosevelt's Rough Riders and glory.

# CHAPTER THIRTY-TWO

As Ryder traversed the street, people passed by him. He tipped his hat in respect to women. And the women in turn looked away from him, but not before staring, glaring, or spitting on his boots, the ultimate insult.

All he could do was sigh, remain respectful, and keep moving.

After all these years, after running away from Emily, after leaving her alone at the altar, after running off to war and returning a hero for the rest of the land but not for the town of Brannan, he was still a pariah, a coward, an unfit man, unworthy of respect.

Ryder passed by one of the town's two saloons. He turned onto the corner street that led toward Doc Welsh's clinic. Coming down the boardwalk toward him was a group of young men. He recognized one of them as Ben Walker, one of Emily's brothers.

"Hello, Ben," Ryder said as he stepped into the street to let the four cowboys walk by.

Ben stopped. The others stopped, too. The board walk was four inches high, which put Ben above Ryder. Emily's brother glared at him.

Of a sudden, Ben threw a left punch at Ryder, connecting with the right side of his head, mostly mashing his ear. Ryder staggered, his ear ringing. Pain shot into his jaw.

Another punch, from Ben's right, flashed at Ryder. Ryder stepped in, caught Walker's right arm. He pulled Walker forward, as he spun around, and Ben sailed over him, landing in a cloud of dust on his back, the wind knocked from him.

Ben's friends watched him fall, then as one, they tackled Ryder. They ended up on the ground, wrestling, three men struggling to punch Ryder, while he struggled to get away.

Ryder managed to get up, but a cowboy grabbed his ankle and pulled it out from under him. He fell.

The man who had his boot tried to climb over it and jump on Ryder. But Ryder's other boot kicked out. The man cried out and rolled sideways, off of Ryder and away. Blood spewed from his nose and mouth.

Ryder regained his feet. The other two cowboys, also up, stepped toward him, fists tight, hate in their eyes.

One rushed Ryder. He stepped sideways and drove his knee into the man's stomach. With a loud grunt, the man collapsed into the dusty street.

The other cowboy grasped Ryder's shoulder, spinning him around and struck him in the stomach with his left fist. Ryder bent over, the wind knocked from him.

The cowboy stepped in and with his right hand clasping his left fist brought them both down hard on Ryder's back. Ryder pancaked into the dust.

"Leave him, he's mine!" Ben shouted.

The cowboy who had taken Ryder down was about to kick him in the face when Ben bellowed at him. He lowered his boot and spit on Ryder, then stepped back.

Ryder lay in the dust, his eyes blinded by the dirt in them. One ear bled, ringing loudly. He was dazed but not done fighting.

Tears filled Ryder's eyes, washing some of the dust away. Blinking repeatedly to create more tears, his saw Ben's booted feet step closer. Unlike most of the cowboys hereabouts, Ben wore spurs. His left foot turned so Ryder could see the spur close to his left eye.

"This is what happens to rapists," Ben said. "We brand them beneath the eye."

"Sometimes we even get the eye," said the man who nose Ryder had broken, now on his feet.

Ben started to strike, but Ryder's arm wrapped around the boot. Before Ben could shake him free, Ryder rolled sideways into him, slamming him into the dirt once more.

Walker screamed curses as he crashed back into the dust.

Ryder continued rolling sideways over Ben, driving the elbow of his other arm into Ben's stomach, just beneath the breast bone. The wind again was knocked from him.

The other three cowboys attacked, kicking at Ryder.

Ryder scrambled away, avoiding most of the kicks, though a couple struck his arms as he deflected them.

"What's going on here?" a voice cried out.

The cowboys stopped kicking and turned around. A man in a grey suit, with a light grey hat and shiny boots, stood on the boardwalk.

"None o'yer business, Mixon," one of the men said.

"It's my business when anyone beats up a stranger," Mixon said.

"He ain't no stranger," Broken Nose said. "He's one of them Manns."

"Yeah," said the one Ryder had kneed in the stomach, "he's the bastard sonuvabitch who raped Ben's sister."

"No, he didn't," Mixon said. "He did what you boys try to do with the local girls every Saturday Night around here. That's no crime and certainly not one to beat him up for."

"It is," Ben said, getting to his feet. He began brushing the dust from his clothes. "An' you'd do worse if he or someone like him did it to one of yer girls."

"No, I wouldn't. I'd kill whomever did it. My girls are only twelve and thirteen. Keep that in mind when you boys start sniffing around them again."

"It ain't none of your affair," Ben said.

"I say it is."

"An' what if we mess you up some?" said Broken Nose.

"Then I'd be throwin' yer asses in jail," said Deputy Rixx, as he came around into the side street. He'd just crossed the street with a shotgun from the jail. The shotgun was in case he needed to get someone's attention.

"It ain't yer business neither, Rixx," Ben said, still brushing the dust from his clothes.

"An' how the hell d'you figure that? Ain't I the deputy?"

"Yeah. But this is personal. We're not committin' any crime here," Ben said.

"All depends on whether or not you cut him with yer spur."

"We was just foolin' with him," Broken Nose said.

"Didn't look like it from where I set over at the jail."

"You boys better get going home," Mixon said. "Your mothers will be lookin' for you."

Broken Nose wiped the blood from his nose onto a dirty shirt sleeve. "You got no cause to talk down to us like that. We was havin' fun till you showed up."

"Wasn't fun for me," Ryder said, standing. He brushed the dust from his clothes, found his own hat by the boardwalk and brushed the dust from it, too.

"Four-to-one is kinda cowardly," Mixon said.

"You would know," Ben said.

"What do you mean by that?"

"He means that yer gonna get it when Mann find's out what you did to his brother," Broken Nose said.

"Shut yer face," Ben snapped at his friend. He found his hat, which had been black a few minutes before but was now a dusty gray. "Let's get outta here."

"I didn't mean no harm, Ben," Broken Nose whined.

"Shut up." Ben began slapping his hat against his thigh. Dust rose from both the hat and his pants. He walked past Mixon, giving him a dirty look. His friends followed him.

Out on the main street, Ben turned and glared at Ryder. "This ain't over with."

As Ben walked away, Ryder said to Mixon and Rixx, "Why does everyone keep sayin' that to me?"

"Because they mean it," Rixx said. He turned to Mixon. "Why don't you take him down to Doc? I got peace keepin' to do."

Mixon grasped Ryder's upper arm and said, "I will."

As the two moved down the street toward where Doc Welsh's office was, Ryder sighed.

"What's with that?" Mixon asked.

"Everyone seems to hate me," Ryder replied.

"Why shouldn't they? You haven't done much good around here."

"Can't anyone ever forgive me?"

"Some, maybe. But most see you as trouble. And from what we've heard of you as being an Arizona Ranger, you sound pretty dangerous."

"Bad reputation?"

"The worst."

Ryder frowned.

# CHAPTER THIRTY-THREE

A S THEY PROCEEDED DOWN the dusty street, they heard Deputy Rixx call out to them. "Hey! Take this one with you."

They turned and saw Rixx dragging Broken Nose with him. "He needs Doc's help, too."

"I'm fine an' I ain't goin' with them."

"You'll go with them or you'll have a busted nose the rest of yer life."

"So? It'll give me a reputation."

"Yeah. Of bein' ugly," Rixx said, grinning. He held the young man's arm. Of a sudden, Rixx released his grip on his prisoner and shoved him down the street. "Make sure Doc make's his face pretty again. Well, as pretty as ugly can be!"

With a loud snort, Rixx turned around and walked back toward the jail. Mixon, Ryder, and Broken Nose could hear him laughing all the way back to the sheriff's office.

"I ain't goin' to no doctor's office," Broken Nose said.

"Suit yourself, Mister Allan. Guess you found out you weren't as fast or as tough as you thought," Mixon said.

"I'm faster than you, Walt. I'm faster'n both of you," Allan said.

"Faster than what, runnin' or gunfightin'?" Ryder asked.

"I can out-fight you an' out-draw you an' out-run you!"

"An' out-brag me, too," Ryder goaded him.

"Looks like he out-spoke you, Allan," Mixon said.

"I was on the ground. If I'd been on my feet, I coulda taken him!"

"So, everything being equal, with you both on the ground, he still out-fought you," Mixon taunted Allan.

"Tain't so. If'n I was on my feet an' if'n he was on his feet, I'da pounded him into the ground."

"I believe it would've been the other way around," Mixon said.

"You tweren't there," Allan snapped. "Sides, he started it."

"I started it?" Ryder said. "Ben threw the first punch."

"An' you had it comin'. After what you did to his sister. It's a wonder you ain't in jail for it, waitin' to hang like yer brother."

Mixon's face turned white.

But Ryder's face turned red. "What d'you mean about me belongin' in jail? An' what d'you know about my brother's hangin?" he demanded.

Allan stepped back a couple of paces. He began looking around for someone, anyone, to rescue him.

Ryder closed the gap. He grasped Allan's shirt and swung him to his left, toward the boardwalk. He hauled Allan onto the boardwalk, climbing up as he did so. Then he slammed Allan into the wall behind him.

Ryder's hands slipped up from his grip on Allan's shirt, finding Allan's throat. He leaned in close, his hands tightening around Allan's windpipe.

"Better tell him something," Mixon said.

"Get Rixx!" Allan croaked, as Ryder choked him.

"Why should I be in jail?" Ryder hissed.

"Everyone knows you raped Ben's sister," Allan moaned, Ryder's hands tightened on his throat, making speaking difficult.

"Raped her?" Ryder demanded. "I loved her! I still do."

"Then why'd you run away?"

Ryder backed away, releasing his hands.

"I don't know."

"Everybody knows why," Allan gasped.

"What do they know?"

"That yer a coward. That you an' yer brother are two of a kind, both murderin' cowards."

Ryder threw a right cross at Allan. It landed with such impact that Allan was thrown sideways along the wall, crumpling on the board walk.

Ryder's knuckles ached and he flexed his fingers. He leaned closer to Allan. "We're not cowards or murderers."

"The jury said elsewise," Allan replied, blood bubbling from his mouth. He leered up at Ryder. "Why don't you ask Mixon? He was on the jury. It took them only a bit to convict him. If'n he twasn't guilty, why'd they hang him?"

"You stay there," Ryder growled at Allan. "You move an' I won't need a gun to kill you. You understand?"

Allan saw the look in Ryder's eyes and nodded. As Ryder walked away, Allan knew that death was near, and he didn't want to die.

# CHAPTER THIRTY-FOUR

THE LOOK IN RYDER'S eyes and on his face terrified Mixon. He glanced back up the street toward the sheriff's office. Deputy Rixx was nowhere to be seen. Mixon knew that if Ryder wrapped his hands around his throat, he wouldn't be able to call out for help before his wind was cut off.

However, Ryder stopped a couple of steps away. He took a couple of deep breaths and his features softened. Slowly, Mixon relaxed, as did Ryder.

Ryder approached Mixon. "You were on the jury?"

Mixon swallowed some spit so his voice wouldn't croak as he replied to Ryder. "Yes."

"Why'd you convict my brother?"

"Initially, I didn't want to. I voted for not-guilty. But the others insisted Riley had done it. The evidence seemed thin to me, but Bill Nolan an' Ike McGuire reminded me that Riley had confessed, that he had claimed he wanted to kill something an' that when Mr. Gleason came into his sights, he fired."

"Did my brother actually say that? That part about Gleason comin' into his sights an' then firin'?"

Mixon started sweating. "I-I don't really remember."

"What do you remember?" Ryder demanded, his voice cold. He had to take another deep breath to calm himself down.

Mixon swallowed. "I remember your mother screaming when the verdict was announced. I remember Miss Walker crying out. Someone else sobbed. I remember the shocked look on your brother's face and the achievement in Rixx's and Carlson's eyes. I remember the hard look on Mrs. Gleason's face. I remember how my heart sank. I remember so many things, but I don't remember your brother's exact words.

"But he claimed he was guilty. An' after the judge's verdict condemning him to the gallows, he looked relieved. I don't know why but I reckon he was glad to have it over, even if it meant his death."

Ryder was swamped with emotion. He wanted so much to strike Mixon, to beat him unconscious. But he held his rage back. He kept control of himself. Getting tossed in jail for assaulting Mixon wouldn't solve anything.

"Why'd you change your mind? Why didn't you hold to your guns?" Ryder demanded.

Though it was cool out, Mixon sweated profusely. He wanted to run away. His eyes shifted ever so slightly as he glanced left and right, trying to figure out the best way to run, to flee from Ryder. But he controlled himself, taking a moment or two to breathe.

"I..." he began, "I was adamant at first. The facts didn't add up. Why did Riley think he was guilty if it was an accident? But Nolan, McGuire, and the other jurors were just as adamant. They reminded me of Mrs. Gleason's impassioned plea. Of how she felt firm that Riley had murdered her husband. In the end, that was what convinced me.

"But looking back, especially as I watched a thirteen-year-old boy stumble his way up the steps to the gallows, I doubted my own choice. When Doc Welsh presented his evidence, Judge Garson, at the request of county prosecutor Herman Fields, kept Doc's testimony short, only confirming that a rifle slug had killed Gleason. Judge McHugh, who retired a few years back, represented Riley. But try as he might, he couldn't convince Judge Garson to let Doc present all of his findings. So I didn't know until later, after they had hanged your brother, that Doc had some evidence that might have saved him."

"What evidence?"

Mixon stepped back from Ryder.

"What evidence!"

"I don't really quite know. We were in the bar, getting drunk. That is, most of us who regretted hanging a boy, when Doc said the wound was wrong. But I got so drunk that Rixx threw me in jail and I spent a couple of days there until I sobered up. Since then, I don't really remember much more than what I told you."

"You sure?" Ryder said, stepping close and grasping the lapel of Mixon's coat.

Mixon twitched. "I'm-I'm-I'm sure."

Ryder cursed. "Then let's get down to Doc's. Right now."

"Yes."

Ryder turned to collect Allan. He wasn't where he left him. He spotted him creeping along the wall, almost back to the main street.

Ryder glanced around the dirt street, spotted a rock, grabbed it and hurled it at Allan. It ricocheted off the wall and struck Allan, knocking him down. Before Allan could rise, Ryder reached him.

Ryder grabbed him by the back of his collar and yanked him up. "Where you goin'?"

"I was thinkin' it might be better to let you two work things out while I went an' got a drink."

"With all that blood on your face an' your nose bent that way?"

Allan grinned. "The ladies will like it."

"I doubt it. Come on, the Doc's awaitin'."

Ryder dragged him back down the side street. Allan kept trying to twist out of Ryder's grip.

"What's the matter? You weren't afraid of me when you an' your pardners were around."

"No. No. Hell, no! I can take you anytime I want."

"Go ahead," Ryder said.

"I don't want to."

"You want your face fixed, right?"

"Yes. That's right. But, aw, hell. The ladies love broken noses. Makes a man look tough."

"Not on that face," Mixon said. Though nervous, he walked with Ryder down toward Welsh's office.

"Shut yer mouth, you cowardly son of a..."

Ryder jerked Allan's collar. "Be polite."

"How can I be polite when he's insultin' me?"

"Your face is an insult," Mixon said.

Even though Ryder was angry, he managed a little smile.

"Stop makin' fun of me!" Allan whined.

"Shut up!" Ryder snapped.

Allan shut up. So did Mixon.

They reached Doc Welsh's office. The door was locked. A note posted inside the door's window said, "Back soon. Seeing a patient."

Ryder sighed. He turned to Mixon. "What do we do with him?" referring to Allan.

"We can't let him go," Mixon said. "He needs medical help."

"I'm fine the way I am," Allan protested.

"Not if I punch you a few more times," Ryder said.

"That'll be the day."

"There were four of you before," Mixon said. "Now there's just one of you."

"So?"

Ryder's head spun around. He glared into Allan's eyes. Allan glanced away. "All right. I'll stay here."

"Like hell you will. You're comin' along."

"Where?" Allan asked. He didn't know what Ryder might do.

"How about Judge McHugh's office?" Mixon suggested. "He's only a block away on this street. Not far from Old Joad's stable an' blacksmithy."

"Good idea," Ryder said. "Let's go see the judge. An' when we're done, we'll stop in to see Joad. I haven't seen him in years. How is he?"

"Old," Allan said. "That's why they call him 'Old' Joad."

Ryder grunted. He dragged Allan along with him. Mixon followed. When they reached McHugh's office, he was out, too. So they continued down toward Joad's smithy, though Allan walked now. Ryder was tired of towing him.

The town's main street was for the stores, saloons, hotels, restaurants, and the sheriff's office. The secondary streets on either side of Main Street housed the churches, various offices, the stables and the smiths. Besides two blacksmith shops, stables and churches, there were law offices, Doc

Welsh's clinic, a cartwright's shop, a carpenter's shop, and a few other shops. There was also the gunsmith's shop.

Outlying the secondary streets paralleling the main street were the streets with houses, including two boarding houses.

At the end of the street, on the outskirts of town, stood Joad's Stable. About thirty feet beyond that was Joad's Blacksmith Shop.

As Ryder and his companions passed the stable, it seemed different to Ryder. It didn't smell like a stable, with the scents of straw, of barley, oat, and alfalfa hay. Nor did it smell like horses and horse manure. Instead of smelling musty and mangy, dusty and dirty, it smelled of metal and oil.

Ryder frowned, perplexed. He and the others walked on, toward the building beyond.

The black smith shop had a roof, a stone chimney poking through it. The smithy was open on three sides, with thick wooden beams set far apart and well away from the fire whose thick smoke swept up the chimney. Ryder could feel the heat from the fire.

Two men worked in the smithy. One was a tall, muscular man with thick blond hair and skin bronzed by the sun. He had his shirt off and sweat glistened on his face, arms, chest and back.

The other man was even taller and bigger. His shoulders were huge by comparison to the blond man's. This second man's skin was a dark black and also glistened with sweat. He, too, was shirtless. And his hair was similar to the bronzed man, but instead of blond, it was white.

Both men wore their hair cut short. But while the bronzed man was clean-shaven, the black giant had a closed-cropped white beard.

Both were pounding away on metal. It was so loud that Ryder, Mixon, and Allan had heard it all the way from Doc Welsh's place.

Some of the clanging, banging blows were painful to Ryder's ears and he grimaced every time one landed.

"Hey, Joad!" Ryder called out, loudly.

"He can't hear you," Allan laughed, his voice almost drowned by the noise. "He's deef."

"What?" Ryder cried out. He covered both ears with his hands.

"I said, he's deef!" Allan bellowed back.

"You don't need to yell," Ryder yelled back. "I ain't deaf."

The banging and clanging stopped. The big black man strode out. "Ah ain't deef, t'either! Ah was listenin' to the metal singin' to me."

Ryder looked at Joad.

Joad ignored him. "Whatcha want, little man?" he said to Allan.

"I don't need nothin'," Allan bellowed out, his ears still ringing from the banging metal.

"Ah told yew, Ah ain't deef. No need ta yell."

"I ain't," Allan started, stopped. He opened his mouth and twitched his jaw about, then stuck his little fingers into his ears and massaged them. Removing his fingers and in a less loud voice, Allan said, "I ain't yellin'."

"You were a moment back," Mixon said.

Ignoring Allan, Joad turned to Mixon. "Whatcha need, Walt?"

"I don't need anythin', either," Mixon said.

"Den whatcha stoppin' me foh?" Joad demanded.

Mixon pointed at Ryder. "He wanted to see you."

Joad turned and looked down at Ryder. Everybody, even the big blond, bronzed giant inside by the fire, was smaller than Joad.

"Ah doan know yew. Whatcha want?"

"It's me, Joad," Ryder said.

"Yew sound fahmiyah, but Ah still doan know yew. Take yer hat off."

Ryder removed his hat.

Joad peered at him. He leaned down and looked closer. "Rydah, dat yew?"

Joad had come out carrying a twenty-pound sledge hammer in his right hand. He dropped it. The sledge hit the packed dirt with a dull thud.

Joad stepped closer, leaning down and wrapping his huge arms around Ryder. Ryder was as a small child in a grown man's arms as Joad lifted him up in the air.

"Rydah! Rydah! Ah thought yew was daid. Ah haven't seen yew in yeahs. What happened ta yew?"

Ryder grunted. His shoulders and arms were being crushed into his ribs and lungs.

"Oh, sorry Rydah." Joad carefully set him down.

Allan snickered.

Joad glared at Allan. "Whatcha laughin' at, little man?"

"Nothin'."

"Doan be laughin' an' snickerin' at Rydah. We been best friends almos' all his life, since he t'were five yeahs old."

"Six," Ryder gasped, catching his breath.

"Ah'm sorry, Rydah. Ded Ah hurt ya?"

"I'm good," he wheezed.

Joad waved for the bronze giant to come out. The big blond man set his hammer down, backed the fire down a bit, and came out.

"Rydah," Joad pointed toward the bronzed man, "dis heah's Toh Neelsin. Toh, this heah's mah friend, Rydah. Rydah Mann. His daddy brought him heah when he was a small thin'. Dat musta been twenty yeahs ago."

"Just about," Ryder coughed.

"He was such a small thin'," Joad said.

"Everyone's small to you," Tor Nielsen said. "Even me."

"Dat so!" Joad laughed. While he had a deep voice, Joad's laughter bubbled out of him like a mountain stream over rocks. His laughter was light and friendly and captivating.

Mixon, Nielsen, and Allan laughed. Even Ryder laughed, though at the moment it was more of a whisper.

"Ah was a jiyant ta him."

"You were a mountain," Ryder wheezed.

"Dat so, dat so!" he exclaimed, bubbling with laughter. "He stared up at me an' Ah looked down at him. An' then, whatcha think happened? His little hand lifted up ta me an' he gave me a piece of candy. The last piece he had."

"Pa only bought me two pieces," Ryder said, his breath back within him. "That's all he could afford."

"Dat so? Half'n his treasuh. Dis little white boy, he gives me half his treasuh. An' from den on, we was friends."

"We still are," Ryder said.

"We is, we is!" Joad stopped and thought. His eyes grew sad. "Ah was sorry ta heah 'bout yer brother. Ah never knew him, but Ah wish Ah had."

"I wasn't around enough to bring him out to meet you. I should've."

"Dat so. Whatcha been doin' all deese yeahs?"

"I went off to Cuba durin' the war. An' then I became a Ranger down in the Arizona Territory."

"Dat so? Dat's mah Ryder." Joad looked at Nielsen and the others. "Ah neevah had no little ones o' mah own. But Ryder was like the son Ah always wanted. His daddy was willin' to share 'im with me. He was heah so often it was like he was my own little man. Ah's so proud of yew, boy."

Ryder looked at his feet. He wasn't embarrassed or afraid, but ashamed. Ashamed for how he had hurt this town and how he had hurt so many people that loved him.

He knew why Joad hadn't had any children of his own. It wasn't because there weren't any black women around to marry him.

Ryder knew Joad's story. He had escaped from his master when he was ten, by then as big as a full-grown man. He had made it all the way from Alabama, crossing Louisiana, into Mississippi, and then crossing the Mississippi River into Texas, stealing food, killing small animals for meat, and keeping hidden from white people in general. Many slaves at plantations helped him along, especially when they discovered that the man they saw before them was still a boy, giant though he be. By the time he made it into Texas, the Civil War was over. And he was twelve.

In Texas, he joined up with a wagon train going west to New Mexico. He worked as a servant for a white family from Louisiana. In Western Texas, Comanches attacked the train and everyone was murdered. But Joad hid under a wagon, scraping a hole into the hard dirt deep enough to hide in. His finger nails scraped away, his fingers bloody, he pulled a canvas and some broken pots over him and lay underneath the wagon.

He watched while the boys his age were scalped and then murderer. He heard the cries of the women and girls. When it was done, the warriors set the wagons on fire. But for some reason, the fire in the wagon above him went out. After the Comanches got drunk and passed out, he managed to get away. He made his way across Texas until he reached the New Mexico Territory. Ryder's grandfather found him, starving, sick, and worn out.

His grandfather took him in. When Joad was healthier, his grandfather arranged for Joad to become the local blacksmith's apprentice. When the blacksmith died, Joad took over the smithy.

When Ryder was fourteen, he used to tease Joad about not being married or having any kids. Ryder only did it because he was nervous and scared about dating himself.

One day, Joad, with tears in his eyes, explained that he could never have children. His master, whom he had killed, had cut his personal parts off, he said, like he was a horse or a sheep. His master had said it was so he would stop growing. But he still grew. So, a few months later, when his master wasn't looking, he struck him in the back of his head with a shovel. His master went down and Joad kept striking him until he was dead.

Then he ran.

After learning that, Ryder never made fun of Joad again.

He never thought of Joad as another father, but he often wished Joad was an uncle, or better yet, his big brother.

Ryder changed the subject. "What you workin' on? All that bangin', you can hear it all the way down to the other side of town.

"No doubt," Joad laughed. "We is smoothin' metal foh a new side to an attamible."

"A what?" Mixon asked.

"An automobile," Ryder explained. "How long you been workin' on automobiles?"

"Almos' three yeahs. Toh's been teachin' me. Toh has duh stable an' forge at duh t'other end o' duh town. But Ah have duh bettuh forge. So we cleaned out mah stabile an' made it inta a bahn foh attamibbles. We have foah o' dem in dare an' we're workin' on a t'other one now."

Ryder nodded. He glanced at Nielsen.

"He knows more about metal than I do," Nielsen said. "It talks to him. The engines talk to me, but the metal talks to him. After all these years of competin' with each other, now we're partners."

"Dat so," Joad said, bubbling with laughter. "Now we're friends. Funny how thin's work out, tain't it, Rydah?"

"It is."

"How long ya gonna be heah?" Joad asked.

"Until I find out what happened to Riley."

"He was hung. That's what happened," Allan said.

Ryder glared at Allan, but said nothing. Allan looked down.

"Boy, ya best be watchin' yer mouth," Joad said to Allan. "Neeveah know when somebody's gonna be knockin' yer tathe out."

"He needs his nose fixed first," Mixon said. "We took him down to Doc's clinic, but he was gone."

"Ah was wonderin' 'bout all that blood on his face," Joad said. "Toh, git him some clean rags an' some wateah. Boy, after yer done washin' up, Ah'll set yer nose for yew."

Allan stepped back. "No."

"Show some grit," Mixon said, grabbing Allan's arms from behind. Allan twisted free and spun, throwing a wide right hook at Mixon's face. Mixon stumbled back, taking the blow on a shoulder.

"That's enough," Ryder said.

Allan dropped his shoulders in surrender. He glanced at Ryder and Joad, then walked away.

"You okay, Walt?" Ryder said.

Mixon rubbed his shoulder. "I think so."

Nielsen came back with a bucket of fresh water and some clean rags. He took them over to Allan. Allan washed his face, careful of his nose.

Joad approached, wiping his hands on a couple of dirty rags. He stuffed the rags in a hip pocket and then placed his gigantic hands on either side of Allan's nose. Joad's hands completely covered Allan's face.

Joad gently brought his hands close to Allan's nose, until they engulfed it. After he made contact, Joad's giant hands made a small twitch, followed by an audible crick. When Joad stepped back, Allan's nose was straight again.

Joad looked at the bruises on Allan's face, around the eyes and nose. "What happened ta duh rest o' yew?"

Allan pointed at Ryder.

Joad looked at Ryder.

"We were figthin'. He tried to hit me. I hit him first."

"Ya ded a good job," Joad said. He turned back to Allan. "All dun. Have Doc tape yer nose."

Allan nodded. He looked at Ryder.

"You can go," Ryder said. Then, to Mixon, "Make sure he gets to Doc's place."

"I don't need a baby sitter," Allan said.

"I'd rather stay here, if you don't mind," Mixon said.

"I don't need a baby sitter, either," Ryder said.

"Dat so!" Joad proclaimed, a big, friendly grin on his face.

Mixon nodded. "Okay. Take care of yourself, Ryder."

"I will."

As Mixon started to leave, he saw that Allan was well away. Before Mixon passed the car barn, Allan had turned up the side street toward the jail. Mixon decided he would take a round about way home. He turned down the first street leading away from the city's center.

# CHAPTER THIRTY-FIVE

RYDER WATCHED MIXON AND Allan disappear down the street. Once they were gone, he turned back to Joad. "What d'you know about my brother's trial?"

"Don't know nothin' 'bout dat. Dey's wouldn't let me in. But Ah watched dem hang him. Made mah heart hurt harder dan when mah momma died. Dat be more'n fifty yeahs ago."

Ryder nodded. "You know anythin' else about what happened to him?"

"Ah knows dat dare was a lot o' blood all over that buckboard. Toh an' Ah cleaned it up foh Missus Gleason. Dare was too much blood foh a man who bled out while his horse wandered inta town. It took his horse twenty minutes ta get ta town. Mister Gleason woulda had ta have his whole head blowed off ta bleed dat much. Ain't dat so, Toh?"

"Yah, that is so. No man could bleed that much in just twenty minutes. Not unless a mountain lion or bear had gotten to him."

"I don't understand," Ryder said, shaking his head. "Why's that so important?"

"Cause a man woulda had ta been shot long befoh dat."

"That's right," Tor Nielsen said. "He must've bled for at least an hour before getting' into town."

"An hour?" Ryder wondered. "How could that be? If Riley shot him when he did, how could he have bled that long? Did his horse wander around for forty minutes before heading into town?"

"No suh, dat tain't so. Blood dripped from dat buck board. Dare was a trail all the ways ta town."

"Drip, drip, drip," Nielsen said. "A little here an' a little there. That horse kept coming, carrying a dead man into town. He didn't wander anywhere."

Ryder turned to Nielsen. "Were you at the trial?"

"Yah. Joad asked me to go so I could tell him all about it."

"Was the blood trail mentioned?"

"Yah."

"Did you tell McHugh about there being too much blood?"

"No. Doctor Welsh mentioned it to him. He knew the moment he saw the wagon that there was too much blood."

"Then," Ryder began, "did McHugh or Welsh mention it at the trial?"

"No. The judge from Las Vegas wouldn't let them talk 'bout that."

"Why not?" Ryder demanded. "My brother's life was on the line. Why wouldn't he let the truth come out?"

Nielsen shrugged. "I don't know. The judge, I tink his name was Garson, said something about it not being important to the trial. I tink that's right. The prosecuting lawyer, Mister Fields, said this to Judge Harland and the judge agreed with him. He said that the jury didn't need to know 'bout it and Judge Harland agreed with him. I don't know why. I'm just a blacksmith and a mechanic. I don't know these legal tings."

Ryder's face twisted full of anger and hate. He stomped around for a few minutes, wishing he knew what to do.

"Yew okay, Ryduh?" Joad asked, concerned.

"Not in the least."

"Why not?"

"Because this Judge Harland an' that attorney named Fields railroaded Riley for murder. An' Rixx an' Carlson were part of it. But, why? Why convict a thirteen-year-old boy for murder? Why frame him? Why make him believe he was guilty? Why, why, why!"

"Ah don't know, Ryduh, but Ah's worried 'bout yew."

"Don't be worried about me, Joad. Be worried about those sonsabitches who hanged my brother."

"Whatcha gonna do?"

"I don't know, yet. I don't have enough evidence. But I'm goin' to get it."

"Ah'm sorry we upset yew, Ryduh. Why don't yew set a spell with us?"

Ryder stopped and breathed. When he had calmed down enough, he stretched his hand out to Nielsen and shook the big blond giant's hand. Then he reached out to Joad.

Joad's hand wrapped around Ryder's hand like a grown man's hand wrapped around a little boy's hand. "Ah's worried 'bout yew."

"Don't worry about me. I'll be fine."

"Dat may be so, but Ah's still gonna worry 'bout yew."

"I know."

"Anythin' Ah can doos foh yew, let me know. Ah's heah foh yew. Always."

"I know. I'll be okay."

"Yew shur?"

Ryder nodded. "Yep. Just stay outta things. I don't want you gettin' hurt."

"Ah knows. Ah's a big, strong man, but Ah's also colored an' dat makes me a tahgit. Ah'll be careful. Yew be, too."

Ryder nodded and turned back down the street.

Joad watched him go. He wiped his eyes with a red bandanna he kept in a pocket. Then he and Nielsen went back to work.

# CHAPTER THIRTY-SIX

RYDER HAD MUCH TO think about. How could he reconcile what Sheriff Carlson had told him this morning about Riley claiming he was guilty with what Dell Jarrett, Walter Mixon, and Joad had told him? The evidence was mounting up in favor of Riley's innocence while it also mounted up against Rixx and Carlson's desire to close the case, and with the prosecuting attorney, Herman Fields, and Judge Garson's railroading of Riley to the gallows.

While he felt resentment toward Mixon for convicting Riley, he understood why he did it. Ryder had once been on a jury and knew all about the pressure jurors could put on a member to vote their way.

It seemed more and more likely someone wanted Riley to die for someone else's killing Gleason. But who was that someone? Carlson or Rixx, maybe? Or maybe it was Rixx's hot-headed brother, Tony?

Tony could be the killer. He was one of those young gunmen who loved the power of a pistol. They fed on killing and on out-drawing their victims. Tony Rixx seemed more like the logical killer and maybe his older brother and the sheriff were covering up for Tony's involvement in murdering Gleason.

But Tony Rixx had friends, cowboys who loved violence as much as Tony did. And there was also the fact of how fast Tony really was, probably much faster that Ryder. Plus, his big brother was clearly watching out for him.

He couldn't just confront Tony. That was a quick trip to an early grave.

And what if Tony wasn't Gleason's killer? What if he was all that he seemed to be, a gun-happy man who loved killing people?

Then who else could it be?

It certainly couldn't be Ben Walker. Or could it? No, why would Ben want to kill Gleason? For revenge against Ryder? No. Ben and his buddies were more of the beat-you-up kind of guys. Revenge was more personal that way.

What about Mrs. Gleason?

Ryder thought as he walked. Why would Mrs. Gleason want Riley to hang, other than her desire for revenge against him for killing her husband? Did she kill her husband? Had she wanted him dead? But, why? It was unlikely and improbable that she killed her husband.

What about the prosecuting attorney, Herman Fields? What kind of a man was he? Had Gleason cheated him or hurt him in some way and could he have shot Gleason? Could he have done it about the same time and on the same morning as when Riley was out hunting? Could he have then just taken advantage of Riley's emotional state to get him convicted for murder?

Ryder had learned from some of his fellow Rangers that where murder was concerned, there were no coincidences. But how could there not be? Could Fields have followed

Riley around until the right circumstances put him in the right place when Fields murdered Gleason?

No, that was too wild of an idea.

Maybe Fields just got lucky, just happened to have murdered Gleason when Riley was out hunting. Luck was often a major factor when surviving a gunfight or running up a hill against entrenched Spanish defenders. Ryder knew this from personal experience, both from Cuba, and from the gunfights he'd been in during the last couple of years.

But why would Fields have murdered Gleason? That was the real question. Without motivation, how could Ryder prove Fields guilty?

With Tony Rixx, proving guilt was easy. Tony had a bloodlust. He enjoyed killing and he enjoyed violence, especially hurting people. Tony didn't need any other motivation.

But that was also Tony's defense. Just because he enjoyed killing didn't mean that he had killed Gleason.

What it came down to, finally, was that maybe none of Ryder's suspects were really Gleason's killer. Maybe Sheriff Carlson's and Jeff Rixx's desire to convict Riley was just laziness. Ryder had seen such behavior in a lot of small-town sheriffs and deputies since becoming a Ranger. Perhaps Fields' and Judge Garson's behaviors were similar, just cynicism and laziness.

Or, worst of all, maybe Riley really was guilty.

That last thought made Ryder sick and angry at himself for even considering it. His brother was too good of a person, too innocent a boy, to have done something like that.

Wasn't he?

Angrily, Ryder shook his head. He didn't want to think about any of this anymore.

He continued on past the side street leading up to the sheriff's office. He continued two more blocks before turning onto another side street that led back to the main street. He came out beside a clothing store just a block from the Guzmans' Hotel.

At the hotel, he scraped his boots off before going inside. He hoped the Guzmans were home and that he could get a late lunch with them. He'd had enough of the people of Brannan for one day. He intended to remain in his room for the rest of the day, hiding out from people's lies, their questions, and conflicting information.

"Hey, son, want some lunch?" his father asked as he went in.

Surprised to see him, Ryder walked over and shook his hand. "Sure, I'd like some lunch. So long as it's here an' not anywhere else in Brannan."

"Oh," his father said. "The Guzmans are out until tonight. How 'bout we go down to the café?"

"How 'bout not?"

"Have you been lookin' into Riley's death?"

"Yep."

"Good. Tell me what you know."

"I know too much. The more I find out, the more confused I get. I just want to get away from town for a while. Maybe go for a ride. Want to come along?"

"Sure. What about lunch?"

"I have some hard tack an' jerky in my saddle bags upstairs. I'll fill my canteen."

"Uh, uh."

"Why not, Pa?"

"My teeth ain't what they used to be. How 'bout I go down to the café an' get us a couple of sandwiches?"

"Sure. I'll get my canteen an' fill it up an' then I'll go down to Nielsen's stable an' get my horse."

"You do that. You been wrasslin' with people in the dust again?" He pointed toward Ryder's clothing.

"Just a little disagreement."

"Sure. Didn't think of flashin' your badge?"

"It ain't any good here in New Mexico. Besides, sometimes it leads to gun play an' I'd rather be tradin' punches than bullets with people. A punch can only travel as far as the end of your arm, but a bullet travels a might further. There's too many innocent people, includin' kids, wanderin' around town to be throwin' out lead."

"You got a good head on you, son."

"Thanks, Pa. Go get your sandwiches while I get my horse an' some water."

"See you down at the stable."

"Let's make it outside of town. I don't want anyone causin' any trouble."

"You expectin' some?"

"You never know."

"Then I'll meet you a half mile outside of town."

# CHAPTER THIRTY-SEVEN

**R**YDER WENT UP TO his room. He decided to remove his dusty, sweaty shirt and put on a clean one. But looking at his hands and smelling how he smelled, he decided to go down to the bathing room to see if there was any water there.

There was a pitcher of water, a bowl, soap, and various clean towels for bathing. Pouring water into the bowl, he dropped a cake of soap in and watched it float around. When the soap seemed soft enough, he removed it. Rubbing it under his arms, over his front and down his back, he set it aside. He soaked a small towel and washed his torso, arms, and armpits. Then he washed his face and hair and toweled off.

Returning to his room, he left his dirty shirt beside the door. He knew Dolores Guzman would wash it for him.

They were good people. Like family to him.

Back in his room, he combed down his wet hair. Then he grabbed a plain, pale blue shirt and put it on, tucking it into his pants.

Removing his gun belt, he pulled out his pistol. He inspected it. Even though he'd been rolling around in the dusty, dirty street, it hadn't seemed to suffer any wear. Nor did it appear to be dirty. Most of the dust had been confined to his face and hands, while most if was kept from his body by his coat. None had reached his pistol.

In the West, and especially in the territories, a man's pistol and rifle were his life. Even more so for a law man. But the West was changing, becoming more civilized. Someday, maybe sooner than later, few would wear guns. More people would be safe, except for those victimized by outlaws.

But for now, and maybe far into the future, for a lawman a gun was the difference between order and disorder, between peace and chaos, between life and death. And the better care you took of your hardware, the safer you and the innocent were.

So, though he knew he was running late to meet his pa, he took time out to inspect his pistol. He flipped the cylinder to the side, removed each of the five bullets from their chambers.

Certain the cylinders were clean, and having inspected each shell, he returned the five rounds to their homes. Then he checked the sixth slot. A smart man knew better than to carry six rounds. In all that fighting and wrestling today, if he'd had a sixth round in the chamber, it could have gone off and shot him in the leg. Or missed him and shot someone else.

In a prolonged gun fight, where he might fire all five rounds in his pistol, he most likely would reload six. He had yet to experience such combat, except in Cuba. In the territories, three shots proved adequate enough. Usually, it took but one.

With the cylinder still loose, he blew down the barrel. No dirt or gunpowder came out the end. After the fight with McAvoy, he had cleaned his revolver. He was glad it had remained clean.

He spun the cylinder to make certain it rotated well. Then, with the cylinder still to one side, he checked the trigger, making certain it worked as well as everything else. Finished, he closed the cylinder and secured it. He stuffed his pistol back into its holster, but only after he was sure the holster was clean and free from debris.

Next, he examined the shells he carried on his gun belt. He found two that were dented. He removed them and placed each of the damaged ones in one of this coat's pockets. He'd give them to the local gunsmith to dispose of. He still had sixteen reloads, more than enough for anything short of a small war.

Putting his gun belt on, then his coat, then his hat, he headed downstairs. He grabbed his canteen as he exited his room.

He filled his canteen in the kitchen. Then he was off, down the street to Nielsen's stable, where he found his saddle and No Name.

Petting No Name's neck and side, he led her out of her stall. He spoke to her with soothing words, explaining that they were going to meet his pa, outside of town. While he spoke with her, he tossed a blanket across her back. Next he tossed his saddle across her, fastening the belt firmly, but not too tightly, beneath her belly.

No Name seemed in good spirits as he led her outside of the stable. Bob was right. Your horse was your best friend, equal to your human best friends, if not superior to them.

Tor Nielsen's grandson, Franz, was outside, unloading loose hay from a wagon. "Where you off to, out to see yer ma, maybe?"

Ryder shook his head. "Just goin' for a ride. Met your grandpa today."

"Quite a man, ain't he?" Franz said.

"Yep. I like him."

"Thanks. I'm sure glad he and Old Joad became partners. Our incomes have improved quite a bit since."

"Glad to hear it."

"When will you be back, Mr. Mann?"

"In a couple of hours. The town's air has gotten a little stale for me."

Franz grunted. He watched Ryder recheck the straps underneath his horse. Ryder then settled his saddle bags on his horse and tied his canteen to the saddle horn.

Ryder swung onto No Name, patted her neck, and started away.

Franz waved as Ryder rode off. He liked him. He had heard some terrible stories about Ryder, but he liked him and didn't care whether the stories were true or not. He seemed like a good man and the world needed all the good men it could get.

After Ryder disappeared down the street, Franz went back to forking the hay out of the wagon.

# CHAPTER THIRTY-EIGHT

RYDER GUIDED NO NAME out to where he and his father planned to meet. He occasionally glanced back to make certain he wasn't being followed. He wanted anyone who might be following him to know that he was expecting him, but no one came.

He arrived before his father did, so he dismounted from No Name, both to rest her and to be less obvious to anyone trailing his father.

After a while, he became concerned that his father was late. He pulled out his watch. It was about a quarter after one. He kept an eye back toward town, though he also frequently looked around to prevent anyone from sneaking up on him.

Ten minutes later, he saw his father riding out from town. Five minutes after that, Ryder spotted two men following him.

A few minutes passed and his father rode up. "Ready to go?"

"Yep." He swung into his saddle. "We got company."

"I'm aware. Where's your rifle?"

"Didn't think I'd need it."

"Who says you will? But if you do, I got both my Winchester and your grandpa's Henry. You remember how to use the Henry?"

"Never forgot. Every repeater's just about like the next one."

"Just about. Let's go."

"Where we goin'?"

"To where it all started."

Ryder nodded. They were on the road that Gleason's horse had followed that Sunday morning, with Gleason dead in his buckboard. The day that poor Riley thought he had killed him. Though, now with riders following them, and with what little Ryder had learned, he was fairly certain Riley had been innocent and that someone else wasn't.

The road cut deep into the ground, wore down by more than half-a-hundred years of wagons, horses, and cattle. They rode along, as the road dipped into draws and gullies, climbing up the high side of each earthen wave. Every time they crested, they glanced back. After a while, the riders disappeared.

"Think we lost them?" Ryder asked.

"Do you?"

"Nope. They're probably paralleling us."

"There's a fancy word. Where'd you learn that?"

"From the President, before he was president."

"Ah, Colonel Roosevelt. I never got a chance to ask you what you thought of him."

"He led from the front, just as he does now as president. He fought beside us an' had our backs. He's a genuine hero, leader, an' man."

Roger Mann nodded. "My opinion of him, too. Tough way to become president, though, by the death of your boss."

Ryder nodded, too. "But he's man enough for the job."

"He is."

As they dropped into another gulley, Ryder said, "Why don't we stay down here an' see what happens."

"Naw," his father said. "We got a mile more to go. I checked the embankment where Riley fired from an' I found nothin'. But that was two days after the shootin'. Rixx an' Carlson had already found the only shell."

As they climbed out of the gulley, up ahead and to the right, Ryder spotted a man on horseback, looking back at him.

"There's one on the left, too. They look like some of the men that work for the Gleasons," Roger said.

"What are they doin' out here?" Ryder asked.

"Nothin'."

"Except keepin' an eye on us."

"They probably don't want us messin' things up."

"How so?"

"How'd you feel if you sent an innocent boy to the grave, an' then some jackass started lookin' into it?"

"The same as I feel now," Ryder replied.

"How so?"

"Angry."

"Why?"

"Riley didn't do it."

Roger halted his horse and leaned toward Ryder. "How do you know that?"

"I don't know, not for certain. But there's too many things that don't add up. An' no one would be followin' us if Riley had been guilty."

"What doesn't add up?"

"The trial. Dell Jarret told me that the prosecutin' attorney an' the judge wouldn't allow any evidence that might've cleared Riley."

"I know. I was there. Maybe they thought such evidence wouldn't clear his name but would cause a lot of anguish among the Gleasons."

"I saw Joad today. An' his partner, Nielsen. They both said there was too much blood in the buckboard for a man shot so close to town."

"Some people bleed more than others."

"Ain't you supposed to be on my side?" Ryder demanded.

"I am. You lost a brother, but I lost a son. An' I gotta make sure that you're sure."

"I still gotta talk to Judge McHugh an' Doc Welsh. They might have some evidence that could prove Riley was innocent."

"An' what if you find that he wasn't?" Roger asked, anger in his voice.

"Then there's nothin' I can do to help ma."

"I reckon not."

"But I know that he is."

"How?"

"A feelin'."

"That's no proof of innocence, at least not for the courts."

"I know. But it's all I got. When you're out huntin' killers, feelin's are sometimes the only thing that'll save your life. I learned that in Cuba. After you've survived bein' shot at enough times, you get to know when someone's sneakin' up on you or gettin' ready to back-shoot you. It's a feelin' of somethin' not bein' right, an' I got that feelin' right now about Riley an' his hangin'."

"Then keep diggin'," Roger said.

"Yep. Did anyone ever find that coyote he said he shot?"

"The day after they locked Riley up, I came out here. I saw a bunch of vultures a couple hundred yards beyond the gulley, out in the grass. But when I got there, there was no way to know if that was the coyote Riley shot or not. Or if it was even a coyote."

Ryder blurted out, "I shoulda been here for him!"

"You shoulda. But what could you have done, shoot your way into the jail an' out again? That'd make everyone in town hate you all the much more."

"They already hate me. More now than they did back at the beginning."

His father sighed. "Sometimes people hate because they're afraid. But more often they hate because it gives them a sense of power over others. An' sometimes they hate just because they're angry."

"Which one is it for the people in town?"

"All three, I reckon. Or maybe it's just jealousy. Jealousy's even more deadly than fear or anger."

"So why did they hate Riley so much?"

"Maybe we're lookin' at if from the wrong direction," Roger countered. "Maybe it isn't about Riley but somebody else."

Ryder halted his horse. "What d'ya mean?"

"Who had it out for Vernon Gleason?" his father replied, continuing to let his horse drift down the road.

"I don't follow."

"He's dead. If Riley didn't do it, an' you an' I both know he didn't, then who murdered Vernon an' why?" Roger said over his shoulder, his horse meandering along.

Ryder nudged No Name forward. "I don't even know where to begin. Who should I talk to?"

"How 'bout the ones you've already talked to? Except for Carlson an' Rixx, of course."

"Why not them?'

"They won't admit they're wrong. Not all lawmen are as honest as you, son."

"So I've noticed. But I'm not really sure I'm a lawman."

"Why not?"

"Because my job is bringin' in killers an' other vermin. Alive, if possible. Dead, if more reliable."

"That's what most lawmen do."

"But what laws am I enforcin'?"

"The law allowin' innocent people to live their lives without bein' murdered or molested."

"I'm just one man. How can I do that with a whole town?"

"Who says you have to? Can't you ask for some help from your Arizona Ranger friends?"

Ryder shook his head. "I hardly know any of them. Besides, there's not that many of us. Twenty-six, in all. Twenty-seven, with me. An' the Territory's thinkin' of cuttin' it down to twenty-six. It's all it can afford. I might be outta a job soon. Besides, we're only lawmen in the Arizona Territory, not New Mexico, nor anywhere else. We're local boys, not Federals."

"I didn't know that. This is the first time you told me 'bout anythin' you've been doin' in a long time."

"I know an' I'm sorry, Pa. Mostly, it ain't worth talkin' about."

"So I reckoned."

They road on for a while in silence. The road rose up until it was just a few inches below the prairie around them. Looking about, they saw that the two cowboys who had been paralleling them had disappeared.

"Wonder where they got off to?" Roger asked, referring to the riders.

"Hopefully, nowhere where they can cut us down."

"There's no place like that for a couple of miles," Roger replied.

"Where you want to eat lunch?" Ryder asked.

"I was thinkin' 'bout the cemetary."

"No thanks."

"Afraid of seein' Riley's grave?"

"Afraid of seein' Emily."

"Why would she be there?"

"She was yesterday."

"You were out there?" Roger asked.

"Yep. I wanted to see Riley's grave. I wanted to talk with him. An' I kinda wanted to see if ma was around. I miss her."

"I know," Roger said. "Was she?"

"No. Just Emily. An' our daughter."

"I'm sorry 'bout that, son."

"She hates me so much."

"You hurt her."

"I didn't mean to. I wanted to go to war. I wanted adventure. I wanted to know life before settlin' down."

"You wanted to run away."

Ryder pulled up his horse. Roger did the same.

"Why would you say that?" Ryder demanded.

"Be honest, son. She was never right for you. That same feelin' you told me 'bout knowin' when somethin' ain't right, you felt it then. You knew she was wrong for you."

"Then why was I marryin' her?"

"You got her with child. You were doin' the honorable thing. But you didn't love her. Not really."

"I loved her. I still love her!"

"Did you?"

"Yep."

"Then why'd you run away?"

Ryder looked away, out at the rolling hills. "I don't know. Because I was afraid, I guess."

"Every man's afraid of gettin' married."

Ryder glanced at his father. "You, too?"

"Me, too."

"Why?"

"You know the answer. Marriage is a big thing. It's confinin'. But it's also excitin'. Bein' a husband, settlin' down, raisin' a family. That's a lot of responsibility. More responsibility than leadin' men into battle. More than huntin' down killers. More than anythin' else.

"A man that stays an' loves his wife an' children, a man that is faithful an' never strays, a good man, a loyal man, a happy man, who puts his family first, is a greater hero than anyone else. What's Abe Lincoln, or Davy Crockett, or even Teddy Roosevelt, compared to a good father?"

"Then I'm none of those things. I ran away. I'm not a good man. I'm just a coward."

"No, son, you're a good man, you're all of those things."

"Then why did I run away? Wasn't that the act of a coward?"

"Did you run away in Cuba?"

"Nope."

"Have you, as an Arizona Ranger, run away from any man you've had to bring in?"

"Nope."

"Are you runnin' away from your duty to your brother an' mother now?"

"Nope."

"Then you're not a coward."

"Then why'd I run out on Emily?" Ryder demanded.

"You ran because you knew she wasn't the right person for you. You were doin' the honorable thing, givin' your future child a name, keepin' people from callin' it a bastard. But a marriage without love ain't no marriage at all. Two people married to each other who don't love each other, might get along for the children, but if they don't love each other, then the children are keen to it. Sometimes, a mother or father will hate a child because the child's keepin' them married to the wrong person. Hate's even worse than havin' no father at all."

"I wish I'd known this long ago, Pa. Maybe I wouldn't have bedded Emily. Maybe I wouldn't have had to run out on her an' have everyone hereabouts hate me."

"Sometimes we have to suffer to gain wisdom, son. We don't listen to our elders when we should. We think we know life an' don't need to learn anythin' else. Learnin' is a hard thing."

"Then why did Ma want me to marry Emily?" Ryder asked, confused.

"Your mother always liked Emily. She would've been happy to have her for a daughter. But she an' I both knew you two weren't right for each other."

"What d'you mean?" Ryder asked, staring at his father.

"Emily's a sweet girl. When she wants to be. But she holds a grudge forever. Remember that boy that insulted her older brother when you were both ten? She never forgave him for that insult. A few years ago, when his horse threw him an' he broke his neck, I heard her whisper over his grave after the funeral that God punished him for his wicked ways. There was ice in her words."

"He was a wicked child."

"No, he wasn't," Roger countered. "A might loud-mouthed an' brash sometimes, but basically a good man. But she holds grudges like mothers hold new babies. She will never forgive you for runnin' out on her."

"I know," Ryder said. "But I still love her."

"It's a good thing to do son, but she has someone strong enough for her now. They're gettin' married soon, before Christmas, I think."

"What's his name?"

"Berry Farrell."

"What's he do?"

"He's a merchant."

"I never thought she'd go for a mercantile man."

"He's right for her. He has the patience an' strength to love such a strong woman. You need somebody lest fickle, less inflexible an' more forgivin'. Somebody sweet an' kind, like Becky Jarrett, for instance."

"Becky Jarrett! She's just a kid. Hell, she just told me today that she loves me. We've only known each other for a day an' already she loves me? How can she love me in just a day?"

His father smiled. "She's loved you since she was thirteen."

"How d'you know that?"

"Dell told me."

"Why would she do that? Why pretend to love me?"

Roger shook his head. "She's not pretendin'."

"It doesn't make sense."

"You were always nice to her."

"I'm nice to a lot of people."

"Even the ones you fight? The ones you kill?"

"That's different."

"So it is. We can't understand why God makes one person love another, but sometimes the right people get together an' sometimes the wrong ones do."

"But Ma loves Emily."

"She does. But she doesn't want her for a daughter anymore."

"I suppose she wants Becky."

"Maybe. But she mostly wants you safe an' happy."

"It didn't seem that way when I got into town the other night."

"She's in a lot of pain. Her baby was hanged in front of her."

"How am I gonna make this better?"

"You can't change people. People can only change themselves."

"What kinda answer's that?" Ryder demanded.

"You gotta move on, son. Find out who killed Vern Gleason an' you might find out why Riley was hanged. Your ma loves you. That love's still inside her, buried beneath a lot of pain, but still there. Give her time."

"What about Emily?"

"Let go of her."

"I don't know if I can."

"Try. You lose any friends in Cuba?"

Ryder nodded.

"You still mournin' them?"

"I miss them."

Roger sighed. "I miss Riley. I mourn him now. I may get over it someday. But I'll never forget him. I'll always miss him."

"So will I."

"If you find someone to love more than Emily, you'll be able to let go of her."

"Like Becky Jarrett?" Ryder complained. "She's just a kid. How could I love a kid?"

"That's for you to find out."

Ryder frowned. He pointed toward a couple of oaks off to the left. "Let's eat there."

"Sounds good."

# CHAPTER THIRTY-NINE

DISTURBING DREAMS FILLED RYDER'S sleep. He dreamt of disappearing people, disappearing houses, disappearing trees, disappearing deserts and prairies and mountains. In his last dream before awakening, great beasts wandered the world, gobbling up men, women, and children alive, until all that remained was a desert surrounded by either choking dust or choking smoke. And as he wandered the desert, lost and alone, without even a monster to kill him, he wondered where he was and why.

He awoke in the morning, cold and hungry. He got up, visited the water closet down the hall, then washed up, dressed, put on his pistol belt and pistol, and went down stairs.

Smelling bacon, beef, potatoes, and eggs from the Guzmans' kitchen, he went there.

"Good morning, Ryder!" Dolores Guzman called out. "Merced, set a plate for him."

Merced, frying bacon and beef steak, went to get Ryder a plate, some flatwear, a napkin, and a cup for coffee. He nodded at Ryder and briefly smiled.

"We haven't seen much of you lately," Dolores said. "Where have you been? What have you been doing?"

"Visitin' people. Askin' questions."

"Questions?" Merced asked.

Ryder nodded.

"Sit down, sit down," Dolores said. Turning to her husband, she asked, "What's ready?"

"Everything."

"Then bring it," she said. She scraped a huge pan full of sliced fried potatoes onto a plate. On another plate, she scraped scrambled eggs, all yellow and buttery and white. And on a third plate, she placed flour tortillas. She brought first the eggs, setting them on the table and pulling from her apron's pocket a large serving spoon. Then she brought the potatoes, producing a second large spoon for them. Then the tortillas.

While Mrs. Guzman served her plates, Mr. Guzman delivered his plates of bacon and beef steaks. He also brought a large pot of coffee.

"Sit, sit," Dolores said.

"Not before you, ma'am," Ryder said.

"Your mother taught you well," Merced said.

"Not my ma. My pa taught me manners."

Both Guzmans stared at Ryder in disbelief.

He smiled, wryly. "Well, my pa taught me to never wear my hat indoors. An' to never sit down before ma sat at the table. But ma taught me the rest."

Merced laughed. "That's what I thought. Sit down, woman, sit down. Men are waiting."

She chuckled and sat, her husband holding her chair.

After Dolores sat, Merced and Ryder sat. Ryder made certain that Merced sat just before he did.

"What'll you have?" Merced asked.

"Everythin', if you please."

Dolores smiled and looked at her husband, tears in her eyes. "It's just like having the boys back."

Merced nodded. He passed the bacon and beef to Ryder. While Ryder forked meat onto this plate, Merced poured him coffee. Dolores passed the eggs, the potatoes, and the tortillas.

Ryder filled his plate with food. He was hungry. He'd had lunch with his father and then they had ridden a little more in silence. Ryder left him at the road to their ranch, then moseyed back to town. It was dark when he returned and after unsaddling No Name and brushing her down, he guided her into her stall and returned to the hotel. Too tired to eat, he went to bed.

Where demons and dreams haunted him all night.

"You're hungry," Merced said.

Ryder nodded, eggs and potatoes filling his mouth.

"Good to see you eating so well," Dolores added.

Covering his mouth with his palm, Ryder mumbled, "Everythin' tastes great."

She smiled and ate her food with more daintiness.

Later, plates covered with crumbs, cups refilled with steaming coffee, Merced asked, "What kind of questions have you been asking?"

"The kind without answers."

"What do you mean?" Dolores asked.

"Do you mean more questions than answers?" Merced inquired.

Ryder nodded. "For every question answered, there's many more questions to ask. An' no answers."

"About the hanging?" Dolores asked, her voice trembling.

Ryder nodded again.

"Who have you talked to?" Merced requested.

"My pa, Joad, Sheriff Carlson, Dell Jarrett."

"Three out of four good choices," Merced said. "What did your father say?"

"That I should look at it from a different way."

"How?" Dolores asked.

"From the way of why would anyone want Mr. Gleason dead."

Merced nodded. "Your father's a wise man. What have you come up with?"

"Not much, yet. At lunch yesterday, I asked him if he knew who would want Mr. Gleason dead. He said I should find who hated him the most."

Dolores nodded. "He was not a nice man."

"Twenty years ago, he was," Merced said. "But time and this country ages a man, and men change with age."

"How did he change?" Ryder asked.

"He became cold and hard."

"He was rude to his wife," Dolores added. "Cruel to his children."

"How so?" Ryder asked.

"He has four children," Dolores explained. "Three sons and a daughter. He struck his daughter in public a few weeks ago. And the way he stared at his sons, it made me shiver. It was like he hated everyone."

"Why did he strike his daughter? What's her name?"

"Suzy. He struck her for talking to your brother."

"Why?"

"He said he didn't want his daughter getting with child by slutting around with your brother," Merced said.

"Merced, please," Dolores chided.

"It needed saying."

"They're just kids," Ryder said.

"Twelve is old enough to marry," Merced said.

Ryder shook his head. "That just gives Riley a motive to murder him."

"Gleason also broke Brenda's arm last year," Merced added.

"Brenda?"

"His wife," Dolores filled in.

"For what reason?" Ryder asked.

"For defending his daughter," Merced said.

"How do you know?"

"It happened in front of the Mercantile Store. Everyone saw it, even us."

"What happened?"

"He threatened to beat his daughter for talking to another boy," Dolores said. "He had removed his belt and was going to whip her with it. When her twin brother, Nate, tried to interfere, he knocked him down and whipped him. Then when Brenda screamed for him to stop and stood in front of Suzy to block him, he grabbed her arm and twisted it hard enough to break it."

"Other motives," Merced said.

"How so?"

"Why would a loving father abuse his children so much? Maybe Brenda shot him," Merced suggested. "Though the evidence does make it more likely Riley shot him."

Ryder stared at Merced.

"Could it have been a robbery?" Dolores asked.

Ryder glanced at her.

"Maybe someone met him on the road just before he crossed in front of Riley. Maybe he shot Mr. Gleason," she suggested.

"Then the buggy would have been stopped," Ryder said, "so the killer could rob Gleason."

"Maybe the robber scared the horse along, throwing pebbles at it," Dolores added.

"Then what was taken?" Ryder asked, glancing from Dolores to Merced.

Merced shrugged. "We heard of nothing being stolen."

"Then it can't be a robbery."

"Maybe Riley spooked the killer and he fled," Dolores suggested further.

"Why?"

"Why, why, why?" Dolores wondered. "Why do you say 'why' so much?"

"It's a useful tool."

"Tool?" Merced and his wife both asked.

"A useful question," Ryder explained. "When interrogatin' someone, you ask certain questions, such as how was the deed done, or where did it happen, when did it happen, how did it happen, questions like that. Why is the most important question, as it leads to motive. Why would the killer shoot Gleason an' then let the horse run away? If it was for robbery, why didn't the killer rob him afterward?"

Dolores sighed. "I just thought it might be a good reason why Mr. Gleason was killed."

"So complex, is life," Merced said. "Who knows why he wasn't robbed, if he was even robbed. I cannot believe your brother murdered Gleason. Someone else must have done it. But who and why, I do not know nor can I say."

The conversation dried up. Ryder stared at the crumbs on his plate. Then he finished his coffee, wiped his mouth with his napkin, and stood.

"Going?" Merced asked.

Ryder nodded. "There are people to talk to today, two of which are Judge McHugh an' Doc Welsh."

"Must you take that?" Dolores asked, pointing at his pistol.

"Men attacked me yesterday. It was a fist fight. But what if one of them had decided to draw on me. I coulda died."

"And if you had your gun, would you have shot him?" Dolores softly demanded. "Would you have killed Emily's brother Ben?"

"I had my pistol. But how d'you know about the fight?"

"It is a small town. Everybody talks," Merced said.

"And would Emily hate you any less if you had killed her brother?" Dolores asked.

Ryder shook his head. "No," he said, his voice smaller. "She'da hated me all the more. But better to be alive than dead."

"That's what our son Emilio thought," Merced said. "He lived by the gun and died because of it."

"But was Ernesto also carryin' a gun when he died?" Ryder asked, his voice cold.

"No," Merced shot back. "But how would his having carried a gun have saved him from the drunken cowboy who shot him in the back?"

"It wouldn't. But having a pistol handy often keeps people from shootin' at you. People respect guns an' fear them. Who wants to get shot?"

"Who indeed?"

Both men stopped arguing as Dolores sobbed. They looked at her. Merced's face grew harder, for a moment. Then it softened. "I am sorry, mi corazon," he said to her.

"I'm sorry, too," Ryder said. He stood there, gazing at these two people who had been such good friends to him since his return. He sighed and undid his gun belt. He handed it to Merced. "Take care of this for me, please."

"I will. Be safe."

"I hope so."

# CHAPTER FORTY

AS RYDER DESCENDED THE steps in front of the Guzmans' Hotel, he tightly buttoned up his coat. It was a much colder day than yesterday. With his coat closed, no one would know whether he was carrying his pistol or not.

Anyone drawing on him would have an easy target, but an impossible job of explaining why they shouldn't be hanged for murdering an unarmed man. Most gunslingers would first make sure whoever they shot at, at least was armed. Murder was murder, and killing an unarmed man was murder, wherever you went in the world.

But at the same time, if he let his instincts move his hand toward a gun he didn't carry, that would benefit his killer. Such motion would provide a much-needed shadow of doubt for anyone intending to kill him.

He didn't know if anyone would try to kill him today. But after his fight yesterday, with Ben Walker and his friends, Ryder realized that his hometown was as violent and unforgiving a community as any other in the world.

He felt naked. Yet he understood why Dolores Guzman wanted him to proceed unarmed. One Mann had been hanged for murder already. She didn't want another Mann to die, whether someone else started firing first or not. The court and sheriff in this town were as cold as an ice storm in December. Even if he was justified in shooting anyone shooting at him, it only took one stray bullet to take an innocent bystander's life. And if that bystander was a child, woe to the shooter, even if he was defending his life.

A stiff wind was blowing leaves and small branches, bits of paper, and even an odd piece of clothing here or there, down the street.

Ryder kept his gun hand on top of his hat as he scurried across the street. He had no intention of wandering down the main street. Besides, those that he sought were on the next street over.

He hoped that Doc Welsh and Judge McHugh were in today. He wanted answers and he was growing tired of wandering around, wondering what to do next.

Detective work was new to him.

In the war with Spain and the war with killers, Ryder considered himself more soldier than lawman. His job was to remove the lawlessness from the world, not figure out who was guilty and who was not.

However, he had to admit, it was a lot quieter and safer asking questions than shooting at someone who shot back, who wanted to take your life before you took theirs.

There was only one real problem with going around town unarmed: Rangers weren't supposed to go anywhere unarmed, not even to an outhouse, not even to church, not even when bedding a woman. A Ranger was supposed to always have his gun at hand.

Ryder made it across the dusty, windy street without a problem. He continued down toward Doc Welsh's clinic, the wind at his back, pushing him along.

He was pleased when he found the clinic open. He was less pleased when he entered and saw Emily and a strange man standing there, backs toward him, holding hands.

They didn't see him enter. But Welsh did.

"Ryder, I'll be with you in a moment," he said. "Close the door, if you'd be so kind."

Ryder turned and closed the door. Turning back, he saw Emily, wearing a bonnet over her brown hair, looking over her should at him, eyes glaring with contempt. The man with her, of medium build and height, also looked over his shoulder. His eyes were just as cold as Emily's.

Removing his hat, Ryder nodded to Emily. She looked away. So did the man with her.

He didn't mean to listen in, but the foyer to the clinic was small, with barely enough room for all of them, including Welsh.

"She'll be fine," Welsh said. "Just a twisted knee. She'll be okay in a few days, enough time before walking down the aisle with you on your wedding day."

"Good, good," the man said. His voice was loud, not booming, but deep, deeper than Ryder's.

"Your daughter's a strong girl. But keep her off of her knee for a few days. I know she'll want to run around but her knee needs time to get better," Welsh said.

"Any medicine I can give her?" the man asked.

"Love. Patience. And be there for her when she complains about wanting to do things for herself. And find her a place downstairs until her knee gets better. Give it a week. And bring her back sooner still."

The man nodded.

"I'll get her for you," Welsh said, disappearing through a door behind him.

The moment the door clicked closed, Emily spun around. "What're you doing here?" she demanded, her voice colder than the coldest winter day.

"I have some questions for Doc," Ryder replied.

"About what?" Emily demanded.

"About Riley," he said. He turned to the man. Extending his open hand, Ryder said, "You must be Barry Farrell."

"How d'you know who Ah am?" Farrell asked, a slight Texas twang to his voice.

"My Pa told me about you."

"And what did he tell you?" Emily interrupted before Farrell could speak.

Ryder stood there, his right hand still extended, his left hand holding his hat. "That he's a good man. And that he's a merchant."

"What's wrong with that?" Emily snarled.

"Nothin'," Ryder replied. He still held his hand out.

Farrell looked at Ryder, at his open hand, and at Emily. He reached out and grabbed Ryder's hand. He gave it a solid squeeze, one that often brought lesser men to their knees.

But Ryder returned the grip with a firm, though not harsh, clasp. "Pleased to meet you."

"The same," Farrell said, releasing Ryder's hand. "That's quite a grip you got there."

"Yours, too." Ryder flexed his fingers and after a moment, so did Farrell.

"I'm sorry about what happened to your brother," Farrell said.

"Thanks."

"If there's anything I can do to help, let me know."

"Nothin' that I know of, except let Emily tend to Ma for now."

"Done. You been out there yet?"

"Some. But my work's here right now."

"How so?" Farrell inquired.

"I'm tryin' to find out what really happened."

"And what have you found out?" Emily demanded.

"That maybe Riley didn't do it. That maybe Mrs. Gleason might have."

"Why would she do that?" Emily asked.

"She may have hated her husband enough to do it. He broke her arm last year an' frequently beat Nate and Suzy."

"That's no motive," Emily said.

"Hate's a powerful thing."

"Then maybe I should shoot you. I hate you as much as anyone can."

Farrell turned to her. "Em. That's enough," he said, voice soft and warm and kind.

Emily glared at her future husband, then her face softened and she glanced at the floor for a moment. When she looked up again, avoiding Ryder's eyes, she said, "Sorry, Barry."

"I want you to set a good example for Tilly," Farrell said. "I don't want my little girl growing up hating people."

"I don't hate people. I just hate that particular man," she said, pointing at Ryder.

Farrell tilted his head. Emily frowned and turned away. "I'll go get Tilly," she said, stepping through the door Welsh had disappeared through.

Farrell turned back to Ryder. "Aside from everythin' else," he said, "she's ragin' mad that you beat up her brother yesterday."

"Did Ben tell you he threw the first punch? Did he tell you he was with several others an' they were all beatin' on me? Did he tell you Deputy Rixx broke it up?"

"He told us Rixx broke it up. He didn't say anythin' about anyone else."

"Maybe you should ask Ben how many others helped him jump me."

"Maybe so."

"Poppa!" a little girl's voice chimed. She came through the doors in crutches. "I don't need these stupid things. I can walk by myself."

"If Doc says you need them," Farrell said, "you need them."

"I don't care what he says. When no one's looking, I won't be using them."

"Your father said to use them," Emily said, sweetly and supportively and softly. "Don't you care enough to do what he says?"

"He doesn't always know what's good for me."

"Hush, now," Farrell said. "Let's get goin'."

"Who's this?" Tilly asked, looking up at Ryder.

"Just somebody I met."

"You ain't that monster that beat up Uncle Ben, are you?"

Ryder looked down at her. "Maybe."

Tilly dropped one crutch and grabbed the other in her hands. She swung it at Ryder's shins. He hopped backward, crashing into the door.

Welsh came out at the sound of the crash. As Tilly raised the crutch to bash at Ryder's head, Welsh grabbed it from her hand.

"Don't you want to walk at the wedding?" he demanded.

Tilly grimaced in pain and anger. "Yes, sir."

"Then you do what I told you to do. And you leave this poor man alone."

"He's a monster. He beat up Uncle Ben."

"He's not a monster," Farrell said. "In fact, if it weren't for him, I wouldn't be marryin' Em and you wouldn't be havin' her for your ma."

Tilly stared at her father. "But..."

"Your father's right," Emily said. "Whatever else you may think he is, he brought your father and me together. Now, let's get you back on those crutches and get you home."

Tilly sighed. "Okay, Emily."

"Don't you mean 'mother'?" Ryder asked, stumbling up. "She's your mother now, if you want her to be."

Emily and Tilly both stared at Ryder. Tilly turned to Emily, whose face immediately softened. She knelt in front of the girl.

"You still want me for your mother?" Emily asked.

"More than anything!" Tilly exclaimed.

"Then I am."

Tilly whooped and left her crutches again, for Emily's arms.

After a few moments of hugs and kisses, Emily helped Tilly into her crutches. She looked at Ryder. Her eyes bore anger, even hatred, but were also filled with wonder. She smiled, just a little, the corners of her mouth up-turning for a moment.

Ryder nodded.

She nodded back.

Turning, he opened the door for them. Farrell, Emily, and Tilly exited into the wind.

The family that he would never have disappeared into the dusty day. It was the family that Emily deserved.

After they left, Ryder closed the door.

# CHAPTER FORTY-ONE

"**N**OTHING LIKE A LITTLE excitement to get the heart going, eh, Ryder?" Welsh said. Welsh was shorter than Ryder, by a good five inches. He had a pot belly and a grayish-white beard. He wore a bowtie and his coat fit his arms and shoulders, but not his waist. He wore wire-rimmed glasses. His face was a ruddy red, but his hands and throat were deeply tanned.

Ryder turned away from the door. "You're a peculiar man, Doc."

Welsh laughed. "What can I do for you, Ryder?"

"Walter Mixon said you have evidence that Riley didn't kill Gleason. I'd like to know what it is."

"I think that Judge McHugh and I should explain it to you together. Let me get my hat and lock up. No one's here right now and I'm not expecting anyone anytime soon."

Ryder waited while Welsh disappeared from the foyer. A moment later, Welsh returned wearing his hat.

"Let's go," Welsh said, opening the door and stepping out into the cold wind. With his left hand, he immediately crushed his hat to his head to keep the wind from taking it from him while he waited for Ryder to exit his office. Once

Ryder was out, Welsh locked the door and started down the street. He kept his hat tight to his head.

Ryder followed him. He held onto his hat, too.

The wind pushed them down to Judge McHugh's office. They knocked on the door. McHugh opened it.

"I've been expecting you, Ryder. I'm glad you brought Doc with you," McHugh said, his deep voice friendly.

"It's the other way around," Ryder said. "Doc brought me."

"To be honest," Welsh began, "the wind brought us here."

"So I see," McHugh said.

They entered and McHugh closed the door. He directed them toward his desk, a large, dark brown thing covered with stacks of books and piles of paper. A simple, cushioned, high-backed chair stood behind it.

It was cold out and the wind made it feel even colder. But the inside McHugh's office was well-lit and warm. In one corner stood a narrow wood stove, a pot of coffee on it. The heat from the wood stove made the room tolerable. Further heat was provided by several kerosene lamps.

"I won't ask what I can do for you because I know. What has Luke told you?" he said, referring to Welsh.

"Nothin'."

"I see." McHugh sighed. "Well, I'll let him go first an' then I'll tell you what we think happened."

"What we know happened," Welsh said.

"We have no proof. It's all speculation," McHugh said.

"I have proof."

"But not enough."

"Get to the point," Ryder snapped, tired of all the bantering. He'd just done the toughest thing he'd ever done, letting go of Emily and letting her know it by announcing to Farrell's daughter that Emily truly was her mom. He now knew what he didn't know yesterday, or even this morning, that there was no turning back, no returning to the past. Emily loved someone else and that someone was Farrell, and especially his daughter, Tilly. Ryder could never compete with that. He could never win her back. He had to go on, no matter how hard it was.

He was angry now, angrier than he had ever been. He felt like he had let go of his future and now there was nothing left to live for. He was angry at himself for letting go of Emily, even if it was the right thing to do. He was also angry at himself for having abandoned her in the first place. Lastly, he was so angry at himself, that he was furious for not returning sooner, for not making amends, for being afraid, for being a coward. A man who could charge up an enemy held hill, even though surrounded by his fellow Rough Riders and other solders, while bullets hissed past and bombs blew men to bits, but couldn't confront the woman he loved was no man at all, but just a coward.

And Ryder was also angry, not just at himself but at the people of Brannan, for their unkindness and hard-heartedness toward his brother when they turned their backs on Riley, when they accused him of murder. He had no patience left for friendly banter. The joy, the hope, the life was gone from his heart. His heart still beat, but now it was cold.

"What d'you have to tell me?" he demanded.

Welsh looked at Ryder's hard, cold eyes. "The bullet hole was wrong."

"How so?" Ryder's voice was cold, hard.

"When a bullet goes through a man's body, as the .44 caliber slug that penetrated Vernon Gleason's body did, it makes a small hole where it enters but punches a bigger one out the other side. The bullet does that because as it passes through the body it's shoving everything in front of it out of the way," Doc explained, matter-of-factly.

"I know that."

"The small hole was in Gleason's chest and the larger hole came out his back, close to his spine," Welsh said, cool and to the point.

Ryder stared at Welsh for a moment. Then he said, "How's that important?"

"From where Riley stood, he could only have shot Gleason if he had shot him in the back," McHugh said. "But Gleason had been shot in the chest."

Ryder stared at McHugh, then at Welsh.

"Riley didn't shoot Gleason," Welsh said, slowly and carefully.

"He was innocent," McHugh said.

"Then why'd they hang him!" Ryder's bellowing voice was so cold, so angry, so hard, that both men flinched when he spoke.

"That's where it gets worrisome," McHugh said. "You see, Judge Garson an' Prosecuting Attorney Fields had a secret meeting. We had already presented this information to them. And then they met. Afterwards, Garson forbade us to talk with anyone about it or even mention it. When Luke tried to tell some of the jury members, Garson charged him with contempt of court and had Sheriff Carlson confine him in his house. I then had a choice. Garson could confine me to my house, too, or I could try to defend Riley but keep my mouth shut."

"But he couldn't keep his mouth shut," Welsh said. "So he was placed under guard at his house, too."

"And who guarded you?"

"Carlson had deputized some of the townsfolk," McHugh said.

"Who?"

"Joe Nolan, Ike McGuire, Jim van Dyke, Tony Rixx, Owen Gleason," McHugh said.

"McGuire?" Welsh exclaimed. "He was on the jury!"

"I know," McHugh said. "After the trial, Deputy Rixx and McGuire came over and took over watching me. Later, just before the hanging, Rixx's brother, Tony, replaced them as my guard.

"Tony played with his gun a lot and said it was a shame that an honest man like me had to lie about Riley being innocent. He also said that it was sad that the truly innocent suffered when someone lied about who was innocent and who wasn't."

"What?" Welsh exclaimed. "Did he mean your wife?"

"No. If Tony's anything more than a cold killer, he's blunt. He meant my grandchildren. They live in Santa Fe, you know. He named all six of them, including my five-year old granddaughter. He said kids die any of a hundred different ways, from snake bite, spider bite, even from stray bullets."

"So you let them hang my brother because you were afraid for your family?" Ryder demanded.

"They're my grandkids! What did you expect me to do? What would you have done?" McHugh yelled at him. "The oldest is my first grandchild. She's fifteen. Rixx described her to her toes. Her face, the way she smiles, how she laughs, who her friends are, what color dresses she prefers. He said how easily someone could steal her in the middle of the night from my son's house. How sad it would be if someone beat her, abused her, killed her. How could I choose between your brother and my granddaughter?

"But I did. I did! Oh, Ryder, it's so easy to judge from the bench when the law's on your side. But when it's not? When the men entrusted to protect you don't? When they threaten you? And not just you, not just your wife or children, but your grandchildren?"

Ryder glared at McHugh. He turned to Welsh. "And you?"

"I was just kept prisoner. No one would harm the only doctor around for fifty or sixty miles. Owen Gleason guarded me, most of the time. He was determined to keep me from spreading the word about who actually killed his father. But he never threatened me. He felt sorry for Riley. He said it would kill his mother if Riley wasn't convicted for murdering his father. But he didn't threaten me, just kept me away from everyone for two days. It was a blessing that no one needed me during that time."

"Why would Fields want my brother dead?" Ryder asked.

"The real question is, who was Fields protecting," Welsh said.

"What d'you mean?"

"He means, that Fields was protecting somebody. Somebody that maybe he loves. Would you kill to protect Emily Walker from hanging?" McHugh asked.

Ryder turned away. He looked at the door leading out of McHugh's office. He had just surrendered Emily to another man. But did he love her enough to keep her from hanging? He loved Riley enough that if he had been here, he would have killed to save him. He supposed he still loved Emily enough to save her for the family she would soon have.

"Well?" Welsh jumped in, "Would you?"

"I would have killed to save Riley. I suppose I could kill to save Emily."

"But who was Fields protecting?" McHugh asked.

"We both know the answer," Welsh said.

"That was a long time ago. And we gave our word never to speak of it again."

"Speak of what?" Ryder demanded.

"Fields and Mrs. Gleason snuck around for a couple of years. But that was years ago," Welsh said.

"You had no right to tell anyone that," McHugh said.

"As much right as you had choosing between Gloria and Riley."

"Gloria?" Ryder asked.

"His oldest granddaughter," Welsh said.

"That was different. Tony Rixx wouldn't have stopped there. He planned on killing me. He said it be would sad how my house would burn down around me while I slept in my bedroom. How my wife and our servants and I would all die horrible deaths. And then he asked, who would save my Gloria?"

"I don't know what happened to that boy," Welsh said. "He was such a sweet child when I delivered him."

"Why would Fields want to protect Mrs. Gleason? Did he think she did it?" Ryder asked.

"Maybe," McHugh said. "But that relationship was over long ago."

"Not exactly," Welsh said.

"What d'you mean?" Ryder asked.

"Nate and Suzy are Fields' children. They didn't belong to Vernon," Welsh explained.

"How would you know?" McHugh demanded of the doctor.

"From when they were born and when they would've been conceived. Gleason was up in Colorado for several months when the two of them were sneaking around. Why do you think Gleason beat the twins and their mother so much? He wasn't a stupid man. He could figure it out when they were born and back track nine or ten months to know he wasn't around."

"That's when he started hating them," McHugh added.

"So Mrs. Gleason killed her husband?" Ryder asked.

"We have no proof of that," McHugh said. "For all we know, it could have been some stranger, who then robbed him."

"Was he robbed?" Ryder asked.

"Yes. He had a silver watch that he inherited from his father," McHugh explained. "No one knows what happened to it."

"So, a stranger could have killed Gleason?" Ryder wondered. "Or it could've been Mrs. Gleason?"

"Or one of her older sons. They've loved Suzy and Nate ever since they were born, and their mother, too," McHugh said.

"So, four possibilities," Ryder said. "Joad said there was too much blood in the buckboard. What does that mean?"

"That he most likely was long dead when he reached the drop where Riley shot over him at his coyote," McHugh said.

"Long dead?" Ryder mused. "How long?"

"At the rate the horse walked, maybe three miles."

"Then Gleason was shot close to his ranch," Ryder suggested.

Welsh nodded in agreement.

"Anyone else I should add to the list?"

"How about Tony Rixx?" McHugh said. "Rixx hated Gleason and vice versa."

"Why?" Ryder asked.

"Because Gleason's son, Owen, was friends with Tony."

"I see."

"As good of a suspect as anyone," McHugh agreed.

"You only want it to be him because you're afraid of him," Welsh stated.

"I admit it," McHugh said. "I fear Tony Rixx. Don't you?"

"I do," Welsh replied. "But it can't be him."

"Why not?" Ryder asked.

"Because Tony Rixx is a gunslinger, not a rifleman."

"That doesn't make any sense," McHugh said. "All gunslingers are riflemen."

"Not all," Ryder said. "Some men like to look into the eyes of the men they kill. They enjoy their fear, their suffering, the surprise and sorrow they feel as they die. I've seen it before."

"Watch a lot of men kill other men before you kill them?" McHugh asked, with cold sarcasm.

"No. I've seen some lawmen who are like that. And a couple of the men who I fought alongside with on San Juan Heights were like that."

"I forgot you were a Rough Rider," Welsh said.

"So, Tony Rixx is out, then," McHugh said. "Too bad. I'd like to see him get what he deserves."

"That's hardly the kinda talk for a judge," Ryder scolded.

"I'm not a judge anymore. Just a scared old man with too many precious grandchildren to lose."

"Besides," Welsh began. "He's only human. No judge is God, even if the state grants such powers to him. Men are strong or weak depending upon what they have to lose. And when it comes to family, all men are weak."

Ryder nodded. "So, what do we have then?"

"Probably one of the Gleasons," Welsh said. "And I'd hate to see that family suffer anymore."

"The way Brenda Gleason argued for Riley's guilt, I'd say it wasn't her. She was defending someone she loved more than herself and was willing to sacrifice someone else for that person," McHugh said.

"So, her son Owen," Ryder suggested.

"Or her son, Nate," Welsh said.

"How sad it will be if it's him," McHugh mentioned.

"How so?" Ryder asked.

"Because he's only thirteen," Welsh explained. "And he was Riley's best friend."

"So," McHugh began, with a sad sigh, "this town will hang another thirteen-year-old boy. We'll be known as the town that kills its children."

"What are you going to do, Ryder?" Welsh asked.

"Find out which son murdered his father."

"What if it's neither?" Welsh asked.

"Then who could it be?" Ryder countered.

"How about Fields?" McHugh asked.

"I don't think so," Welsh said. "He was protecting his kids."

"Oh, dear God, what if it was Suzy?" McHugh said.

"Then that would be the greatest tragedy of all," Welsh said.

"Why?" Ryder asked.

"Because Riley and Suzy were sweet on each other."

Ryder went to the door. "I hate this town," he said.

"They'll hang her, if she's guilty," McHugh said.

"And what about Fields? And Mrs. Gleason?" Ryder asked.

"They'll go to prison for perjury," McHugh stated, flatly.

"So that whole family will be destroyed?" Welsh lamented.

"If you take Nate or Suzy in," McHugh said, "you can count on Owen and his brother coming after you, Ryder. And since Tony's his friend, he'll be after you, too."

Ryder nodded. He started to open the door.

"You know," Welsh began, "I despised you for running off on Emily Walker, Ryder. I hated you for almost five years. But now, seeing what you did for Emily back at my office, and knowing what you have to do now, I feel sorry for you. I admire you for letting go of Emily. But, whether it's revenge or justice for Riley, you're about to kill a family. As surely as if you shot each of them with your pistol."

"Which you may have to do," McHugh added.

"One last thing, Ryder," Welsh began. "Tony Rixx is a close up killer. He can't hit much beyond twenty feet. But less than that and he's death itself."

Ryder nodded again. "Thanks for the warning, Doc. And for your sentiments. You, too, judge."

"Wait. I'll walk with you, if you're heading back toward my office," Welsh said.

Ryder waited.

# CHAPTER FORTY-TWO

I F WALKING WITH THE wind at their backs was hard, walking into the wind was almost impossible. Dust blew into their eyes, into their noses, into their mouths. Ever step forward was like wading through an overflowing stream, with wind instead of water trying to knock them over. Every loose piece of clothing flapped with the wind. They removed their hats and stuffed them in their clothing. Flying grit stung their faces.

They tried talking, but the wind stole their words away. They trudged and stumbled their way back to Welsh's clinic, where they unlocked the door and tumbled inside, barely closing the door against the gale.

Both men coughed and gasped. Welsh produced glasses of water and they rinsed their mouths and swallowed the grit, having no place but the floor to spit, which they didn't do.

"I think it's getting worse," Welsh said.

Ryder nodded, but said nothing. His thoughts were focused on the man he had seen leaning against a building on the side street opposite McHugh's office. The man's hat was drawn over his eyes, his coat tight against his body. The wind whistled past him, but the wall was on the downwind side and provided protection.

The man had looked familiar, though Ryder was unable to see his face. His thinness, his height, the way he stood, reminded Ryder of someone. And though the man obviously sought shelter from the wind, why was he there, when he could be safe inside a saloon, a hotel, a restaurant, anywhere but out in the weather? What was his business, his purpose?

"Thinking about what you're going to do next?" Welsh asked. "How you'll exonerate your brother? Have you thought of what cost it'll bring to the Gleason family, the town, to yourself?"

"None of that matters," Ryder said.

"None of it matters? How can it not matter? If it's Nate or his sister, Suzy, whichever one, he or she will hang. Another child strung up. And for what? Justice? Or revenge?"

"The truth is all that matters."

"The truth!" Welsh exclaimed. "What truth? That your brother was hanged when he wasn't guilty? That one of the Gleason twins is guilty? 'Here, you hanged the wrong child. Here's the one that's really guilty. Hang this child instead.'

"You want to see this town die? Become another ghost town. Another home for killers and vermin? Ryder, killing one child was a crime in itself. But killing two? And what if you're wrong? What if you bring in the wrong Gleason twin and the town hangs him or her? Should we hang them both to make sure? How many children do we have to kill to prove the truth that the wrong child was hanged to begin with?"

"My brother didn't deserve to die."

"No, he didn't. But how many must die for the truth? It's fine for the Arizona Territory to hang thirteen-year-old killers or send them to prison for life, but the people of New Mexico are different. Range wars and feuds have been started in this territory for a lot less than killing children."

"The truth has to be known," Ryder declared.

"What's the truth mean to the law?"

Ryder stared at Welsh. "The truth has to mean something, be worth something. Why else have laws? Why have lawmen?"

"Why indeed? But how many innocent lives have to be ruined for the truth?"

Ryder grasped the door handle.

"Where are you going?"

"Out. I need to find my Pa and talk to him."

"And if he agrees with you?"

"Then we'll pay a visit to the Gleasons."

"Nothing I said means anything to you?"

Ryder turned his head to Welsh. "Why should it? The truth will set us free."

"That was Jesus' truth, divine truth. Your truth is the human kind. Vengeful truth."

"Truth is truth," Ryder retorted.

"The Lord's truth was to forgive. To love your enemies. To do good to them that hate you and use you. How is what you intend to do good?"

"I have to do what I have to do."

"Everybody says that," Welsh said. "But most people mean only to get revenge when they say it."

"I'm only looking for justice."

"Again, like most people, you're not seeking justice, you're just using it as an excuse for revenge."

"What would you have me do?" Ryder bellowed.

"Be stronger."

"How can I? My brother's dead!"

"You let go of Emily Walker a little while ago. Do the same for your hate."

"I don't hate anyone. I want the truth to be known."

"To set you free?"

Ryder stared at his hand on the door handle. "Yes."

"How will that free you?"

"I don't know. It just has to."

As Ryder's hand turned the door knob, as the wind pushed the door inward, a shot pierced the howling wind.

Ryder and Welsh looked at each other. As they dashed outside, two more shots sang out. They came from down the street.

# CHAPTER FORTY-THREE

BOTH MEN RAN DOWN the street, bareheaded, their hats stuffed inside their clothing. As they neared McHugh's office, a man in a black coat, his black hat tied by a string to his chin, ran out.

He saw them racing toward him. In his left hand he held a pistol. From his hip, he fired at them.

Ryder's arm stretched out and shoved Welsh sideways, away. Meanwhile, he dodged the other way. As he fell, he felt the bullet sizzle through the wind past his face.

The man turned and ran down the street. When two shapes appeared from Joad's place, he fired at them, too. One fell and the other disappeared around a corner.

"Who was that?" Welsh asked, breathless.

"Tony Rixx. I saw him leaning against a downwind wall earlier but didn't recognize him then. He hid his face too well." Ryder got to his feet, though the stiff breeze tried knocking him down. Bracing against the wind, he helped Welsh up.

"McHugh!" Welsh exclaimed.

McHugh's door banged in the wind. They rushed inside. McHugh's desk chair was tipped over backwards.

He lay in it, dead. He had a revolver in his hand. There were two bloody wounds in his chest.

"He must've gotten off the first shot," Welsh said, kneeling beside him. "No one with two holes in his chest could've shot back."

"Little good it did him," Ryder said. He fingered a splintered bullet hole in the door's frame.

"Tony shot at someone else, didn't he?" Welsh asked, standing.

"Yep. Joad, maybe."

They hurried out, Welsh closing McHugh's door behind him. Down at the smithy, they found Joad and Nielsen, sitting on the ground beside the car barn. Joad held his right ear. Blood trickled from his hand.

Leaning close, Ryder asked, "You okay?"

"Ah is," Joad said, standing up with Nielsen's help. "If'n Ah had any granchillen, Ah's could tell 'em 'bout how Ah got part o' mah ear shot off. But, o' cos, Ah doan."

"Maybe someday you'll be an uncle and you can tell your nieces and nephews," Ryder said, while Welsh inspected Joad's ear.

"Den Ah be happy!" Joad gushed.

"Flesh wound," Welsh said. "He'll be okay."

"Ain't you happy now?" Ryder asked.

"Sho' is, whiles yew's around."

"What's goin' on here?" Sheriff Carlson demanded, out of breath and hatless. He had grabbed his gunbelt and bolted out of his office at the sound of gunfire, Deputy Rixx trailing a few steps behind him.

Welsh looked up from where he knelt beside Joad. "McHugh's been shot."

"How bad is it?" the sheriff asked.

Ryder turned to the Carlson and Rixx. "He's dead."

Carlson flinched. "Dead?"

"Who did it?" Deputy Rixx demanded.

Welsh stood and looked him in the eyes. "Tony."

"Can't be!" Rixx spat back. "I was just talkin' to him not ten minutes ago."

"I'm sure you were," Ryder said. "He shot at us. I felt the slug burn by my face."

"Ah's saw 'im, too. He shot part o' mah ear off!" Joad said.

"Can't be," Rixx repeated.

"It's so," Ryder said. "He dodged down the side street past the smithy, away from Main Street."

Carlson glanced at his deputy. "Get 'im."

"But it can't be him," Rixx countered.

"Get 'im. Now!" Carlson bellowed.

Deputy Rixx nodded and trotted off toward the side street.

"Show me McHugh," Carlson ordered.

Welsh led the way back to the McHugh's office. As Welsh opened the door, a gust of wind whipped through it, scattering loose papers everywhere. Carlson and Ryder followed Welsh inside.

The sheriff rubbed a hand through his dusty and windblown hair. He went over and stared down at the retired judge's body.

After a moment, he turned and looked at Ryder and Welsh. "What happened?"

"What d'you think happened?" Ryder snapped at him. "Tony told McHugh he would kill him if he ever spoke to anyone. An' now he's kept his promise."

Carlson glared at Welsh. "You had to go an' blab, didn't you? You knew what would happen if the two of you talked an' now McHugh's dead."

"You should be, too," Ryder growled.

"Don't you dare talk to me like that," Carlson growled back.

"Why not? You're as guilty as Tony Rixx. You let an innocent boy die. It's as if you shot McHugh yourself."

"It's not like that."

"Why isn't it like that?" Ryder demanded.

"I did what Judge Garson told me to do."

"So easy, isn't it?" Welsh gently said, "to blame someone else for your own sins."

"Did you want me to disobey the Court? My job is to uphold the law. To see to it that justice is done."

"Justice!" Ryder stepped over to Carlson, stopping inches from him. "You call it justice to hang the innocent?"

"Other lives were at stake."

Ryder spat in Carlson's face. The sheriff flinched. His hand brushed his coat, finding his gun handle. But Ryder clamped his own hand on top of Carlson's. Carlson tried, but couldn't draw his pistol.

"I ain't carryin'," Ryder snarled. "Gunnin' me down would be just like what you did to my brother, murder."

"You ain't innocent," Carlson hissed back.

"Maybe not, but you ain't, either." Ryder let go and backed away.

Carlson drew his gun and cocked the hammer back.

Welsh said, "If you shoot him, you'll have to shoot me. And there's not another doctor around for sixty miles. If someone just happens to shoot you, there won't be anyone around to save you."

Carlson slowly eased off the pistol's hammer. Once the hammer was back down, Carlson re-holstered his weapon. "This ain't over yet."

"It ain't. But you still have to bring Tony in for shootin' McHugh," Ryder said.

"If'n he's guilty."

"He is," Ryder said.

"Your word ain't proof."

"We'll see."

"We will." Carlson shoved past Ryder and left McHugh's office. Ryder shut the door after him.

# CHAPTER FORTY-FOUR

"WHAT NOW?" WELSH ASKED Ryder.

Ryder shrugged. "Don't know."

"You going after Tony?"

Shaking his head, Ryder said, "No. I don't have my pistol with me. An' besides, he's probably long gone by now. He may have had a horse stashed somewhere nearby. I doubt Deputy Rixx will bring in his brother, even if he finds him. An' with this wind, any tracks Tony left behind are already gone. We don't even know where he's goin'."

"You don't think he's going to Santa Fe to murder McHugh's granddaughter, do you?" Welsh asked

"Nope. That's days and days of hard ridin' away. Even if he went over to Las Vegas and took the train, that's still a couple of days of ridin' followed by a day of sittin' on a train. We could warn McHugh's son by telegraph long before Rixx got there. He'd be runnin' into a trap. Even as stupid as killin' McHugh was, I don't think Tony's so stupid as to travel all the way to Santa Fe to murder a girl for no good reason."

"He has a reason," Welsh countered. "He told McHugh that if he talked, what would happen to his granddaughter."

"Tony got what he wanted. He scared McHugh into keepin' quiet an' lettin' my brother die for someone else. Killin' that girl wouldn't accomplish anythin'."

"I suppose you're right. So what will you do now?"

"Go back to the hotel. Get my gun. Then go visit Mr. Fields."

"Why?"

"Why get my gun or why visit Fields?"

"Both."

"So I don't walk into an ambush without my gun. An' to find out why Judge Garson did what he did for Fields. An' find out who Fields is protectin'."

"After you're done talking to Fields, I suppose you'll be heading out to the Gleason ranch?"

"Most likely."

"And then what, justice?"

"I don't know. But I want the truth. I want to know why my brother died. Why his life was less valuable than someone else's."

"Need help?"

With a gesture, Ryder pointed at McHugh's body. "I'll be fine. Do what you have to do."

"I have one more question for you, though," Welsh said.

"Ask away."

"Why aren't we dead? Why didn't Tony's bullet kill one of us?"

"He wasn't tryin' to kill us."

"Seemed like he was."

"That was just panic fire, to scare us off."

"Tony's too good of a shot for that," Welsh countered.

"Then it was the wind an' dust in his eyes," Ryder retorted.

Welsh nodded. "Maybe so. In this weather, just seeing is hard enough to do."

Nodding and opening the door, Ryder looked out. Looking downwind was easy. Looking upwind was more difficult, what with the sharp, cold air, and the blowing sand and dust. His hat was still safely tucked inside his shirt, beneath his overcoat.

No one was out there that he could see.

He stepped into the wind. Behind him, he heard the soft thud of McHugh's door closing as Doc Welsh pushed it closed.

Trudging forward into the wind, grit and cold air stinging his face, burning his eyes, Ryder found himself groping forward through the wind, barely able to see.

He made it to a building and ran his hands along the side of it, tracing his way toward the downwind side. Once he found the corner, he swung around it. The wind was considerably less on the leeward side.

Leaning his face against the wall, he fumbled in his pockets until he found a hanky. Pulling it out, he worked his tongue in his mouth to create spit. Then he licked a corner of the cloth, wetting it, and daubed his eyes until he got the grit out and he could see again.

He removed his crumpled hat from his shirt. Shoving it tight on his head, he took the handkerchief and wrapped it over the top of his hat and tied it down underneath his chin. The hat was tight and uncomfortable, but more or less secure. Then he stepped back into the wind, but this time on Main Street.

Few, if any people, moved about. The only ones braving the wind were like him, the ones who had someplace to go and needed to get there.

Head down, the wind whipping his hat's brim, he struggled forward, occasionally tripping on a loose board in the boardwalk. He stumbled off the walk into a side street.

He decided to cross the street. He glanced into the wind, watching out for traffic, seeing none. When he reached the other side, he tripped, trying to negotiate the beginning of the board walk.

He crashed into the boardwalk, his elbows stinging from the impact, the air rushing out of his lungs. He coughed and gasped and tried to breathe, tried to rise. He found both difficult.

He couldn't get up.

Then he felt hands helping him up. As he got to his feet, Ryder saw two men standing beside him. Both wore dusty, full-length coats. They ushered him through a door. Inside, he recognized them.

"You," he gasped, hissed, concentrating on regaining his breath. "Thank you."

"The least that I could do," Barry Farrell said. "You blessed my family."

Ryder nodded. He looked around. He was in a clothing store. He looked at the other man. It was Ben Walker, dark bruises covering his face.

There was no anger in Ben's face, but only confusion.

"Where you heading?" Farrell asked.

"Guzman's."

"We heard shooting," Ben said.

"Tony Rixx murdered Judge McHugh," Ryder said.

Neither man said anything.

"I've gotta get goin'," Ryder announced.

"Careful of where you step," Ben said, cautious friendliness in his voice.

"It's blinding out there today," Farrell said.

Ryder nodded. He stepped back out into the wind.

# CHAPTER FORTY-FIVE

RYDER JUST BARELY MADE it back to the Guzmans's Hotel. He had walked the remaining blocks, his head down, with his hat's bent brim deflecting most of the dirt and grit.

Climbing the steps to the porch, he stomped his boots, shaking the dust from them. Afterwards, he opened the door and went inside. The hotel was mostly dark, the exception a lit kerosene lamp on a long pole over by the front desk. At the desk he found a note from the Guzmans saying that they had gone out and would be back later on.

Opening his coat, Ryder retrieved his watch from his shirt pocket and glanced at it. It read Eleven Forty-two.

He sighed. He wanted someone to talk to. No, he needed someone to talk to. He had a lot of mixed-up thoughts and emotions and he needed someone to listen to him. He wanted that someone to be his father. But with the ferocity of the wind and all the flying sand and dirt, he knew riding out to the family ranch was out of the question. If he could barely make it across town, there wasn't any way either his horse, or he, could make it out to the ranch, a few miles away.

The hotel was empty, lonely. The wind howled, whistled, whimpered, and whined outside. Sometimes the wind would shriek as it worked its way through tiny cervices in the walls and between windows and their frames.

It was also cold inside. Wind like this was too dangerous for anyone to start a fire. Even though every chimney and stovepipe had a metal hat on it that caught and kept sparks from flying up and out, from flying the wind in search of dry grasses and dryer wooden buildings to set on fire, to punish and destroy the self-righteous citizens certain they were safe from destruction.

Ryder wasn't one of those citizens. He knew the danger of warming himself through fire on such a windy day.

The good thing about such wind was that it tended not to last long. It either preceded a storm, or proceeded from one. Ryder figured the wind preceded a storm. All he could do was keep as warm as possible and ride the wind out.

He found a candle within a holder and lit it, protecting its flame with a hand. Climbing the stairs, candle in hand, he located his room. Inside, atop his dresser, he found his pistol in its holster, coiled like a rattle snake waiting for its next victim.

With care, he placed the candle on the far side of the dresser, then moving nearer to his weapon-belt, he gently lifted the belt and wrapped it around his hips, closing the buckle and adjusting the belt.

Satisfied, he drew his pistol, sliding it in and out of it's pocket several times, making certain it moved swiftly and with purpose. Then he inspected the pistol's ammunition, making certain that he had five bullets in their five chambers, with the sixth chamber empty and lined up with the pistol's striking hammer. He would have no accidents with his own body, nor with someone else.

Then he located and inspected his spare bullets and stuffed them in his coat's pockets.

Finished, he made a bed on the floor with his back leaning against the end of the room's bed. Anyone coming to kill him would shoot at the bed first, expecting him to be there, giving him the chance to shoot from the floor. Then he went to sleep, the candle still flickering on the dresser.

# CHAPTER FORTY-SIX

HE AWOKE ON THE floor. His room was dark, but not too dark. He was cold and sat up, shivering. The wind whistled but no longer moaned, no longer slammed the hotel, no longer squeezed through the crevices.

Ryder gained his knees, stood. He checked his pistol. All was well. He made his way to his window, drew back the curtain. The wind was soft, quiet, friendly. A light gray overcast covered the sky. The sun was a soft white button, poking through the overcast.

He saw people walking down the street before the hotel. Horses carrying riders meandered by. A small, ungraceful motor car putted along.

His watch said Eight O'clock. It couldn't be Eight. The sun set hereabouts well before Six. He must have slept all night. How was that possible?

His stomach rumbled. His throat, mouth, tongue, lips felt dry, parched.

He heard voices downstairs. He recognized two of them. The Guzmans.

He heard more voices. Sheriff Carlson. Deputy Rixx. And his father's voice.

He left his room, walked down the hallway. At the stairs, he carefully, cautiously, quietly, descended. He stopped at a little landing that turned left and then led to the foyer and the front desk. At the foot of the landing were three more stairs.

The voices came from the main dining room, behind the stairway. The first two stairs were quiet as he stepped on them. But the last creaked as he stepped to the floor.

"What was that?" Rixx exclaimed.

"Me," Ryder replied. As he moved around the stairs and into the open, he noticed three hats on the hat rack by the door, one of which was his father's.

"Come over here," Carlson ordered.

Ryder obliged him. His coat was closed, his pistol hidden.

There was a fireplace in the dining room and a big fire burned brightly in it. Though the hotel was still cold, Ryder felt the heat from the fire.

"Where ya been?" Rixx demanded.

"Upstairs, sleepin'."

"Why?"

"No one was here. I was cold an' tired. So I slept." As Ryder spoke, he kept walking. Around the table, which was between him and everyone else. He moved toward the fire. He was cold and sought its warmth.

"Stop!" Carlson snapped.

Ryder raised his arms until his elbows were even with his shoulders. He turned around. "Why? I'm cold. I just want to get warm."

Ryder noticed that Carlson and Rixx both had their hands on their pistols. He glanced at his father, who was looking at the lawmen, their backs to him. His father's hand was on his pistol, too.

The Guzmans stood beside Roger Mann, but were to his left, in front of the open door into the kitchen.

"Where ya been?" Rixx repeated, his voice edgy.

"I told you I was sleepin' upstairs, in my room."

"Where's your gun?" Carlson asked.

"My rifle or my pistol?"

The response seemed to confuse Carlson.

"Both," Rixx said.

"Upstairs," he lied.

"Search him," Carlson said.

"Why?" Ryder asked.

Rixx started forward. But Ryder's voice startled him. And he stopped, surprised.

Roger Mann said, "My son told you where he was. An' where his guns were."

Both men turned to look at Ryder's father. They noticed his hand on his gun.

"Now, be careful, Roger," the sheriff said. "This ain't none of your affair."

"He's my son," Roger snarled. "He is my affair."

"Ya might git the sheriff, but I'll git ya," Rixx said.

"An' I'll get you," Ryder said. With one hand, Ryder unbuttoned his coat, while his other hand drew his pistol. When Rixx and the sheriff turned around, they were stunned by the sight of Ryder's pistol, in his right hand, pointing at them.

Rixx sneered and started to say something.

"Shut up!" Ryder growled. "Sit down. At the table. I want to see your arms stretched out on that table."

"Boy, ya gittin' into a lotta trouble," Rixx said, sitting down, his back to Ryder, his arms stretched out over the table.

"Really? Where's your brother? McHugh's killer."

"He's gone," Rixx said.

"It's your job to bring him in."

"He's my brother. I'd have to kill him. I couldn't do that."

"Why not?" Ryder hissed. "You murdered my brother."

"He was guilty."

"He was not. And you know that."

"He was…"

"You know he was innocent. You an' Carlson an' that visitin' judge knew my brother was innocent an' you hanged him. You knew the truth an' you wouldn't let it out. It was your job to protect him. The law protects the innocent. But you didn't. Neither of you did. You let an innocent boy die."

"It was out of our hands," Carlson said, sitting at the table, arms also stretched across it. His fingers twitched.

"You knew that he was innocent?" Roger Mann asked. His voice was cold, colder than death. "An' you still hanged him?"

Ryder glanced at his father. Roger had drawn his gun. Ryder watched as Roger's thumb cocked back the gun's hammer.

"Don't do it, Mann," Carlson said, his voice trembling. "You'll be guilty of murder."

"Compared to you, it's justice," Roger replied.

Rixx's right hand darted under the table, where his pistol rested in its holster.

With a long step, Ryder covered the distance to Rixx, poking his pistol into the back of the deputy's neck.

Rixx froze.

"Why do you bring this violence into my home?" Dolores Guzman shrieked. "What kind of men are you!"

Merced wrapped his arms around his wife, who began weeping. "Why are you doing this?" he demanded. "This is my home and none of you belong here."

Roger Mann looked down at his pistol. He uncocked the hammer and replaced his gun in its holster. "I'm sorry, Delores. I'm so sorry."

"Go away, please," she sobbed. "My sons are dead because of men like you."

Roger nodded.

"Yer're goin' to jail for this," Rixx gloated. "We'll wipe out the whole Mann clan."

"Why?" Merced demanded. "Why threaten our friends in our hotel?"

"Because Ryder killed Herman Fields," Rixx said.

Dolores moaned, sinking to the floor. "What is wrong with this town?"

"The Mann family, that's what," Rixx said.

"Why is my family the problem?" Ryder asked. His pistol's barrel still rested against Rixx's neck.

"Cause ya killed Fields. After we found Field's body, we sent for Welsh an' he told us ya were goin' ta see Fields."

"How d'you know Tony didn't do it?" Ryder asked.

"Witnesses saw him ridin' outta town."

"So, it can only be me?"

"That's right. We came ta git ya. An' ya daddy got in the way. Ya are both gonna hang for this!"

"Hang for what?" a voice called out for from the front door.

Every one turned to look at the source of the question. Welsh stood there, hat in hand.

Ryder stepped back to see who it was. He continued covering Rixx.

Rixx leaped up and spun around, drawing his pistol.

Ryder shot him.

# CHAPTER FORTY-SEVEN

"**Y**A SHOT ME! YA dirty sonuvabitch, ya shot me!" Rixx squirmed on the floor. He had dropped his pistol.

Ryder stepped over and retrieved the deputy's gun. He tossed it over to Merced Guzman, who caught it.

"What do you want me to do with this?" Merced asked.

"Put it in the kitchen. Someplace where he can't find it," Ryder replied.

As Merced turned around, Ryder's father said, "Wait a minute."

He moved forward. Carlson still sat at the table, his hands on it. Roger bent over and took the sheriff's pistol from its holster. "Sorry about this, Caleb, but I cannot have you killing my son. One son dead by your hands is one too many."

"You're gonna rot in prison for this, Roger, if you even survive at all. Who's gonna care for your wife now?"

"Me," Roger said. Straightening, he moved back to Merced and handed him the sheriff's pistol. "Someplace safe an' hard to find."

Merced nodded. He glanced down at his wife, sitting on the floor, weeping. He didn't move.

Roger frowned. He stepped over and offered an outstretched hand to Dolores. "I'm sorry for this. You lost three sons an' I lost one. But we can't let the wolves win. One form of evil is just as bad as another."

Dolores nodded. Still weeping, she took Roger's hand and let him pull her up. She removed a hanky from her dress and wiped her eyes. "I understand."

Roger let go of her. She went over to her husband and took the pistols from him. "I will take care of these."

Dolores disappeared into the kitchen.

Merced turned to Roger. "My wife is strong."

"So are you," Ryder's father said.

"And you, my friend."

Meanwhile, Welsh marched over and knelt beside the deputy. He examined Rixx, removed one of his boots. "What a big baby you are, Rixx," Welsh exclaimed. "He shot you in the foot. He didn't even put a bullet in you. He just grazed your foot. You're going to need a new boot and clean socks.

"Speaking of socks, pew. Don't you ever wash your socks or your feet? You smell like you've been walking in pig shit."

Rixx stopped bellowing and grabbed Welsh's jacket lapel. "It hurt's like hell an' all ya are doin' is insultin' me? What kinda doctor are ya?"

"The only one you've got." Welsh stood. He saw Dolores reentering the room. "Mrs. Guzman, could you bring some warm water, some soap, a clean cloth, and some alcohol, please? And some strips of clean cloth for a bandage?"

Dolores nodded.

Welsh looked down at Rixx. "I need you to get up and into a chair. Are you man enough for that?"

Rixx glared at him. "Goddammit, Welsh, ya are gonna go to jail fer this."

"Why?" Welsh responded. Then he said, "When I came in, you said someone was going to hang for something. What were you talking about?"

"Fields," Carlson said. "Ryder killed him."

"How do you figure that?"

"Who else could it be?" Rixx hissed. He managed to climb into the chair he had occupied minutes before.

"What about your brother?"

"He was seen leavin' town after shootin' at ya an' Mann."

"And you think that's proof that he didn't do it?"

"Proof enough," Carlson said. "Which only leaves Ryder."

"Well, I got some news for you," Welsh said. "Fields has been dead for more than a day. He must've been killed while Ryder was visiting me in my office."

"You sayin' Ryder was with you when Fields' was killed?" Carlson asked.

"I am. And since Ryder and I spent the better part of yesterday morning together, I'd say it was impossible that he could have killed Fields."

"We only have ya word," Rixx said.

"His word's good enough," Carlson stated.

"Then I got shot fer nothin'?" Rixx whined.

"Better than you killing an innocent man," Welsh retorted. "Here, over here, Mrs. Guzman."

As Mrs. Guzman walked past, Carlson turned around and stared up at Roger Mann for a moment or two. Then he glanced down at the table top. Looking back up, he said, "Can I git up?"

"Sure. If you're not goin' to misbehave."

"I won't."

Welsh knelt before Deputy Rixx. "Okay, I want you to remove your sock. I'm going to wash your foot. And after I'm done, I'm going to pour a little whiskey on your big nasty wound and then bandage it up. And I want you to clean your other foot and your socks and air out your boots because the next time you get shot in the foot, if your feet aren't clean, I'm not going to take care of you. Got that, mister tough guy?"

"Why're ya makin' fun of me in front of everyone?"

"Because you..." Welsh grimaced and shook his head. "Because I don't like you, that's why."

"Why dontcha like me? What've I ever done ta ya?"

"If you don't know, then you're dumber than I thought."

Ryder had smirked throughout the discussion. With Welsh's last statement, he laughed.

Welsh looked up. "Well, I don't think that was all that funny."

"I do," Ryder said.

# CHAPTER FORTY-EIGHT

THE SHERIFF HAD LEFT, assisting his "wounded" deputy out the front door. Welsh told the lawmen he'd bring their weapons around later, less they were tempted to use them. Carlson agreed to that, while Rixx protested. But Carlson was sheriff and Rixx was only his deputy.

"Someday, when I'm in charge, I'll git even with ya two," Rixx said, as Carlson opened the door for them to leave.

"That's if the town council votes you in," Welsh said.

"And if I recommend you," Carlson added. "We don't need any vendettas."

"I don't know what that means," Rixx said. "But we ain't even yet, Mann, an' I won't give up till we are."

"You murdered my brother," Ryder said. "You'll never be even with me."

"We'll see 'bout, uh…" Rixx grunted as Carlson yanked him out the door and down the steps. "Take it easy, sheriff, that smarts like hell!"

Welsh closed the door and the Guzmans, Ryder and his father, and of course Welsh, returned to the dining table.

"Why would Tony Rixx murder Mister Fields?" Dolores asked, somewhat recovered from the ordeal.

"Because Herman was his father," Welsh said.

"What?" everyone exclaimed.

Welsh nodded. "You never wondered why Fields never married? He liked women."

"I just thought he had a secret lover," Roger said.

"He had a lot of secret lovers. Half the children born around here in the last twenty-five years or so are his," Welsh said.

"I did wonder why so many gringo children looked so alike," Merced commented.

"He got around, didn't he?" Roger said.

"Then why did Tony kill him?" Ryder asked. "Did he know?"

"Maybe. Tony's been lonely for a long time," Welsh explained. "His mother died when he was young. His father, the man he thought of as his father, died or disappeared when he was four. And for the last few years, his brother's been working with the sheriff so much that he hasn't had any time for Tony. Loneliness can be as deadly as a bullet. It kills the spirit long before it kills the body."

"Maybe Tony killed Gleason," Roger suggested.

"Why would he do that?" Dolores asked.

"Maybe Gleason told him Fields was his father. Maybe he rubbed it in to hurt Tony," Merced suggested. "Gleason and Tony hated each other. Maybe he told Tony nobody wanted him, not his brother, not his real father, not anyone. Maybe Tony hated both Gleason and Fields, one for telling him and the other for not telling him."

"We already ruled him out as a suspect," Ryder said.

"Why?" Roger asked.

"He's a close-in killer," Welsh said.

"So?"

"He likes to watch his victims die," Ryder explained.

"We know he likes killing people," Merced said. "Why not use a rifle? Wound him just enough to die slow and then ride up and watch."

"Tony likes to kill close in," Welsh reminded. "With a rifle, he might get lucky and kill his victim right out. No gloating that way."

"Did Mister Fields ever tell Tony he was his father?" Dolores asked.

"To the best of my knowledge, no," Welsh said.

"Then why kill him?" Dolores wondered.

"Out of hatred an' revenge," Ryder suggested. "If Gleason told him the truth, maybe he went to Fields an' demanded to know if it were true. An' maybe Fields rejected him."

"That'd be enough for most men to kill someone," Roger said.

"In any event, Tony killed him," Welsh said. "And Fields was our best hope of finding out who was really guilty."

"Why?" Roger asked.

"Because Fields convinced the court to protect him or her from bein' tried for murder," Ryder said.

"Are you tellin' me that the court actually railroaded my son?" Roger demanded. His face was cold, hard, like the winter ice found in frozen mountain lakes.

"Yeah, Pa."

"Somebody's gonna pay for this!" Roger growled.

"They already have."

"Who? Who has paid?"

"Fields an' McHugh."

"McHugh? He defended Riley. How'd he pay?"

"Tony killed him."

Roger replied with a perplexed look.

"McHugh and I both knew your son was innocent," Welsh explained. "But the judge removed us from the court to shut us up. He had the sheriff place us under house arrest. But Tony threatened McHugh. Told him intimate details about his teenaged granddaughter in Santa Fe. Told him how if McHugh spoke up he'd kidnap, molest, and murder her. So McHugh kept quiet."

"He had to protect his kin, just like I wanted to protect mine," Roger said, frowning, nodding. "But why were you quiet?"

"They wouldn't let anyone near me. And I was watched like an owl hunting a mouse. I was the mouse. I couldn't get away."

Again, Roger nodded. He stared at the table, then looked away, toward the blazing fire.

"How could the men we trust the most to protect us do such evil things?" Dolores demanded. "How could this happen?"

"They say justice is blind," Welsh said.

"It's as blind to the guilty as it is to the innocent," Roger said. "But I don't understand why Tony killed McHugh."

"He's a cold-blooded killer, Pa," Ryder said.

"Maybe so."

Dolores turned to Ryder "What I don't understand is what you meant when you said 'him or her'?"

"That slipped past me, too" Roger said. He asked his son, "What did you mean by that?"

Ryder glanced first at Dolores, then at his father. His expression was confused and sad. "It could be either one."

"Either one?" Roger demanded.

Before Ryder could speak, Welsh piped up. "Gleason was killed miles from where Riley shot at him."

"Near him," Ryder corrected.

"Yes, of course. Near him."

"What d'you mean by that?" Roger demanded.

"He means, Pa, that Gleason may have been killed somewhere near his house an' the horse took off pulling his buggy."

"By whom?"

"His wife?" Merced interjected.

"By either Nate or Suzy. His daughter or son," Ryder said.

"What!" Roger exclaimed.

"Madre de Dios," Merced whispered.

"From as soon as they could walk," Welsh began, "Gleason beat them. And when they got older, especially his daughter, he beat them more."

"And his wife," Dolores added.

"And his wife."

"Why? Why beat them? Why would they kill him?" Roger demanded.

"Because Fields may have been their father," Welsh said. "And maybe Vernon knew."

Roger and Merced sat back, stunned. But Dolores said, "Or maybe they just wanted to be free from his brutality."

"You knew?" Welsh said to her.

"I knew."

"How?"

"By how far she was along when Mr. Gleason returned from Denver. And by my cousin."

"Your cousin?" Welsh asked.

"She is a gossip. She sticks her face into everyone's business," Merced explained.

"It is true," Dolores said. "Mister Gleason had a lover in Denver. He had no interest in his wife or her children."

"Then why did he beat them?" Ryder asked.

"Pride," Roger said. "False pride. He cheated on his wife but couldn't handle her cheating on him."

There was silence for several moments. Then Roger asked his son, "What are you goin' to do?"

"I don't know," Ryder replied.

"What d'you mean you don't know? You know. You'll take them in. You'll exonerate your brother," Roger growled.

"And watch one of them hang for their father's murder?"

"Justice must be served, son," Roger said. "If not for our sake, then for your poor mother's sake."

"And watch another child hang for Gleason's death?" Welsh asked.

"If need be."

"Did you know that your son was in love with Suzy Gleason? That her father forbade her from ever seeing him?" Dolores asked. "Or that Nate was your son's best friend? What would your son say if you helped hang the girl he loved?"

Roger jumped to his feet. "I'm a decent man, Dolores Guzman. But my boy was hanged just a few days ago. My wife is crazy with grief. How can I save her, if the truth doesn't come out?"

"You've been my strength and council my whole life, Pa," Ryder said, "but how will it help Ma to watch another child hang?"

"What can I do? Where was I when my son was in jail? Why did I believe in the integrity of the law when I should've rescued him?"

"Where was I when my brother was hanged?" Ryder asked.

Roger sat back down. "What can I say? I want my son back."

"So do I, Pa. So do I."

"What are you going to do, then?" Merced asked Ryder.

"I don't have any authority in this territory," Ryder said. "But I'm a lawman. Of sorts. I believe in justice. There's still a few hours of daylight left. I'll ride out to the Gleason ranch an' find out what the truth is. Then I'll bring the guilty to justice."

"And if it's Suzy?" Welsh asked.

"Justice must be done." Ryder stood. He left the table and went up to get a little more ammunition. When he returned back downstairs, everyone was gone.

He hadn't eaten yet, but strangely he wasn't hungry. Nonetheless, he got some food from the kitchen. Some flour tortillas with cold beef stuffed in them. Some cheese. A couple of apples, one for himself and one for No Name.

Rifle in hand, pistol hidden by this coat, food in a saddle bag, he left the Guzmans' Hotel and walked toward the stable a few blocks away.

# CHAPTER FORTY-NINE

IT WAS COLDER OUT now, colder than when the wind wailed and whipped through the town the day before. And it was darker outside, more like night rather than midday.

The stable was dark, too. Ryder found a kerosene lantern and lit it. He didn't find the stable hand.

He approached his horse. No Name looked at him, her eyes bright. He petted her side, neck, her face. As he placed a blanket on her back, he said, "I wouldn't take you out on such a dismal an' dark day if I didn't have ta. You're a good horse an' I don't ask you to do anythin' I ain't willin' ta do."

Picking up her saddle, he laid it carefully on her back, petting her as he talked to her. "This is nasty business we're goin' into. I don't know how it'll turn out an' I wish I was anywhere but here today. But at least I'll have you with me."

Once the saddle was on and the straps cinched tight, he found some grain and gave her a handful. When she was done eating, he put her bit in her mouth. Then he gathered some more grain and slipped it into one of his saddle bags.

When he led her out, he turned off the lantern's flow of kerosene to the flame, snuffing it out. He left the lantern outside the stable.

He patted No Name once more. "I know you probably don't understand my words at all, but I bet you get my feelin's. I have to ride out to the Gleasons an' decide which child is gonna die an' it won't make a damn bit of difference. My brother's dead. Why bring someone else in for murder, to die wigglin' at the end of a rope when it won't bring my brother back?"

After swinging into his saddle, he leaned over and patted No Name's neck again.

As he rode out of town, he glanced up at the dark and cold clouds. He'd never seen a more dismal day in his life. Nor had he experienced a colder day. It ate at his bones and his being, knowing where he was going and what he had to do.

Justice was blind, Welsh had said. And justice had to be served, his father had said. Ryder knew justice must be done. But what was just and what was revenge? What good was the law, if in serving it lives were destroyed? But Riley had died for someone else's deed. Was that just?

He remembered Pastor Jarrett once mentioning in a sermon, back before the war with Spain, back before he ran out on Emily on their wedding day, a line from the book of Micah which said, "What does the Lord require of thee but to do justly, to love mercy, and to walk humbly with thy God?"

And as he rode along, his heart ached and his conscience condemned him.

What was justice, without love, without mercy? Was what he planned justice or revenge? Was it done in humility or with arrogance?

As he rode on, he wondered if he had the strength to do what was right. The strength to obey the law, to bring the guilty to justice. The strength to be merciful.

But what was right? The Law was right. But did he have the right to be the Law? Did he have that right?

Justice must be done. The Law was the Law.

A mile passed. Then two. He fished a tortilla out of his saddle bag and ate it, then ate his apple. The Rough Riders had taught him to never fight on an empty stomach. A little food in your stomach gave it something to do besides twist up inside you as you moved into danger.

The clouds lightened, just a little.

More miles and he came to the side road into the Gleasons' ranch. He took a deep breath, stopped, patted No Name on the neck.

He bowed his head and prayed The Lord's Prayer. But he couldn't get past the part that said, "forgive us our trespasses, as we forgive those who trespass against us."

He couldn't forgive himself for betraying Emily, for running off to war, for not coming back when their baby girl had died, for being a coward. Nor could he forgive himself for not returning home immediately when his mother needed him. Where was he when his brother was condemned and hanged?

He may have brought many men to justice as an Arizona Ranger, and he may have stood in battle beside his fellow Rough Riders, but where was his courage with Emily? Where was his courage with his family?

How could he ask others to forgive him, when he couldn't forgive himself?

Ryder had a job to do and he better get to it. He had to find out who murdered Mr. Gleason and he had to bring the killer to justice. It didn't matter that his brother had paid the highest penalty for a crime he didn't commit. Justice must be done. The Law must be served. The killer had to be brought to justice.

Ryder rode down the Gleasons's road.

# CHAPTER FIFTY

THOUGH THE GLEASONS'S HOUSE was set half a mile from the main road, its side road twisted and turned between various low hills, making the trip longer. Rough, rocky outcrops covered the hills. Straggly, thorny bushes bunched around the outcrops. Small oaks, no more than ten feet tall, dotted the hills.

All of this created excellent hiding places for someone planning on ambushing Ryder. It might also have provided cover for whomever had murdered Mr. Gleason.

Ryder was nervous. Tony Rixx, or anyone else, could be hiding anywhere around him. Up ahead, to the left and around another turn, stood a long, low ridge, thirty feet back from the road and twenty feet high. Anyone could be lying flat on the top, legs drooping down the reverse slope, watching through the dry grasses as he rode by, aiming a rifle at him.

Many times, he had been in places like this. Many times, he had shots fired at him and only by chance, by luck, had he survived. But there was always a chance, in his line of work, that a bullet would find and kill him.

He passed the long ridge and all the hills without consequences. And yet, the small hairs on the back of his neck twitched. He felt watched. He felt danger.

He felt death nearby.

Around the last bend stood the ranch house, the barn, and various outbuildings, corrals, pens and sheds.

The ranch house was tall, two stories, with a steep roof and a wide porch all around the base of it. The upper floor had lots of open windows, all good locations for snipers. They'd be far inside, hidden from the outside and yet close enough to see anyone approaching.

There was a large barn, tall, also with a steep roof. On the end that faced him, near the peak, a hay loft door was open. He spotted movement up there.

He took a deep breath and let it out slowly. He had learned from the other gun fighters and lawmen who made up the Arizona Rangers how important it was to control your breathing. If you focused on breathing, then your fear couldn't terrorize you.

Ryder noticed everything as he neared the house.

In front, on either side of the steps reaching up to the porch, stood two hitching rails. At the one on the right stood three horses, saddled, rifles in their boots. Rolled-up blankets were tied behind each saddle, while further back saddle bags bulged with contents.

Off to the left was a flower garden, full of dead flowers. Past the garden, towards the barn, stood a tall hand pump, its spout aimed at a trough full of water. Around the pump lay three empty wooden buckets on their sides.

On one side of the barn was a chicken house, surrounded by a tall wire fence. Chickens wandered within the fenced area. On the other side, away from the house, sheep were penned in. Beside them, in a corral, several unsaddled horses wandered about.

In the distance, beyond the house, he saw cattle. Some in small groups, most in one large group. With the gray sky, he barely saw the cowboys working the cattle.

As he passed the barn, he heard mooing. At least one cow, maybe more, awaited milking.

Pigs roamed about freely.

Nearing the house, he heard the barn door bang open. Turning around, he saw a young boy, no older than Riley had been, burst out and sprint past him toward the house. "Ma, Ma!" the boy cried out.

He stopped twenty feet from the house and dismounted. He rubbed No Name's face, patted her side, whispered for her to relax. He said it more for himself than for her.

The front door opened.

Out came a woman, wearing a gray dress. Her head was bare. Her hair was gray, but some bits of brown streaked it. She held a double-barreled shotgun in her hands. The barrels looked big enough for wagons to roll through.

"Hold it right there, mister!"

"I'm Ryder Mann, Mrs. Gleason."

"I know who ya aire! What d'ya want heah?"

"I've come to find out the truth."

"What d'ya mean by the 'truth'?"

"I've come to find out who killed your husband an' why my brother was hanged for a crime he didn't commit."

"Who says yer brother didn't murder mah husband?"

"Doc Welsh an' Judge McHugh."

"An' how do they know that?"

"Welsh said the bullet that killed your husband came from the front an' went out his back. He also said he'd lost too much blood to have been killed close to town. He said it musta happened closer to home."

"Lies. All lies." She turned to the youth beside her. "Go git yer brothers. Tell 'em ta hightail it back here, pronto. An' tell 'em ta git any of the hands that aire around an' bring 'em back lickity-split."

"Yes'm," said the boy, who Ryder realized must have been Riley's friend, Nate. The boy darted to the nearest horse, unwound its reins from the hitching post, swung into the saddle, and galloped away toward the cowboys in the distance.

While Mrs. Gleason watched her youngest son ride away, Ryder edged away from No Name.

His movement caught the corner of her eye and she spun around, raising her shotgun menacingly. "Ya move 'nother notch, Mann, an' Ah'll blow ya ta Kingdom Come!"

Ryder froze.

"Git yer hands up high."

Ryder complied.

"Who d'ya think ya aire, comin' out 'ere an' threatenin' mah kin?"

"I haven't threatened anyone."

"Yeh, ya have, boy. Ya come to take one of mah boys away fer murder. Well, Ah ain't lettin' ya do that. They aire good boys an' they ain't done nothin' wrong."

"I never said they had."

"But ya been thinkin' it, ain't ya?"

Ryder nodded.

"Thought so. Yer brother was a good boy. But he was in the wrong place at the wrong time. Takin' one of mah boys back fer hangin' won't bring yer brother back. Yer brother's gone. Tain't nothin' ya can do 'bout that."

Ryder nodded.

"Then why ya out here?"

"The law is the law. Justice must be served."

"Justice? That's a laugh. Where was justice when Vernon was beatin' mah children? Where was the law when he almost beat Suzy ta death? He broke her nose an' cracked her ribs. If'n it tweren't fer Nate an' Owen findin' there sister, she'da died. Ah says he got what he deserved, what the Lord intended fer 'im, leavin' her out there fer the coyotes ta find."

"You shouldn't use God for an excuse to commit murder."

"Murder? Hah, Vernon got what he deserved. He hated that girl an' what she'd done ta him twasn't murder, twas self-defense."

"Suzy? She killed Mr. Gleason?"

Mrs. Gleason glared at him. Her eyes and her mouth tightened up. "Ah ne'er kilt a man in mah life, an' now lookit what ya done. She don't deserve ta spend the resta her life in prison or danglin' from a rope. A mother has ta protect her children. Ah can't let ya go now. Yer mother's gonna loose both her sons this week."

"I heard that Riley and Suzy loved each other. Why'd you let him die? If everythin' you say about Mr. Gleason's true, why didn't you come forward an' tell the truth? Why didn't Suzy come forward?"

"Cuz Vernon beat her half ta death."

"If he had beaten her half to death, how did she kill him?"

Before Mrs. Gleason could answer, four men road up. Two of them were the men who had followed Ryder and his father the other day. The other two were Mrs. Gleason's sons. He recognized Nate and Owen.

"What's up, Ma?" said the second of the two men who had trailed Ryder and his father. Before anyone could say or do anything, he had his pistol out, pointed at Ryder. "Want me ta shoot 'im, Ma?"

"No, Victor."

"Why not?"

"Any shootin' will be done by me. If'n anyone has ta dangle, it'll be me."

"I can kill 'im, ma," Victor said. "No one'll know what happened ta 'im."

"My pa knows I came this way," Ryder said. "So does Doc Welsh an' the Guzmans. You gonna kill four more people to keep me quiet?"

"Shush!" Mrs. Gleason exclaimed.

Victor moved his horse over to Ryder. His right hand, holding his pistol, was pointed at Ryder's head. "Ah'll kill 'im right now, Ma. Ya won't have nothin' ta worry 'bout no more."

"Behave yerself, boy!" Mrs. Gleason growled.

Ryder moved. Victor's horse was beside him. He drove his shoulder into the horse's side, while at the same grabbing Victor's stirrup. He heaved the booted stirrup upward, sending Victor tumbling over the horse, slamming him hard into the ground.

Victor's gun went off, firing skyward. The shot and the cowboy's tumble, plus Ryder's shoulder impacting the horse's side, frightened the horse. It almost stomped the fallen cowboy before running off.

The gunshot, and the combat, frightened Ryder's horse, too. No Name raced after Victor's horse.

A loud bang split the air.

"Hold it!"

Ryder turned to see Mrs. Gleason, her face red with anger and fear. She had blasted one of her shotgun barrels into the air. Quick as a rattlesnake, she aimed it at Ryder again.

"Owen, Nate, see ta yer brother. Harry," she said to the hired hand who wasn't one of her sons, "Watch 'im."

Harry drew his pistol and pointed it at Ryder.

The Gleason boys dismounted. They were immediately at Victor's side. "He's okay, ma," Nate said. "Jist got the wind knocked outta 'im."

"I outta kill ya fer that," Mrs. Gleason said.

"Don't worry none, ma," Victor gasped. "Ah'll do it fer ya. With pleasure."

"No, ya won't. Owen, git 'im inside. An' take his gun from 'im."

"Yes'm," Owen said. He took his brother's gun away and gave it to Nate. Then he helped Victor up and took him into the house.

"What am Ah gonna do with ya now?" Mrs. Gleason wondered, staring at Ryder. "Lookit what ya did ta mah boy? An' now dang near the whole town knows yer heah. I can't kill 'em all."

"Maybe you don't have to kill me," Ryder suggested.

"What d'ya mean by that?"

"Where's Suzy?"

"Ya ain't takin' 'er! Ah told ya that."

"I never said I was. I just want to know where she is."

Mrs. Gleason glared at him for a long moment. "She's in the house, gittin' over the beatin' Vernon gave 'er."

"Still? After all this time?"

"Still." Mrs. Gleason's voice was cold and low, rock hard.

"Vern beat the hell outta her," Harry said. "If'n she hadn't killed 'im, I woulda. No man shoulda done that to a sweet little thing like her."

"If she's that weak," Ryder said, "she couldn't have gotten up an' killed her pa, could she?"

"What are ya gittin' at, boy?" Mrs. Gleason demanded.

"She couldn't have done it. She's not the one."

Mrs. Gleason snorted. "Ya don't know nothin', do ya? We found 'er out near the road. She was lyin' in a ditch, half dead. Vernon had beat 'er with his pistol, then with his rifle. It was her gunshot that we heard. Wouldn'ta found her without that."

"What was she doin' out there?"

"Goin' ta meet Riley," Nate said.

Both Mrs. Gleason and Ryder turned and looked at him.

"It's true. She had told me she was gonna run away with 'im."

"Why?" Ryder asked, beating Mrs. Gleason to the question.

"Ta get away from pa," Nate said. "I shoulda gone with her. Pa couldn't have stopped botha us."

Mrs. Gleason lowered the shotgun. "Ah shoulda known. Is that why she took yer pa's rifle?"

"She didn't take it," Nate said. "Pa took it with him in the buggy. I saw him do it. He said he was gonna kill her. An' Riley, too. An' when he got back, he said he was gonna git rid of the last vermin on the ranch. He meant me, Ma. He meant me."

"Where's that rifle at?" Ryder asked.

"What's it ta ya?" Harry, the cow hand, demanded.

"It might give us a clue as to what happened," Ryder said.

"I put it in the coat closet," Mrs. Gleason said.

"I'll go git it," Nate said. He was gone a few moments.

"What d'ya hope ta find?" Harry asked.

"I don't know. Maybe a miracle."

Harry and Mrs. Gleason both frowned.

Nate was back. "Here."

Ryder noticed right away that it was a repeater. In fact, it was a Henry rifle, like the one Ryder's grandfather had carried in the Civil War, the very one his father had given to Riley the night before he went coyote hunting.

Ryder examined the weapon. "There's blood all over the stock an' around the barrel."

"He beat her with it," Mrs. Gleason snarled. "The man Ah married. The man Ah once loved, an' he beat my baby with it!"

"I want to talk to her," Ryder said.

"Ah told ya, she's sick. Half dead."

"It's important."

"So you can take her an' hang her?" Harry asked.

"So I can save her."

The cowboy stared at Ryder. Then he turned to Mrs. Gleason and raised his eyebrows.

"Git back to work," Mrs. Gleason said.

"Yes'm," he said. To Ryder, he said, "Ya better not hurt her. This is the only family I got. The only one I know."

Before Ryder could respond, the cowboy rode off.

"I need to see her. I'll be kind."

Mrs. Gleason aimed her shotgun at Ryder. "No."

"Riley was my best friend, Ma. An' Suzy was gonna run away with 'im. We let Riley hang, Ma. We let him hang. For somethin' he didn't do."

"It's his fault yer sister's lyin' in there, nearly dead."

"No, Ma. She's was tryin' ta git away. He was her hope an' now he's dead because ya wouldn't let us go an' tell the sheriff."

"It was his fault."

"It wasn't, Ma. It's no one's fault. Not even yers."

Mrs. Gleason lowered the shotgun. Turning, she carried the gun to the porch, uncocking the hammer on the barrel still containing a shell. Then she leaned it against a wooden post, both barrels up.

"This way," she said, waving Ryder to follow.

# CHAPTER FIFTY-ONE

REMOVING HIS HAT AND holding it in his left hand, Ryder entered the house. They crossed through a great room, the width of the whole front of the house, with a fireplace at either side, and waxed, hardwood floors. In the back of the room there was a hallway leading to other rooms, while beside it was a stairway rising to the bedrooms above. Up the stairway climbed Mrs. Gleason, followed by Ryder and Nate. At the top of the stairs stood Owen.

"Ma?" Owen asked.

"Ah'm gonna let 'im see Suzy."

"Ya sure?"

"Ah am."

Owen moved aside.

Mrs. Gleason moved down the upstairs hallway, which narrowed and split at the stairs. There were ten doors in all, five on either side. At either end of the hall a large window stood open. A cold breeze blew through the hallway.

The last door on the left led into Suzy's room.

Mrs. Gleason opened it and went in, followed by Ryder, Owen and Nate. Sitting in a rocking chair in the corner behind the door was Victor.

"Ma! What'd ya bring 'im in here fer?"

"Shaddup an' mind yer own business."

Victor glared at Ryder, then he saw his mother's face and he backed down, slouching in his chair.

A thin face, still badly bruised after all this time, shrouded by softly-brushed blonde hair, poked out from the bed's white sheets. A pink bed cover, with little blue flowers, was tucked up under the girl's chin.

Not a girl, Ryder corrected himself. A young woman. He could see why Riley had liked her so much. Bruised though she was, there was a softness to her face, a beauty.

"Suzy. Suzy, honey, it's ma. Wake up, honey. There's a man here ta see ya. It's Riley brother. He's come ta see ya."

Suzy's eyes opened. She squinted. Though the window was open, with the curtains drawn back, and though the sky was dark outside, and growing darker, the room was still too bright for her eyes.

She squinted at Ryder.

"Ah'm hot, Ma. Ah'm burnin' up."

At her words, Owen and Victor both went to a water basin sitting on a table by the girl's bed, across from Mrs. Gleason. Owen found a clean cloth and dipped it into the basin, then wrung it out and took it over to his sister. He gently wiped her forehead. Meanwhile, from a porcelain pitcher beside the basin, Victor partway filled a cup with water and brought it over to her.

Ryder watched, in admiration, as Owen finished wiping her face with the wet cloth and stepped back for his brother. Victor, with one hand, gently lifted her head while with the other helped her sip some water from the cup.

"Honey," Mrs. Gleason asked her daughter, "Ya okay ta answer some questions for Riley's brother?"

"Riley? Is Riley here, Ma?"

"No, honey, t'ain't Riley. It's his brother, Ryder."

"Oh." Suzy's head rolled to her right. She looked up at her brothers, Victor and Owen. Then her head rolled back to her mother, who smiled sweetly at her, then she looked down at Nate, at the foot of the bed. Finally, she glanced at Ryder, standing beside Nate. "Yer Riley's brother?"

"I am."

"Where's Riley?"

Ryder glanced up at Mrs. Gleason. She shook her head. He looked back at Suzy. "He couldn't make it."

"Is he okay?"

"I hope so," Ryder said.

Suzy's eyebrows knotted together, in thought, while she frowned. "Whaddya want ta ask me?"

"When your pa was beatin' you, how was he shot?"

"Oh, Ma, Ma! Is he here to take me away? Is he the law?"

"No, honey, he ain't. He jest wants ta understand what happened ta ya."

"Ah didn't mean ta do it, Ma. Ah didn't mean ta kill Pa. He was hittin' me with it an' I stuck my hands up to grab it, ta take it away from 'im. I didn't mean ta shoot him. Honest, Ma, I didn't mean ta shoot Pa!"

Suzy squirmed over to her mother, grunting as she moved. She lifted a bruised hand to her mother's arm, pulling her down closer, and buried her head in it, weeping and moaning. "Ah didn't mean ta do it, Ma. I didn't mean ta do it."

Victor set the cup on the table and picked up the pitcher. "Ya dirty, no good, sonuva ..."

"Shush!" Mrs. Gleason scolded her son. "Git over inta that chair an' behave yerself. Now."

Victor put the pitcher he intended to hit Ryder with down and sat in the chair.

"Ma, Ma, Ah dint mean ta do it. Ah dint mean ta kill Pa."

"Suzy," Ryder said, "You didn't kill your father."

"Ah dint mean ta do it," Suzy bawled.

"Whadya mean she dint do it?" Mrs. Gleason demanded, turning away from her daughter and glaring at Ryder.

"Suzy, Suzy," Ryder called to her.

Mrs. Gleason held up her free hand and Ryder fell silent. With great effort, she calmed her daughter down.

Ryder came over and knelt beside the bed. He held his hat in both hands, as a sort of a barrier between the girl and himself.

"Suzy," he said, softly.

"Ah didn't..."

"Shhh, Suzy, it's okay. Think. When you raised your hands, when your pa was beatin' you, what happened?"

"He was tryin' ta kill me. He kept screamin' at me that Ah was a slut an' that he wasn't gonna have a slut fer a daughter."

"How was he holdin' the rifle?"

"He held it by the barrel."

Ryder nodded. "Why?"

"He was tryin' to smash mah head in with it."

"An' what happened next?"

"Ah moved mah head outta the way as he tried hittin' me with it. But Ah dint mean ta kill 'im."

"Then what happened?"

"The gun went off."

"Were you holdin' the rifle?"

"Ah had mah arms wrapped over mah face. Ah dint want ta see it comin'."

"See what comin'?"

"My dyin'."

"Was that all?"

"Ah twisted mah head sideways."

"Away?" Ryder asked.

"Yeah."

"Then what happened?"

"The gun went off. Ah dint mean ta kill 'im. Ah dint mean ta kill 'im!"

"You didn't."

"What?" Mrs. Gleason said.

"Ah dint mean ta kill 'im."

Ryder stood. "Suzy Gleason, you didn't kill your Pa. The rifle misfired. It was an accident. He shot himself. It's not your fault."

"Ah dint mean ta..."

"Ya dint do it, honey," Mrs. Gleason said. "It was an accident. Yer Pa shot himself."

"Ah dint mean ta kill 'im," Suzy moaned. Her eyes fluttered and closed. Her breathing was strained. She passed out.

"What d'ya mean it was an accident?" Victor demanded, standing up. "Pa wouldn'ta shot 'imself. He knew how ta handle a rifle."

"Shhh," Mrs. Gleason shushed the room. "Let Suzy sleep." With a wave, she sent everyone out into the hall.

Once outside, the door to the girl's room closed, everyone moved a few steps down the hall. When they all stopped, Victor turned on Ryder and repeated, with vehemence, his question. "What d'ya mean, he shot 'imself?"

Ryder replied with a question. "Didn't your pa teach you to keep from chambering a round in a rifle?"

"Hell, no!" Victor exclaimed. "Pa taught us ta keep a round chambered in our rifles, so as no one could git a drop on us. Pistols, too."

"Why d'ya ask that?" Owen asked.

"Your pa's rifle was a Henry?"

"He was proud of it," Owen said.

"Grandpa gave it ta our Pa," Victor said.

"Henrys don't have safeties," Ryder said.

"So what?" Victor demanded.

"My Pa had his Pa's Henry," Ryder said. "He taught us never to keep a round chambered in it."

"Yer pa's stupid," Victor said, sneering.

Ryder glared at him. His hands curled into fists. But he forced himself to relax. "A chambered round can easily go off in a Henry."

"That never happens," Victor snorted.

"I'm pretty sure it did this time," Ryder said. "An' it's what saved Suzy's life. She was too beaten to shoot your pa. The gun goin' off saved her. He shot himself in the chest an' I think he climbed into the buggy an' tried to git to town for help. But he never made it."

"Then Suzy didn't do it," Mrs. Gleason said.

Owen shook his head. "Poor Pa. He killed 'imself."

"Pa wouldna done that," Victor growled. "He wouldna killed 'imself."

"Who's side aire ya on?" Nate exclaimed. "Would ya want 'im ta have killed Suzy?"

"No, no, Ah jest, Ah jest… Ah jest don't know."

Mrs. Gleason looked at Ryder. "She didn't kill 'im?"

"Nope. An' neither did Riley."

"Oh, my Lord, Ah'm so sorry, Ryder," Mrs. Gleason said, her eyes filling with tears. "Ah let yer little brother die so Ah could save Suzy. How am Ah gonna live with that?"

"I don't know," Ryder hissed, his anger seeping out.

"Ya must hate us somethin' awful," Owen said.

Ryder nodded, unable to say anything. There were no villains here, only victims. No one to blame, no one to hate, no one to take to the sheriff and point and say, "Here's your guilty person. Here's the person you sacrificed my brother for!" No answers and no questions, only despair, fear, sorrow. As he looked at them, he saw in their eyes the same pain, the same regret, even shame, that he felt. And as he remembered little Suzy in her room, broken in spirit and body, he realized he had no right to hate them, either. They saved their sister, while he failed to return in time to save his brother. There was no redemption here, no peace, only grief and affliction. The only justice was the need for mercy. The law was the law, but it had to be flexible enough to forgive, to be merciful.

"What you did, you had to do," Ryder said, choking on the words.

"Yer not takin' us in?" Mrs. Gleason asked.

"For what? For protectin' Suzy?" Ryder frowned. "No. It was an accident. Nothin' else."

"Whatcha gonna do now, Ryder?" Nate asked.

"Go back to town an' tell the sheriff an' his dumb deputy that they hanged my brother for nothin'," Ryder said.

"She don't look good, Ma, does she?" Owen said, referring to his sister.

"Nope," Ryder agreed. "You should take her to town. To Doc Welsh."

"Owen, ya an' Nate git a wagon ready. Make sure it's clean. Hitch up a good strong team," Mrs. Gleason ordered.

"I'll go with them," Ryder said.

"Good. Victor, help me git Suzy ready."

# CHAPTER FIFTY-TWO

IT WAS DARKER OUTSIDE now. Still long before sunset, the clouds were black and heavy and low, the air thick with moisture and cold.

"I hope it don't start snowin' before we git ta town," Nate said, as they walked toward the barn.

"We'll make it," Ryder said.

When they reached the barn, they found Harry, the cowhand, inside lighting up some kerosene lanterns. Ryder's and Victor's horses stood in separate stalls, saddles still on. As they stepped inside, Ryder first, then Nate, followed by Owen, Harry spun around, his hand flying to his pistol.

Ryder's fingers twitched, but there was nothing he could do. His pistol was still hidden underneath his overcoat.

"What're ya doin'!" Nate exclaimed.

"Ya startled me," Harry said. His hand slipped from his pistol.

"You're a bit nervous," Ryder commented.

"Who wouldn't be, with Tony Rixx ridin' around killin' people?" Harry said.

"Where'd you hear that?" Ryder asked.

"From Jed Cummins. He jest got back from town. Says Tony kilt two people yesterday."

"Ain't possible," Owen said. "He's all talk. He never killed nobody in his life."

"He did yesterday," Ryder confirmed. "Judge McHugh and Herman Fields."

"But, why?" Owen asked

"I don't rightly know. It has to do with Riley's hangin'," Harry said.

"It just don't make no sense."

"How well d'you know Tony?" Ryder asked Owen.

"We're friends. Not close. Ah've known 'im fer some years. Ever since his brother took ta deputyin', he an' Jeff have drifted apart. He feels left out, like a cub all by 'imself. Ah know he hates the sheriff fer takin' his brother from 'im, but Ah've never known 'im to hate anyone else."

"An' you say he ain't a killer?" Harry said.

"He is now," Ryder said. "McHugh got off a shot, so maybe it was self-defense, but I don't really think so. But Fields, he'd been killed earlier."

Owen shook his head.

"Whatcha here for?" Harry asked.

"A wagon," Nate replied. "We're takin' Suzy in to Doc Welsh's office. Ryder proved that she didn't kill Pa, that it was an accident."

"How?" Harry asked.

"Vernon tried to smash in Suzy's face with his Henry," Ryder explained. "But she rolled her head outta the way. The gun slammed into the ground. There was bullet in the chamber. It went off. Blew a hole clean through his chest an' out the back. He tried to git to town. He didn't make it."

"Then yer brother was innocent," Harry said.

"He was."

"Ah'm sorry."

"Seems everybody is. But nobody did a thing to save him."

"Let's git the team hitched up," Owen said, avoiding Ryder's eyes. "We gotta git goin' before it starts snowin'."

It didn't take them long to get together a team and hook it to the wagon. When they were ready, Victor and another ranch hand brought Suzy down. Owen and Nate guided the wagon over to the porch.

Mrs. Gleason had blankets and a small mattress laid inside the wagon. Ryder and Owen assisted in lifting Suzy into the wagon. Mrs. Gleason climbed inside, wrapping Suzy and herself in blankets. When it was all done, they headed out. Nate and Owen sat up front, while Ryder and Victor, riding their horses, led the way.

Snowflakes started falling before they reached the main road.

# CHAPTER FIFTY-THREE

T HE GUZMAN'S HOTEL WAS cold the next morning. Ryder wandered downstairs, washed and dressed, and armed. He wore his long coat, unbuttoned, his pistol reachable. He carried his saddle bags and belongings in his hands. He had left the clothes that Delores Guzman had given him, folded on the bed in his room. The bed that he had neatly made. His hat, held by a string around his neck, draped down his back.

As he reached the landing at the bottom of the stairs, he stopped and listened.

He heard sounds in the kitchen. People moving about. Dishes clinked, utensils clattered, food fried. He heard bacon hissing and spitting before he smelled it. He recognized the muffled voices of Dolores and Merced Gleason preparing breakfast.

Upstairs, he heard more movement. There were more guests now. The Gleasons had taken rooms. Suzy had been delivered to Doc Welsh's office last night.

By the time they had reached town, two inches of snow had already fallen. Everyone had crowded into Welsh's office but after a few minutes, he shooed them all out. He let Mrs. Gleason stay, especially after she stated that she wasn't leaving and that there was nothing he could do to make her go.

So, as far as he knew, Mrs. Gleason was still at Welsh's office, while her sons were upstairs.

Stepping around the stairs, he moved toward the dining room. He saw, and felt, a massive fire blazing away in the fireplace. And he saw bowls and plates set around the table. Dainty cloth napkins were folded on the left, while forks, spoons, and knives surrounded the plates. Two pots of coffee pleasantly steamed from a side board.

He stood and stared at the table. Hunger nagged at him to sit down, to wait for his breakfast.

However, he had work to do today.

He had to tell Sheriff Carlson and Deputy Rixx what had happened, that Vernon Gleason's death had been an accident, that nobody had murdered him, that the only murder had been his brother being hanged for a crime that none had committed. That every member of that jury, the prosecuting attorney, the judge, and the sheriff and his deputy, were all guilty of murder, guilty of hanging an innocent thirteen-year-old boy. That his brother's blood was on their hands and that even if they weren't punished on Earth for their sins, as Herman Fields had been, that they belonged in Hell.

They would have to live the rest of their lives knowing they had hanged an innocent boy.

Turning, he started for the front door. He had taken but one step when the door to the kitchen opened. He turned to see who it was, expecting Dolores Guzman to come out carrying a plate of food. But, instead, it was the last person in the world he expected to see.

It was Emily Walker.

The woman who could never forgive him. The woman who loved someone else now. The woman who deserved the happiness that he didn't deserve.

For her part, Emily was surprised and unprepared to see him, too, even though she knew he was here and that she might see him sometime this morning.

She carried a huge platter covered with pancakes. Quickly, she put it down and walked over to him. She stopped in front of him and looking up, asked, "Where are you going?"

"It's time for me to leave."

"Leave? Why?"

"Because I can't do anythin' more here."

"Why can't you?"

"You know why."

"Us?"

"Some of it."

"What else?"

"If I'd been a few days sooner, maybe Riley'd still be alive."

"You don't know that."

"What does it matter? If I stay, I'm goin' to want to kill Carlson and Rixx for hangin' Riley."

"They were just doing their job."

"By hanging a thirteen-year-old boy?"

"It's no worse than leaving your bride at the altar."

How could he answer that? He turned to go.

"Wait a minute," Emily pleaded. "That was harsh and unfair."

"But true."

"Yes, it's true. But you blessed me with a family, with another daughter to love and a husband who will stay with me."

"So?"

"So how can I let you leave without blessing you back?"

"I can't have you."

"You can't. But even if you could, we'd never be happy."

"I know."

"Do you?"

"Yep."

"You've truly changed."

"Not so much."

"You have," she said. "But your parents are on their way in. Pastor Jarrett went out to get them a few hours ago."

"Why?" he asked.

"You proved Riley's innocence. And that it was only an accident."

"It didn't do any good. The town still hanged him."

"It did. And it will have to live with it."

"Good."

She hesitated, aware of the anger he felt. The same kind of anger she had felt toward him for five years. Anger that was now gone.

"Others are coming," she said.

"Who?"

"The Jarretts. Becky's a much better match for you that I ever could be."

Ryder looked down at Emily. "She's just a kid. How can I love her? I don't even know her."

"Open your heart. You'll love her."

"Thanks, Ma."

"I ain't your ma," Emily snapped at him.

"You were our daughter's ma."

Emily's eyes grew wet.

"What was she like, our Hannah?"

"Sweet. Happy. Alive. For awhile."

"I ruined everythin'."

"You did."

"I wished I'd known her."

"I wished you had, too. But I like to think Hannah would've been just like Tilly."

"She's a good kid. I'll think of Hannah that way, too."

"You'll have one someday. Another one. Becky will give you one."

Ryder shook his head. "Nope."

"Why not?"

"I don't deserve happiness."

"How can you say that? Look at all the good you've done."

"I haven't done anythin'."

Emily leaned her head against Ryder. "It's my fault, too."

"How so?"

"I shouldn't have hated you."

Ryder said nothing. He gently pushed Emily away.

"What should I tell everyone? The Gleasons will want to thank you. Doc Welsh says Suzy'll be fine, with much care and rest."

"Anyone tell her about Riley?"

Emily shook her head. "Welsh has asked that we wait a few weeks."

Ryder nodded. He turned toward the door.

"Just like that!" Emily snarled. "Just like the last time?"

"Why not? It's what I do."

"I see you've grown a spine," she said. "You can't run out on all these people. We need a good sheriff around here. You could be that."

"Nope."

"Why not?"

"Because I'd kill Carlson an' his deputy."

She frowned. "People still need you here."

"What people?"

"Becky Jarrett. Your ma and pa. The Gleasons. Joad's coming over, too. He needs you. He needs your friendship."

"Tell them I had to go."

"Why?"

"Tell them I had to be somewhere else."

"Where?"

"Anywhere but here."

"I see. What will you do for food?"

"I have a little jerky and biscuit left."

"Do you have water?"

"I'll find some," he said.

"You have your canteen."

"I do."

"There's a pitcher of water over by the coffee. I can fill your canteen for you. Or would you like some coffee?"

"Coffee would be nice."

"Set your things by the door."

"I gotta get outta here before anyone sees me. If they see me, they'll never let me get away."

"What's wrong with that?" she asked.

"I told you."

"You did."

He fished out his canteen. She took it and quickly marched over to the side bar. A few moments and she filled his canteen. Then, quickly, she wrapped several pancakes and some sliced apples that sat on the table, in a cloth napkin. She brought the canteen and food over to him.

He took the canteen and looped it over his neck. Though wearing a thick overcoat, he could feel the warmth of the coffee through the canteen's metal side.

When she offered the napkin, he refused it.

"Why won't you take it?" she asked.

"I'm not a thief."

"The food was meant for you," she said.

"The napkin wasn't. It belongs to Mrs. Guzman."

Emily sighed. "I'll pay her back."

"Why are you doin' this?"

"I told you."

"I forget," he said.

"Because I want to give you some good. You're letting me have a family. I want the same good for you."

"I don't deserve it."

"You can't refuse."

"Why not?"

"It's a gift."

He stared at her. She stared back. After a moment, he took the napkin full of pancakes and sliced apples and shoved it into an empty pocket in his coat.

"You'll see that she's repaid?"

"I will." Emily reached up and caressed his chin.

"What's that for?"

"For being a good man."

"I was never a good man."

"Well," she said, "maybe you're on the road to becoming one."

He left.

A moment later, Delores Guzman came out. "Did I hear the door close?"

Emily stared at her a moment. "It was just a hungry man. I gave him some pancakes."

"Did you give him enough?"

"I hope so," Emily said.

"Come on. I could use some more help in the kitchen."

Emily waited until Delores returned to the kitchen. Then Emily wiped her eyes with her sleeves. Afterward, she followed Dolores into the kitchen.

# CHAPTER FIFTY-FOUR

RYDER WALKED DOWN TO Tor Nielsen's stable at the end of town. Four inches of snow covered the ground. His boots left muddy footsteps in the snow. The doors to the barn were closed, but Ryder opened one, just a little, and stepped inside. Nielsen's son wasn't there, but in a back room used as an office, he found Nielsen.

"Ryder, come in, come in," Nielsen said. "Shut the door. I have a little wood stove in here. It ain't like the furnace Joad an' I will spend the day workin' at, makin' up fer all the time we wasted in the wind storm. But though this stove's a tiny ting, it warms you."

Ryder nodded and stepped inside, carrying his things with him. The room was noticeably warmer than the barn, and much more so though than outside.

Nielsen looked at Ryder's load. "Set yer things down. You goin' somewhere?"

Ryder nodded. "It's time to leave."

"Why?"

Ryder stared at him.

Nielsen understood. "Joad'll be disappointed. He's lookin' forward to havin' you around for a while."

"I know."

Ryder looked around. The little room had a wooden floor, though it was dirty. It also had two windows, one in a side wall looking into the stable, and one behind Nielsen's desk, revealing the back yard. Near this last window stood the woodstove.

"You could stay."

"Too many bad memories."

"Where you goin'?"

"To meet a friend."

"Where?"

"Out near Las Vegas."

"That's a long ride."

"More or less."

Nielsen nodded. "It's cold out there."

"It is."

"I got a little old tent. It's probably full of spiders, but it's yours if you want it. It'll keep the snow off you."

Ryder nodded.

"Saddle your horse while I find it."

"How much do I owe you?"

"Three dollars."

"That ain't near enough for all the food an' care you've given No Name," Ryder said.

"It's enough."

"I'll pay you more."

Nielsen shook his head. "No need. You've done more for this town than you can imagine. It's not a little thing that you did, findin' out the truth about what happened. It won't bring back your brother, but it proves he wasn't guilty."

Ryder said nothing. He fished three dollars from his pocket and handed them to Nielsen. Nielsen stuffed the money in a pocket of his own.

He followed Ryder out. While Ryder saddled No Name and tied his things onto her, Nielsen found the little one-man tent. He shook it out, scattering half-frozen bugs every which way. After inspecting it, he carried it over to Ryder.

"Don't lose it," Nielsen admonished.

"You expectin' it back?"

"No. But the thought of you freezin' out there on the prairie doesn't give me any comfort."

Ryder nodded again. He took the dusty scrap of a tent and tied it to the back of his saddle. He also tied his blanket to his saddle, over the tent, and led No Name out into the cold.

Nielsen followed him.

Ryder checked that his saddle was secure, as well as his bags and burdens. Before he mounted up, he put on his gloves, the cold making his fingers ache and sting.

Nielsen handed him a little bag.

When Ryder looked at him, Nielsen said, "Some grain and a couple of small carrots for your horse."

"Thanks." Taking the bag, Ryder stuffed it into a pocket different from the one where he carried his pancakes and apple slices. Then he swung into his saddle.

Nielsen extended his hand. Ryder took it and they shook. Then Nielsen asked, "Where to now?"

"The sheriff's office."

"For what?"

"To let the misfits know that they hanged an innocent boy."

"You'll just cause problems."

"Good." Ryder guided his horse out across the main street to the side street beyond. He didn't want to encounter his parents, or anyone else, as they came into town. As he passed between Pastor Jarrett's church and his house, he glanced at the house.

He half hoped that he'd see Becky Jarrett and if he did, that it would make a difference to him. That he might want to stay.

But he didn't see her. He road on by.

As he passed Doc Welsh's office, Mrs. Gleason stepped out. As she saw Ryder pass by, she called out to him.

"Ryder, where ya goin?"

"It's time to move on."

"Why?"

He stopped and stared at her.

"Ah'm sorry Ah dint do nothin' fer yer brother."

"I understand," he said. "You were protectin' your daughter. You thought she had killed your husband."

"But yew proved she dint an' Ah shoulda done somethin' ta save 'im. Ah coulda saved 'im."

"It wasn't your job. It was mine, an' I failed him."

"Ah don't know 'bout that, but Ah do know ya dint fail mah family. Ya saved us all."

Ryder nodded.

"How's Suzy?"

"Welsh says she'll be fine. It'll take a bit of time, but she'll be fine."

"Good." He moved on, turning at the corner and heading towards the sheriff's office.

# CHAPTER FIFTY-FIVE

IT WAS COLD OUT, cold enough to chill both No Name and Ryder. Cold enough to hurt, even with a warm coat wrapped around him and leather gloves warming his fingers. But compared to the hurt he felt in his heart, the cold was nothing. The cold could kill him, just as sure as a bullet could, but he already felt dead inside.

The streets were empty. A few boot prints and a few hoof prints dirtied the snow.

He stopped in front of the sheriff's office, dismounted, looped No Name's reins over one of the railings a bit to the aide of the office. Stepping onto the boardwalk, he walked over and knocked on the door. A muffled "Come in," growled out at him.

Entering, he removed his gloves and hat, placing them on a table by the door.

"Shut the door!" a gruff voice said.

Carlson, Jeff Rixx, and another man, their backs turned to him, sat before a woodstove over by a wall. Turning around, Rixx saw him. Staggering to his feet, he stumbled over to the sheriff's desk, where his pistol rested in its holster. He reached for it.

"I outta kill ya now. Instead, I'll just arrest ya."

"On what grounds?" asked the third man, standing and turning around. Sheriff Carlson also stood and turned about.

"He shot me in the foot. That's assault an' I'm stickin' 'im in a cell until he can come to trial."

"Sheriff, does he need to be tried?" the third man asked.

"He's broken no laws."

"He's still guilty," Rixx growled.

"Is he?" the third man asked.

"Ya, an' I'm gonna shoot him in the foot."

"I think not," Ryder said, opening his jacket and sweeping back the right lapel to reveal his pistol in its holster.

"Ya gonna shoot me? Ya think you're good enough fer that?"

"If he isn't, I am," the third man said.

"Thanks, Bob, but I can take him," Ryder said. "I may not be the fastest draw, but it's accuracy that counts."

"An' intent," Bob said. "Look in his eyes, Deputy Rixx. He's really pissed at you. When a man's that angry, an' that cold, an' I don't mean from the weather, any man challengin' him is a fool."

"You know this man, McCorkle?" Sheriff Carlson asked.

"Yep. We've been friends for years. We fought together in the Rough Riders an' recently in the Arizona Territory town of Holbrook where he killed Mad McAvoy. An' in a few moments, when I swear him in, he'll be a deputy U. S. Marshall. Any man should know that killin' a U. S. Marshal means every other marshal will be after him for the rest of his short life."

"He ain't sworn in yet," Rixx said.

"Ryder, raise your left hand," Bob said.

"Ain't it supposed to be his right hand?" Rixx demanded.

"In this case," Sheriff Carlson said, "I think the left hand is more than appropriate enough."

"Yer supposed to be on my side," Rixx whined.

"Not when yer about to start shootin' up my office."

Ryder raised his left hand, while keeping his other hand inches above his pistol. His eyes never left Rixx's eyes. All the anger and hate he felt for himself and for this town, he channeled toward Rixx, the man who convinced his brother to confess to a murder he didn't commit. The man that at this moment he hated so much.

"Repeat after me," Bob said. "I, your name…"

"I, Ryder Mann…"

"…do solemnly swear to uphold the laws of these United States an' to faithfully execute them to the best of my abilities…" Bob continued.

"…do solemnly swear to uphold the laws of these United States an' to faithfully execute them to the best of my abilities…"

"…so help me God," Bob concluded.

"…so help me God," Ryder confirmed.

"You are hereby a deputy U. S. Marshall, Ryder Mann."

Ryder nodded. He continued staring at Rixx.

"What will it be?" Bob asked.

"You speakin' to me?" Rixx asked.

"Yep," Bob replied.

"I don't know what yer meanin'," Rixx replied.

"He means," Carlson said, "are you gonna back down or try to kill Ryder, an' if you do kill him, then McCorkle can either take you prisoner, which most likely means you'll be tried and hanged fer murderin' a deputy U. S. Marshall, or McCorkle will shoot you dead for the same thing."

"Ain't you gonna do nothin'?" Rixx asked.

Carlson shrugged. "My job is to uphold the law, whether it be the laws of Brennan, the laws of the Territory of New Mexico, or the laws of the United States, which are all one and the same."

"What does that mean?" Rixx demanded.

Ryder's hand moved away from his pistol. He walked over to Rixx, whose hand hadn't moved an inch. He took Rixx's pistol and gunbelt away from him. "It means you lose."

"But he's guilty," Rixx said, turning to Carlson.

"No, he's ain't," Carlson said. "You pulled a gun on him an' he shot you in the foot when he could've shot you dead. In fact, he merely grazed your foot. That's not even a real wound. Are you gonna be jest like yer brother, meanin' that I'm gonna have to fire you, or are you gonna be a real deputy, upholdin' the law, no matter how difficult that is?"

Rixx deflated. He stumbled back to his chair by the woodstove and sat down. "I don't know."

"You better decide soon," Carlson said. "Because even if we upheld the law as we thought it was fit, we still killed an innocent boy."

"We didn't know that," Rixx said.

"We should've. We should've investigated thoroughly, instead of keepin' at him until he confessed for a crime he never committed."

"I don't know what to do."

"Humility, that's a good start," Bob said.

"You're still guilty," Ryder said. "You murdered my brother. He was just a boy, barely a man, if that. An' I'm not goin' to stop until I can prove it an' see you either in prison or hanged for it."

Bob rolled his eyes and sighed. Then he walked over to the woodstove and sat down beside Rixx.

Carlson said to Ryder, "I know that I'm guilty an' I know that there's nothin' I can say to you that'll change your mind, either."

"There ain't," Ryder declared.

"Then I have somethin' for you."

"What?"

Carlson walked over to his desk. He took a key out of a pocket in his pants and unlocked a side drawer. From it, he removed an envelope. He took it over to Ryder and held it out.

Both Bob and Rixx turned to watch.

"What's this?"

"Read it."

Ryder took the envelope. It was addressed to him. He recognized Riley's writing.

He opened it and took out a small piece of paper. He read it. Hands trembling, he crumpled the paper.

Bob stood, not knowing what to do.

Ryder looked around for someplace to sit down. Then he walked behind the sheriff's desk and sat in the chair behind it.

Bob came over and stood beside him. "What is it? Who's it from?"

"It's from my brother. He said he was sorry for lettin' me down. That I was always his hero an' that he wanted to be just like me, but he couldn't. That he knew that Suzy had killed her father, because Nate had sneaked into town, speakin' to him through the window one night an' tellin' him all about it. He asks me to forgive him, but he couldn't let Suzy suffer any more so he's gonna confess to murderin' Vernon Gleason."

Ryder glared at the ceiling. "Why do all teenage boys have to be such romantic fools? An' why did my brother have to go an' do that? An' what made him think I was a hero?"

"What makes you think you're not?" Bob asked.

Ryder turned to Carlson. "You knew about this, what he wrote?"

"No. He told me it was his last will an' testament an' I respected it. He wanted me to give it to you. When we were gonna have breakfast the other day, I was gonna give it to you. But you left before I could."

"An' you know now that Suzy didn't kill her pa?" Ryder asked.

Carlson nodded. "I saw Mrs. Gleason at Doc's this mornin'. Owen came over to my house last night an' told me everythin', includin' how you figured it out. That's when I knew you were right an' that I hanged an innocent boy. An' that I was a murderer."

"I'm not a murderer!" Rixx exclaimed, standing up and almost toppling over. "I was doin' my job. How was I supposed to know that nobody was guilty, that it was just an accident?"

"Didn't you listen to Welsh?" Ryder snarled at him. "Didn't you try to figure out the truth for yourself? No. You took the easy road. You badgered a boy until he confessed to a crime he didn't commit to save someone who didn't commit it, either. But you didn't know because you didn't try. You wanted to watch a boy swing from a rope, that's all you wanted. If anyone does any killin' in here, it should be me killin' you, you goddamned bastard!"

"Calm down, Ryder. Your brother confessed to save the girl he loved," Bob pointed out. "Even if they found evidence to the contrary, your brother still signed a confession. What else were they to do?"

Ryder looked at the paper in his hand. "I don't know."

"He offered his life for the girl loved," Bob said. "Wouldn't you do the same thing for the woman you loved?"

"I already did," Ryder said. "I let her go."

"Then forgive them. They're just lawmen, like us. They did the best they could."

"They coulda done better."

"Everyone can do better."

Frowning, his eyes red, Ryder looked away.

# CHAPTER FIFTY-SIX

SOMEONE KNOCKED AT THE door.

"What the hell now?" Rixx asked.

"I'll get it," Carlson said. He strode over to the door and opened it. A cold blast of air blew inside.

Standing in front of Carlson was one of Tony Rixx's thugs, grinning. "What do you want?" Carlson asked.

In answer, the thug stepped aside.

"It's yer turn, sheriff!" a voice yelled. "Ya took the last person in the world that loved me, from me. An' now I'm gonna make ya pay for it!"

The sheriff looked up. There was a gunshot. Carlson fell backward into the office.

Ryder leaped up, drawing his pistol and reaching Carlson just as Bob reached him.

There was a hole in Carlson's shirt, right over his heart. Blood stained his shirt. His eyes stared, unseeing, at the two deputy marshals.

Bob and Ryder looked up. Outside, on a horse, was Tony Rixx, grinning. "Your turn, Mann!" He aimed at Ryder.

Before either Jeff Rixx or Ryder could aim, Bob drew and fired at Tony. But Tony's horse bucked and the shot missed. His thug stepped back into the door, pistol aimed at Bob. Bob shot him and the man tumbled outside.

Bob ran out, firing at Tony, missing as Tony started riding down the street away.

Ryder also ran out.

At the same moment, Tony turned his horse half around and aimed at Bob.

But before Tony could fire at Bob, Ryder fired at Tony. Tony slumped in his saddle, fell from his horse.

Another man, Tony's other companion, shot from across the street. Bob dropped him.

Ryder walked over to where Deputy Rixx's brother laid face down in the snow. Ryder turned him over. There was a single hole in Tony's jacket, over his heart.

Bob came over, reloading his pistol. He looked at Tony's body. "It's always one shot with you."

"Sometimes. I had to shoot McAvoy several times."

Bob nodded. "He was hard to kill. But you're still the better shot."

"An' you're the faster one. You got two of them."

"One was in the doorway. How could I miss?"

People were coming out onto the street now, wondering what new horror had happened in their quiet little town.

Ryder stood. Bob, looking down at Tony, said, "He almost looks happy. Sorta like he's at peace."

"Maybe he is. From what I heard, he wasn't happy in life."

"It happens."

"It does," Ryder agreed.

They returned to the sheriff's office. The door was still open. Kneeling beside Carlson's corpse was Deputy Rixx.

"Your brother's dead," Ryder said.

Rixx nodded. "Our Pa ran off when we were kids. Ma died when Tony was nine. I did the best I could to raise him, but I was barely a man. He felt lost an' alone when I went to work fer the sheriff. He once asked me who was gonna love him now? I didn't know how to answer him. I shoulda told him that I loved him, but I didn't know how. I shoulda told him. I shoulda."

Bob said, "Looks like you're the new sheriff now."

Rixx looked at them, his eyes red. "Aw, hell, I don't wanta be sheriff. He was like a father to me. I'm not man enough to do what he did."

"You don't have a choice," Bob said.

Doc Welsh, Owen Gleason, and two others ran up to the door, stopping and staring at the bodies outside and inside.

Welsh, disgusted, said, "It's come full circle now."

"I suppose so," Ryder said.

# CHAPTER FIFTY-SEVEN

RYDER AND BOB FOUND a little cleft in the side of a hill big enough for them and their horses. They kept the horses saddled, hoping the saddles and blankets would help keep them warm. For themselves, they built a fire and kept close to it, until it sputtered out. Then they climbed into Ryder's tiny tent. It was a tight fit, but it kept them warm through the night. They survived the cold night and somehow their horses survived, too.

After leaving Brannan, Ryder hadn't said a single word, even while preparing camp. Bob had wanted to meet Ryder's family but after shooting Tony Rixx, Ryder had retrieved his gloves and hat from the sheriff's office, ignored everyone's questions, mounted his horse and had ridden away. Bob had hurried to his own horse and followed Ryder.

After his conversation in the office before Ryder's arrival, Bob knew that Ryder was hurting and he let Ryder lead the way, in conversation and everything else. When they cut cross country, angling back toward Las Vegas, Bob hadn't said a word.

They had made almost ten miles before sunset.

The next day, the air was warmer, the snow melting, the sky a brilliant, cool blue. When they reached the Old Santa Fe Trail, they turned onto it. Las Vegas was only a few hours away.

An hour or so later, Ryder asked, "Am I really a deputy U.S. Marshal?"

"More or less," Bob said.

"What d'you mean by that?"

"I mean you can be a deputy marshal if you want to be, but if you don't, you can still be an Arizona Ranger."

"Where's my badge?"

Bob chuckled. He searched in a side pocket of his coat, guided his horse close and gave Ryder a deputy U. S. Marshal badge. "It's not official, though, until we visit the Marshal's office in Santa Fe. You'll have to take the oath again."

"Why me?"

"Why not?"

Ryder didn't reply.

"You told me that bein' an Arizona Ranger was a short-term job an' you didn't know what you'd be doin' after it was done."

"I also told you I'd be happy to be a cowpoke for your pa," Ryder reminded him.

"An' you said you'd also be happy to have a place of your own someday. How you gonna pay for it?"

"I don't make much as a Ranger. Will I make any more as a marshal?"

Bob shrugged. "Probably not. But I thought you might want to be able to ride into some other territory or state where you wouldn't have to worry about not bein' a legal lawman, like you were here in this territory. As a deputy marshal, the whole United States is your territory."

Ryder nodded. "Does sound better. Deputy Rixx wanted to take me in because I wasn't a lawman here."

"Exactly."

"When did you come up with this plan?"

"When I was up in New Mexico. I telegraphed my boss up in Colorado an' he telegraphed the Marshal's office in Santa Fe. Both thought it was a good idea. So did I."

"An' you just happened to have a badge handy?"

Bob smiled sheepishly. "Well, I thought about it up in Colorado an' my boss let me bring one along in case you were interested an' the office in Arizona didn't have spare ones lyin' about."

"Figured as much. That why you wanted to see me?"

"That an' I hadn't seen you in a long time."

Ryder grunted. They rode on a bit more and he asked, "So, I'll be workin' outta Santa Fe?"

"Maybe."

"What d'ya mean by 'maybe'?"

"Well, this territory's as bad as Arizona an' since Arizona's got all you Rangers an' New Mexico ain't got none, the Marshal Service wants to open up deputy marshal posts all over this territory. One in every county, if possible."

"Where they gonna put me?" Ryder asked.

"Well, you could end up in Oklahoma."

"Oklahoma?" Ryder exclaimed.

"Everyone seems to forget it's still a territory, too, an' just as bad as Arizona an' New Mexico. It also wants to be a state. That's why they had that land rush a few years back."

"I wondered about that. So they might put me there."

"Maybe. But, remember, they might send you anywhere. Maybe even into Texas."

"You heard what that Billy the Kid wannabe Texas Ranger said if I ever ended up in Texas. He said he'd put me in the ground."

"Can't do it. You can go down their now an' he can't do nothin' about it."

"He said he could accidently shoot me," Ryder reminded Bob.

"Not likely. Killin' a deputy U.S. marshal's a federal offence everywhere in the United States. A lotta marshals would go lookin' for him."

"They got a lotta Rangers."

"An' we got a lotta Army. When we need 'em, the Army's there for us."

"So, where will I end up?"

"Maybe anywhere."

"You ever gonna give me a straight answer?"

"Maybe."

Ryder stopped No Name and, turning around, glared at Bob.

"They want you in this county."

"Just me?"

"Me, too. The Marshall Service needs a presence in this corner of the territory. Not just to cover New Mexico but also the Texas and Oklahoma panhandles."

"Whereabouts do they want us?"

"Maybe in Trujillo, or over in Valmora, or up in Wagon Mound."

"Those are our choices?"

"Not exactly. It'll be wherever they wanta send us."

"An' where do they want to send us?'

"Well, possibly Springer, but most likely Brannan."

"I'll throw my badge away before I go back there."

"It's your choice," Bob said.

"It is."

They continued down the road a mile or more before Ryder spoke up again. "What happened up in Springer an' in that little minin' town up in the mountains?"

"Well," Bob began, "Up in Springer, the man they thought was wanted, wasn't the man they thought he was. However, someone shot him thinkin' he was. It was an honest mistake."

"How can killin' a man be an' honest mistake?" Ryder demanded.

"He did look like the man in the wanted poster. But when I got there, there was a telegram for me sayin' that they'd caught that particular character up in Colorado, so it couldn't have been him."

"But what about the guy who killed the other guy?"

Bob sighed. "Sometimes, you just have to exercise a little forgiveness. No harm was intended."

"That's it?"

"No. The judge sentenced him to ninety days of hard labor. He's gonna be bustin' up rock with a sledge hammer to help cover muddy roads. He ain't gettin' off too easy."

"Seems like a small penalty for murder."

"He didn't know the guy he killed wasn't the one on the poster."

"So, he just gets off?" Ryder snapped. "Like Deputy Rixx an' Carlson?"

"Carlson paid with his life. He didn't get off."

"An' neither did Tony Rixx," Ryder retorted.

"He didn't. But the guy that got shot wasn't innocent, either. Turned out he had robbed people travelin' at night an' left 'em out in the middle of nowhere. Some of 'em starved to death or were killed by wild animals. An' he abused some of the women."

Ryder nodded. "So, he got what he deserved, then."

"More or less."

"Then why was the shooter sent to jail?"

"You can't just go around shootin' people without knowin' if they're guilty or not."

Ryder nodded again. "An' the kid up in that minin' town?"

"Turns out he wasn't as fast as he thought he was."

"You?"

"Nope. Some miner got him with a shot gun. Two barrels of buckshot close up."

"Painful."

"Yep."

"I see what you mean by a lot of a desperate people roundabout here."

Bob nodded. "Someone's killin' people up in the mountains an' we might have to look into that, too."

They road on a bit more.

"How much does this job pay?" Ryder asked.

"Not much more than bein' an Arizona Ranger."

"Knew it."

"Then you'll be used to it."

Ryder laughed.

Bob did, too. He was pleased to see his friend laugh again.

They rode on a little more before Bob asked, "Ain't there nothin' for you to return to in Brannan?"

"No. My brother's dead. Emily's marryin' a new man, someone much better than me, an' ma's too tore up from Riley's hangin' to even know who I am. Besides, how can I return to the town that murdered my brother? Hell, I wasn't even there to save him. If I hadn't been such a coward an' had returned when Ma sent me that telegram, I would've been able to save him. But I didn't."

"You proved that he was innocent. The town knows he was hanged for a crime he didn't commit."

"He's dead! What good does it do him that he was innocent?"

"Nothin'. But it might do your ma and pa and you some good."

Ryder stopped and so did Bob. Ryder stared at him. "I don't deserve ..."

"What don't you deserve?"

"I don't deserve to go home. I don't deserve forgiveness."

Bob rode in front of Ryder, blocking his path. "Oh, cut that dead limb off!"

"What?"

"You heard me. That dead part of yer heart that you want to spend the rest of yer life livin' in. It ain't yer fault you didn't get there in time to save him. That telegram didn't get to you because it hadn't found you yet. The moment I found out about it in the telegraph office in Holbrook, I booked passage on the train for you and me. It ain't your fault that you didn't get there in time. It ain't anyone's fault. It's just how things happened. There's nothin' you can do about it so let it go!"

"But ..."

"But nothin'!"

Ryder glared at him.

"Stop punishin' yerself for somethin' you couldn't do anythin' about. An' as for yer girl, Emily, that's over an' done with. So you ran out on her an' everyone hated you for it. You punished yourself a whole lot more than anyone else did. Ain't it time you stopped doin' it an' started livin' your life again?"

"Listen, you have no idea what I went through!"

"Like you're the only one to ever suffer," Bob exclaimed. "In China, I fell in love with my best friend's woman an' neither of us got her. Her family made her marry some fat old ugly bastard an' we both lost out. My heart ached all the way back across the Pacific an' that trip took months.

"This life ain't perfect but if you don't live it, you're wastin' the best part of your life." Ryder stared at the ground for a long while. Bob kept quiet, waiting for his friend to speak up.

"What am I supposed to do?" Ryder asked, still staring at the ground.

"Be a lawman. You're good at it."

"Am I?" Ryder asked, looking up.

"Hell yes you are! You found out that that little girl your brother loved, the one he sacrificed his life for because he loved her, was innocent when no one else even looked her way. Most of the lawmen in the West shoot first and if they make a mistake they blame it on someone else. But you, you looked for the truth an' you found it.

"You showed mercy. Most of the lawmen out here don't even know what that is, let alone how to give it. You're the best lawman I know."

"There's more to it than showin' mercy," Ryder said.

"There is. An' you have it. I fought alongside you in the war an' just recently I fought beside you against one of the worst killers in the West. Without you, I'd probably be dead."

"You're too ugly to die."

Bob laughed. "An' you're too stupid."

Ryder nodded. "I ain't sure if I know how to stop punishin' myself."

"Don't worry, whenever you do, I'll knock you down so you'll know what real pain is."

"You just did."

"I did."

"I don't know how to begin."

"Begin by forgivin' yourself. Be merciful to yourself, like you did for your brother's sweet heart. Like you did for that girl you loved. You said you let her go."

"I did."

"An' what did she do?"

"She forgave me."

"There you go."

"But she's marryin' someone else."

"So what? That frees you up to find someone for yourself."

"If I can."

"Well, don't worry about it too much. You'll get a back full of buckshot from some old, blind miner who can't tell the difference between a deer an' a marshal on horseback before you get to marry some helpless girl who can't find anyone other than some dumb law dog who doesn't know any better."

"You're a lot of help."

Bob laughed again. "I hope so."

"What now?" Ryder asked.

"We go over to Santa Fe an' get you properly signed up. Then we go wherever they want us to go."

"Sounds like a good plan."

"An' if they send us to Brannan?" Bob asked.

Ryder frowned a little. "I wonder if they'll want me back after runnin' out on them again."

"They will."

"An' if they won't?"

"You'll just have to get used to it. But my Pa was so happy to see me come back from the dead. I bet your ma an' pa will be happy to have you back, too."

They moseyed down the road a bit more. Then Ryder said, "I spent a lot of years hidin' out from people, runnin' from my mistakes, just waitin' to die."

"You don't have to do that anymore," Bob said. "You're clean now."

Glancing at Bob, a small smile graced Ryder's face. "Well, we better get along to Santa Fe then, so as I can get officially signed in. The sooner that's done, the sooner I can go home."

"Yep."

They rode on.